Fantasy and reality didn't mix

If they did, she would have written herself a happy ending long before this.

She would have given herself a man who liked the same things she did—home and hearth, children, animals, cold nights and warm fires. She would have given herself a man who valued commitment, fidelity, tenderness, love. She would have given herself a man who loved her for all of herself—not just the bits that were useful to him at the moment.

Those were the sorts of men she wrote about.

Seeing Jack Neillands, and kissing Jack Neillands, had unnerved her, reminded her of dreams set aside, of hopes almost forgotten.

She'd thought herself immune to the temptations of those dreams. She was wrong.

ABOUT THE AUTHOR

For Anne McAllister, ideas for stories are everywhere. She has found inspiration in a variety of sources—a childhood memory, a phone book, even a fortune cookie. In all her stories she writes about relationships—how they grow and how they challenge the people who share them. Anne makes her home in the Midwest with her husband and their four children.

Books by Anne McAllister

HARLEQUIN AMERICAN ROMANCE

186–BODY AND SOUL*
202–DREAM CHASERS
234–MARRY SUNSHINE*
275–GIFTS OF THE SPIRIT*
309–SAVING GRACE

*THE QUICKSILVER SERIES

HARLEQUIN ROMANCE

2721–DARE TO TRUST

HARLEQUIN PRESENTS

844–LIGHTNING STORM
1060–TO TAME A WOLF
1099–THE MARRIAGE TRAP
1257–ONCE A HERO

Don't miss any of our special offers. Write to us at the following address for information on our newest releases.

Harlequin Reader Service
901 Fuhrmann Blvd., P.O. Box 1397, Buffalo, NY 14240
Canadian address: P.O. Box 603,
Fort Erie, Ont. L2A 5X3

IMAGINE

ANNE McALLISTER

Harlequin Books

TORONTO • NEW YORK • LONDON
AMSTERDAM • PARIS • SYDNEY • HAMBURG
STOCKHOLM • ATHENS • TOKYO • MILAN

For Jason
Imagine that.

Published May 1990

ISBN 0-373-16341-X

Chapter One

They were making love when the doorbell rang.

In her mind's eye Frances could still see Ben hovering, his face taut with desire, his dark eyes glittering. She could still feel the thunder of her heart, the moistness of her lips, the need building inside her. She sighed and shut her eyes.

Brrrrrrrrrng. This time more insistent than the last.

"Blast!" Frances muttered and her pencil snapped in half.

Disgruntled, she slapped down the page proofs of her next book, which she'd been reading all afternoon. She was supposed to be dispassionately scrutinizing them for typographical errors.

Instead she'd been swept away into nineteenth-century Maine, into the lives of Ben Cutter and Molly McGuire, into the cold attic room where the heat of their love was all they had to keep them warm.

Frances had central heating to keep her warm, but somehow, ever since she'd created him, Ben Cutter had always done a better job. Even now, when she was only checking proofs and was already halfway through the draft of another book, Ben Cutter still had the power to heat her blood.

The ringing was replaced by loud determined knocking now.

"All right," she muttered. "Hold your horses. I'm coming." She wondered why whoever it was didn't simply come in. She had few neighbors on her secluded woodsy Vermont mountainside. But the ones she did have always knew they were welcome.

Raking a hand through her long, thick hair, she headed down the stairs.

It was a man. She could tell that much from one glimpse through the lace-curtained glass-paneled front door. He stood with his back to the door, staring out toward the barn.

Not Aaron. This man was taller than Aaron, also dark. Nor was it Ebenezer. This man stood ramrod straight and was a good deal less than Eb's seventy-nine. But she had no idea who he was—until he turned.

It was Ben Cutter.

"Ridiculous," she said aloud, arrested where she stood. Utter nonsense. Poppycock.

It was what came of reading too long, she told herself. But she squinted hard once more, staring at this odd apparition, because it really was uncanny, the resemblance.

She could glimpse him in profile now, a tall man with a rangy build, a strong-jawed man with tousled brown hair and a slightly beaky nose. A man with all the features that for so many months had spelled Ben Cutter for her.

How fanciful is that? she chided herself.

Most likely it was an encyclopedia salesman. Or a determined Mormon. But why either of them would be braving a late March snowfall to sell her books or to save her soul, Frances didn't know.

The one thing she did know was that she'd been holed up too long. The increasing pressure of her latest deadline coupled with the page proofs and too many sleepless nights delivering lambs was obviously catching up with her. When she started seeing Ben Cutter in the flesh ringing her doorbell, she knew she needed more companionship than her four-footed friends.

She would have to take Annabel up on her dinner invitation, spend more time in the afternoons working for Eb, or ski over to Ernie and Bert's and do the plumbing she'd promised. Or, and perhaps wisest—because he really did look amazingly like Ben Cutter, she thought as she edged down the steps—she might even have to accept Aaron's standing offer of a drive into Gaithersburg for supper and a movie.

Yes, that's what she would do. She would go out on a date. And the sooner the better.

In the meantime she would put her fantasies back on the pages where they belonged. Determinedly she strode down the rest of the stairs and jerked open the door.

The man turned, and Frances's jaw dropped.

It *was* Ben.

He was smiling at her, a bit bemused. Almost sheepish.

Her eyes narrowed. Ben Cutter wasn't sheepish. Strong, commanding and determined, vulnerable only in his love for the fiery Irish servant girl Molly McGuire—that was Ben.

He'd never been sheepish in his life. She ought to know; she'd created him.

She stared at this three-dimensional manifestation of Ben, totally perplexed.

One corner of his mouth lifted a fraction as if her consternation amused him. "Hi. I'm looking for Frances Moon."

He sounded just the way she always thought Ben would sound, too, his voice deep and resonant. Frances had always known she had a good imagination, but this was amazing.

She swallowed hard, not yet trusting her voice.

"Is she in?" the man who was Ben asked patiently, as if she were slightly dim.

Dumbly Frances nodded again.

Behind her the grandfather clock chimed a quarter hour. In the yard to the side of the house she heard the bells of the goats and the soft *baa*'s of her most expectant sheep. All very realistic and believable. Everyday sounds in everyday circumstances. Completely unlike the man on her porch.

"Could I speak to her, please?" he asked when she still didn't speak.

"You are," she croaked. "I mean, I am."

"You're Frances?" He didn't sound as if he believed in her any more than she believed in him.

That nettled. Frances drew herself up to her full five feet nine inches. "I am." This time her voice sounded normal, albeit a bit belligerent.

He did a double take. She could almost see the gears shifting inside that handsome head of his. Then the smile widened slowly, millimeter by millimeter, and became even more devastating than even she had ever imagined it.

He held out his hand. "It's a pleasure to meet you, Frances. Jack Neillands."

Jack Neillands?

Jack Neillands!

Oh, God, yes. It was all coming back now. The afternoon in her publisher's art department. The head sheet on the wall—one hundred twenty of the world's most handsome men, and Sam Travers, the art buyer, grinning at her and saying, "Take your pick."

But Frances had seen only one: the model with the wry grin and the smoldering eyes. 6 feet, 165 pounds, suit 4OL, shirt 15½—34, waist 32, inseam 33, shoes 10, eyes blue, hair brown, SAG, AFTRA. That model.

To Frances, even then, he hadn't been just another pretty face. The tiny head shot hadn't captured the reality of the man at all, had only hinted at it. But she knew it, knew *him*. He was Ben. Her Ben.

She had stared, captivated. The next thing she knew she was saying, "Him. I want him."

For the cover of her new book, she meant. To be Ben Cutter, her never-say-die, spit-in-your-eye hero, she meant.

To tack up over her computer, to stare at and conjure up heroic and romantic deeds for, she meant.

Just that and nothing more than that, so help her, God.

She certainly didn't mean she wanted him personally.

Not Frances.

Frances had no time for love. Not the mushy man-woman stuff, anyway. Not in real life. Not anymore. She'd tried it once, and that had been enough. It was enough to write about it now, to develop and control it according to the dictates of her imagination, to set it in the nineteenth century and confine it between the covers of a book. It was safer that way, far less painful.

For herself she wanted nothing more to do with it.

All Frances wanted were days of hard work, nights of sound sleep and a life as exciting as a tranquil, deep-woods pond. She wanted her sheep, her goats, her friends, her books, her border collie and her cat. Nothing else.

Certainly not the embodiment of her wildest dreams.

She took another look at the man standing before her. Her eyes slid over the windblown but obviously well-cut hair, the barest hint of whiskery shadow on his jaw. They took in the beat-up leather jacket with the sheepskin lining and the deep blue crew-neck sweater that he wore under it, then skated down the well-worn Levi's to the top-of-the-line hiking boots on his feet.

Gorgeous, certainly. A man to write about, yes. But Frances knew better than to expect more than Ben Cutter's jaw, rangy build and knowing eyes. Jack Neillands was a New York glamour boy if she'd ever seen one!

So what was he doing in Boone's Corner, Vermont?

She knew Sam Travers had a sense of humor. But she never expected it extended this far.

She stared at Jack Neillands again, noticed his hand still outstretched, glimpsed the amusement in those deep, almost navy-blue eyes, and realizing how awkward she must seem, quickly stuck her own out. She felt a jolt when his hard, warm hand wrapped around hers.

She jerked back as if she'd just grabbed the wrong end of a branding iron. Jack Neillands smiled.

"Did Sam Travers send you?"

He blinked. "Who? Sam? No, he didn't." He shook his head.

"Then why...? I mean, you don't...I mean, what are you doing here?" She knew it was almost a wail. She couldn't help it.

"I wanted to meet you."

"You did?" She was astonished. "Why?"

"I heard you asked for me." He hesitated momentarily, as if perhaps he'd made a mistake. "You did, didn't you?"

Frances swallowed. "Well, I—"

"You do know who I am?"

"My model," Frances said, then colored fiercely. "I don't mean 'mine' precisely. I mean, you're...I mean, I'm...I mean I asked for—" She broke off. Silence had to be better than making an idiot of herself.

Jack Neillands, reassured, was grinning at her. "No author ever asked for me specifically before." He shrugged. "It's sort of flattering really. I just wanted to say thanks."

Frances, nonplussed at the thought that she had flattered a man like him, just stared. "And you came all the way to *Vermont* to say it?"

He gave her that sheepish look again. "I was in Vermont anyway. Came up to go skiing, and I had some time, so I thought I'd just sort of...drop by."

There was a long moment's silence while Frances tried digesting that. It wasn't easy. Quite at home with fiction, she was never comfortable with those times when truth became stranger than.

She thought she knew rather how Gepetto must have felt when Pinocchio turned into a real live boy. Gepetto, though, seemed to have had a much better idea about how to handle Pinocchio, than she had about how to cope with Jack Neillands.

"Be polite," her mother always told her. "When someone says 'thank you,' say, 'you're welcome.'"

So she did with a bright smile and expected him to go away.

He stayed right where he was.

She shifted from one foot to the other, wondering what to say now. She always had words when it came to putting them on paper. Reality was a different story.

"It's been a long drive," Jack said. "Forty miles from Killington. Winding roads. Ice. Rugged." He cocked his head looking at her, a slight smile on his face.

He meant she was supposed to invite him in. She felt lightheaded, as if she were dreaming this, imagining it. It was just that she'd been a hermit lately, what with her deadline and all. That was why she was standing here in stupefaction. It had nothing to do with the man smiling at her, nothing to do with a pair of laughing blue eyes and a tantalizing grin.

She made herself concentrate on the barn where she kept her goats, reminding herself that just this morning she had mucked it out, that tomorrow she would do the same again.

Whether Jack Neillands was standing on her front porch or not, goats, not glitz, was what her life was all about.

As long as she kept that in mind, she told herself, she could handle things.

"You'd probably like a cup of coffee, then, before you head back," she said, opening the door wider. "Come in."

"Thanks." Jack stamped his feet on the porch, getting most of the snow off his hiking boots, then walked past her into the entry hall. Immediately Frances wondered if she'd made a mistake.

He seemed bigger than Ben Cutter ever had. More substantial. More intimidating.

Not surprising, of course. Ben was a man of her own making, a man she could control. It would be a damned sight more difficult, she had no doubt, trying to control Jack Neillands.

He untied his boots and slipped them off, leaving them next to hers on the mat just inside the door. Then, wriggling his toes inside his ragg-wool socks, he sighed contentedly like a stray cat taking over the parlor and padded into the living room.

Swallowing hard, determined to be a good hostess to his amazing apparition, Frances followed.

He didn't sit down at once, but stood in the middle of the room, looking around at the pine-paneled walls, the braided rug covering the wide plank floor, the mismatched but homey furniture, the Boston fern that hung from the ceiling almost to the floor, the built-in shelves overflowing with her varied collection of books and periodicals. Then he turned to her. "Nice."

His approval unaccountably pleased her. She smiled and was rewarded with a devastating grin in return. *Be still, my beating heart,* she thought and hastily cleared her throat. "Have a seat. I'll just go get the coffee." And she darted out of the room. She needed a moment's respite, a chance to gather her wits, to stop her pulses racing and her ears from ringing.

"I like your kitchen, too."

Startled, Frances spun around. He was leaning one shoulder against the refrigerator, scratching Dirty Harry's chin as the cat stretched in a contented sprawl across the top of it.

"Harry, get down," she said.

Harry yawned.

Jack grinned. Frances scowled at them both. Harry didn't belong on the refrigerator and Jack Neillands didn't belong in her kitchen.

Still grinning, Jack snagged the cat down and cradled him in his arms. Harry purred madly. It was the only sound in the room.

Jack seemed as comfortable as Harry with the silence that stretched between them, but Frances wasn't. There was an unknown wind stirring the deep, still pond of her life and she was worried about it. *Don't worry,* she told herself. *Later you'll write about it and think it was funny. Later you and Annabel will joke about the day the hero came to life.*

In the meantime, though, she had to give the hero a cup of coffee or he was going to think she was a mindless ditz. Turning away, she filled the coffee grinder with great deliberation.

She wished he would say something. She was no good at small talk herself. It was one of her many failings. Her ex-husband, Stephen, had always been kind enough to point them out to her. This was one of his favorites.

"You never make Mrs. Pottleby-Warren feel comfortable," he'd tell her. Or Mrs. Gretham-James. Or Mrs. Whoever-Whoever. All the partners in the law firm he'd joined seemed to have hyphenated names.

"I try," Frances had maintained. But it hadn't been easy. She'd thought Mrs. Pottleby-Warren was a stuck-up old poot, and Mrs. Gretham-James always made her feel as though her family weren't just farmers, but dirt. Still, this man had come because of her, not because of Stephen's job. Stephen had nothing to do with it.

"You're from New York, then?" she asked Jack.

"Now. Originally I'm from California."

"Ah." She wasn't surprised. Glamour was glamour regardless of which coast it was born on, she thought philosophically. "Is that where you were—what do they call it?—discovered?"

"Yeah," he said, shifting Harry's bulk from one arm to the other. "Sitting on a stool at the soda fountain in Schwab's."

Frances goggled at him.

He laughed. "Isn't that what you were thinking?"

"I, er, suppose. I don't know what I thought, actually," she admitted, spilling the coffee grinds and sweeping them into the pot with her hand. "I mean, I've *never* thought . . . How did you get into it?"

"Just sort of fell into it."

"From Schwab's?" Frances couldn't help smiling.

"After I finished college at Berkeley I enrolled in law school at Columbia and moved to New York."

It wasn't what Frances had expected. College? Law school? She looked at him narrowly, trying to guess if he was putting her on again. But he gave no indication of it.

"I lived with a friend I'd met in Berkeley," Jack went on. "He was starting up his own health-food store so I worked for him while I was in school. And all these models used to come in—" a smile flickered across his face "—to buy their wheat germ and bean sprouts and yogurt. And they used to flirt with me and tell me I was better looking than the guys they worked with." He gave a self-conscious shrug.

Frances could believe that. He was incredible looking, really, especially with that faint flush of embarrassment on his cheeks. "So you applied or whatever it is you do?"

"Sort of. One of 'em I was dating took me around to meet a photographer she knew. He took some pictures for me, and I thought, what the hell, why not?"

A slow grin was spreading across his face almost tooth by tooth. He was wasted on book covers, Frances thought irritably. Television commercials would definitely have been a better medium to capture the full effect.

"Why not, indeed?" she echoed faintly.

"How about you?" he asked her, moving when she did so that he stood only a few feet from her.

Frances blinked. "What about me?"

"Tell me about you." He was focusing right on her, as if she were the only woman in the world. She ducked her head, wishing he'd at least blink. She twisted the dish towel in her hands.

"There's not much to tell." Nothing interesting, at least. Her pedestrian life couldn't hold a candle to his.

"Are you a native Vermonter?"

She shook her head. "I'm from Iowa."

"Farm girl?"

"As a matter of fact, yes." Her unspoken "you want to make something of it?" must've been loud and clear for Jack raised his hands, palms out, as if to say, "No way."

"Some of my best friends are from Iowa."

She looked doubtful. "Oh, yes?"

"Models. Nick Daniels. And Kevin Reinhardt. And there's a girl I know, too—Sandra Cool."

"Sandra *Cool*?"

Jack grinned. "Poetic license. It's really Sandy Kowalewski or something like that. Nobody can pronounce it. Everybody remembers Cool."

Frances laughed. "I bet."

"You guys use pen names, don't you?"

"Some of us." The coffee finished perking. Frances made a production of pouring it into the mugs. "Milk? Sugar?"

"Black." Jack set Harry down, took the mug from her, then leaned back against the counter. "Do you use a pen name?"

She hesitated. "I use a form of my own name."

"Yeah? What?"

Moments like these made her want to crawl under the table, made her wish she'd never succumbed to the momentary flight of fancy that had prompted her to choose the name she'd wanted as a child when she'd complained to her parents about how boring a name Frances Moon was. "I should've been Spanish," she'd complained.

But she wasn't, and now she had no one to blame but herself. She took a deep breath then lifted her chin. "Francesca Luna."

She knew he was trying not to laugh. She could see it in the way his facial muscles were working overtime, in the way a tiny nerve in his cheek twitched. And seeing how hard he was trying made her defiance dissolve.

She laughed, too. "I was a fanciful child. Awful, isn't it?"

"Well…" But Jack couldn't keep a straight face any more than she could. He began to laugh.

Her knuckles tightened around the mug at the full-bodied, masculine sound. Jack Neillands had a wonderful laugh. Better even than his smile.

No fair, she thought. No fair.

"I wish my editor had dissuaded me. But she thought it was great. Exotic, she said."

"Romantic," Jack drawled. "Are your books romantic, Francesca Luna?"

She flushed. "Somewhat."

He grinned. "Sexy, huh? I'll have to read one." He took a swallow of coffee. "Show me one."

She choked, staring at him. He appeared perfectly serious. "The one you're on won't be out till June."

"Show me another. You've done others, haven't you?"

"Yes, but—"

"How many?"

"Six."

"All historical?"

"Yes."

"Frank said mine was set in Maine."

His? Frances felt faintly startled at his proprietary tone. "Frank? Oh, the artist. Yes, that's right, it is."

"What about the rest of them?"

His persistent questions surprised her. "Three have New England settings. I set one in Britain, and I've written two with western locales."

"You get around."

She smiled. "Not really. I read a lot."

"Ah." He nodded slowly, regarding her over the top of his mug with those devastating eyes of his. She wondered exactly what he saw and, in the next moment, knew she didn't want to know.

"So aren't you going to show me?"

"Er, I guess so. If you want."

"I want." And the look he gave her told her that when Jack Neillands wanted something, people didn't say no.

"Just a second. I'll get one." She started out of the room sedately enough. But once she got around the corner, she took the stairs two at a time.

Get your act together, Frances, she exhorted herself. But she felt scattered, shattered—exactly the way Molly McGuire had felt when Ben Cutter was tossed out of the saloon directly into her lap! But Molly was a pithy, competent woman of the '90s, albeit the 1890s. She knew how to handle men like Ben.

Frances was at a loss.

"Shape up," she said aloud. "You can do it." And she could, she was determined. She would make a bit more small talk with Jack Neillands, wave a book under his nose, and then he would drink his coffee, smile his million-dollar smile and go back where he came from.

JACK DIDN'T MOVE an inch. He stood, bemused and entranced, watching as Frances Moon's curvy jeans-clad backside disappeared around the corner and up the stairs. Then he let out a long, silent whistle and shook his head.

So that was Frances Moon.

Talk about surprises. Frances Moon was not at all what he'd expected. Not in the least.

It had been a whim, really, looking her up—the product of a knee twisted on Tuesday's last downhill run and the desperate desire to escape the fawning masses of girls from Brooklyn and Queens who'd descended on him like ministering angels the day after.

His best friend, Carter, who owned the health-food store, thought he was nuts.

"Should've broken my leg," he'd groused when he saw the bevy of females hovering over Jack in the lodge all day.

As far as Jack was concerned, Carter could have them. Jack had come to ski, not to be fawned over. He wanted out. That was when he remembered Frances Moon. Frank had given him her address when he'd said he wanted to drop her a thank-you note.

Who needed a note? he thought. He'd thank her in person.

The more he thought about the idea, the more he liked it. He'd never seen one of his authors before. He knew photographers, artists, art buyers, art directors. He'd even met one or two editors. But authors were an unknown entity. They'd never seemed quite real to him. The books might've been churned out by elves or computers for all he knew.

When Frank had said this Frances Moon person had asked for him specifically, he'd been amazed.

It was always nice to make the money, of course. But why him?

What did he have that any other brown-haired, blue-eyed face didn't have? Lord knew the bookers at his agency didn't see much difference. One handsome face was the same as any other to them.

So what did Frances Moon see that they didn't? He wanted to ask her.

Driving down he'd conjured up Frances Moon in his mind. She'd be about his mother's age, he'd decided. Chubby. With bifocals, house dresses, and gray hair in a bun. Living out her life vicariously. Too far gone to have one of her own anymore.

He started to laugh. Frances Moon was a fox. No doubt about that.

With her long, honey-colored hair and those fantastic cheekbones, she would give half the women he worked with a run for their money. The scattering of freckles across her nose and cheeks undermined any sense of sophisticated elegance, though, making her seem younger than she probably was, which was nowhere near sixty. Late twenties maybe, if that.

She had great eyes, too, that flashed green fire when she was flustered. And he'd flustered her.

He was suddenly interested in far more than simply why Frances Moon wanted to have him on her cover.

He was interested in what she liked for breakfast, for lunch, for dinner. He was interested in what she was doing in this godforsaken part of Vermont, in what she did for fun and excitement.

In what she'd be like in bed.

WHEN SHE CAME BACK DOWN with the book clutched against her breasts like a shield, she found Jack in the living room again, coffee mug in one hand, a book on sheep shearing in the other. He turned and looked at her as she descended. One dark eyebrow lifted quizzically and he held out the book in his hand. "You do a lot of this?"

"A bit," Frances said, glad that her above-stairs pep talk had convinced her heart to stop hammering and her voice to sound calm.

His gaze widened. "It's not just research?"

She shook her head. "No. I've got a flock."

He grinned. "Little Bo-Peep?"

"That's me."

Jack laughed, tilting his head to study her. "Yeah, there is a resemblance. Same subtle curves."

Blushing, Frances thrust the book at him. "Here."

Jack looked at it, his mouth forming the words "Francesca Luna." He winked at her. Frances squirmed. He opened it and began to read.

"You don't have to read it, for heaven's sake," she said.

"Why not?"

"It's hardly your sort of book."

He gave her a curious look. "How do you know what my sort of book is?"

"I don't, of course. It's just that . . . oh, heavens." She didn't mean to be judgmental, but you only had to look at the man, for goodness sake!

Jack shut the book and turned it over, examining the cover carefully. "Cammie Granger," he said. "And Denis Ward."

"What?"

"Your hero and heroine."

"Cammie?" Oh, yuck.

He grinned. "You don't think she looks like a Cammie?"

"No more than I look like a Francesca," Frances said. Whoever she was, she looked as if she were going to fall out of her blouse. She didn't look a thing like she was supposed to, in fact.

"In the book her name was Amelia," Frances told him. "And he was Garrett. She was a straight-laced schoolteacher and he was a know-it-all Texas ranger."

Jack laughed. "In this case she's the know-it-all Texan."

"You know her?"

"I know her well."

Frances didn't ask how well. She could guess. She finished her now tepid coffee in a gulp and started to cough.

"Are you all right?" Jack demanded.

Eyes watering, still clearing her throat, Frances croaked, "F-f-fine." Also foolish. And wishing she was about fifty miles from here. She glanced about desperately for a distraction, something to take his eyes off her. "I need to feed the goats," she said.

"Can I come?" He was stuffing his feet into his boots even as he spoke.

Feeling as if she'd been caught in some fantastic undertow, Frances allowed herself to be swept out the door ahead of him.

"I've never fed a goat," he confided as they walked down the hill. "What do we feed them? Tin cans?" He grinned.

"Hay and goat feed." She stopped to open the gate.

"Goat feed?"

"A commercially prepared, nutritionally balanced mix of corn, oats, molasses, bran, soybean oil and other stuff," Frances recited. "Stop it, Meg." She gently shoved the Nubian who trod on her foot as she entered.

The goat turned toward Jack and, curiosity piqued, butted him in the leg. He scratched her ears. She nuzzled against him ecstatically, then began nibbling his jacket.

Frances watched him, curious as to how he'd react. Stephen had come once, taken one look at her tiny herd, hopped back into his Porsche and shot away.

But Jack just said, "Hi, Meg. Who are the others?"

"Amy, Beth and Jo." Frances shrugged. "I named them after the Little Women."

"Very literary."

"I only have the four. Mostly I just keep sheep. They're easier."

"Of course," he said just as if he knew. It was uncanny how at home he looked standing there against the post with his hands tucked into his jacket pockets, as if he actually were Ben.

The thought was boggling.

"Meg!"

Meg, having taken a fancy to Jack, was noshing in earnest on the pile lining of his jacket. At Frances's voice, the goat cocked her head quizzically, then went right back to her meal.

Frances grabbed the goat and dragged her to the manger, shoving her head toward the feed. "Sorry about that."

"No problem."

"She likes strangers."

"Unlike you?"

Frances's head jerked up. "What?"

"I sort of get the feeling I make you nervous."

So it was obvious? She shouldn't be surprised. Stephen had told her and told her. "You do," she admitted. "It's just that I wasn't expecting you and I'd just been reading the galleys about Ben—the character you...are, er, were. And then you knocked and..."

"I'm real."

That was exactly what Frances was afraid of.

"You were a bit of a shock yourself," Jack said. "I figured you'd be sixty and wear orthopedic shoes. I'm glad you aren't." The devastating grin flashed briefly.

Frances felt her face burn. She turned away to fuss with the goats' food.

"Why'd you ask for me?"

The $64,000 question. Her fingers tightened around the feed sack. "What?" She knew very well what he'd asked. She just didn't know if she could articulate the answer.

"For your cover. How'd you know me? Why'd you ask?"

Frances closed the feed sack and moved toward the door, searching her head for an answer that would make sense. "I was down in New York at my publishers. And I was in the art department with my editor. She was showing me around, sort of walking me through the process of publishing a book. Impressing me with how hard everyone works. And the book I was doing for them, *Cutter's Promise*, was supposed to be—*is* supposed to be my big 'breakthrough' book." She made a doubtful face, but Jack's face showed no doubt at all. He followed her out of the barn.

"Anyway, we were discussing my cover. The first cover I've ever been invited to discuss, I might add. And Sam—the art buyer—he's the one who—"

"I know Sam."

"Well, he asked how I visualized my people. He had a poster in his office. I looked at it, and—" she shrugged, trying to minimize the impact he'd had "—and there you were."

"Me and a hundred other guys. So again, why me?" Dark blue eyes were penetrating her own.

Frances shook her head. She couldn't explain it. "You . . . looked like him."

"What's he like, then, my alter ego?"

He was dogging her footsteps now as she made her way back toward the house. "Persistent." She gave him an ironic smile. "Like you."

"What else?"

She thought about it, about Ben, about what had made him so real to her, about what she'd loved about him, what she'd seen in Jack Neillands's photo. "Strong, demanding. Gentle sometimes. Vulnerable."

"Vulnerable?"

"In his love for Molly."

He was looking at her speculatively. Flustered, she gave him a quick smile. "It's fiction, you know."

"Mmm. Can I read it?"

"You don't want to read my manuscript," Frances said with certainty.

A dark brow lifted. "Why not?"

Frances opened her mouth, tried to form the words—tried to find the words that would express her doubts, her uncertainties, her fear that he would laugh—and found nothing at all.

"I want to read the manuscript, Frances Moon," he told her.

"I—"

"Please."

It was the "please" that defeated her. Her mother had always been a sucker for Emily Post. It must be something in the genes. Besides, she was ninety-nine percent certain he wouldn't even bother. He was probably just being polite.

"If you insist." She got it and put it into his hands, all 547 pages of it. "You can mail it back to me when you're finished. Enjoy." There was a touch of irony in her tone.

But Jack said quite seriously, "I will."

They stood there, each of them holding an end of the manuscript, their eyes locked. The refrigerator hummed. Harry purred. The tap dripped. Jack smiled.

Abruptly Frances dropped her end and stepped back. "Well," she said briskly, "it's been nice meeting you."

"It's been nice meeting you, too, Frances Moon," Jack said quietly and the tone of his voice sent a shiver right up her spine.

She opened the door for him, followed him onto the porch and watched him head down the steps and across the yard to his car.

"Goodbye," she said.

"See you." He got in, shut the door, gave her a grin and a wave.

Frances waved back and stood watching the car until it was out of sight. Then, and only then, did she go back inside, shut the door and sag against it.

"You are an idiot," she told herself and got no argument back. "He is just a man."

But what a man!

What a man, indeed, she chided herself. He might look like Ben Cutter, but that certainly didn't mean he was *like* Ben Cutter.

Quite the opposite in fact. Ben Cutter was a down east wood butcher, a nineteenth-century man content with the simple things. Jack Neillands was a man on the move, an achiever, a doer, a goer. He doubtless lived the same sort of life-style as Stephen did, had the same goals and expectations. In other words, he was the last sort of man she wanted in her life.

"Well, he isn't in your life," she reminded herself tartly. Like Caesar he came and he saw. Unlike Caesar he didn't conquer; he left.

At ten o'clock the next morning he was back.

Chapter Two

Frances stared as if she didn't believe it.

Jack didn't blame her. He hardly believed it himself. Single-minded pursuit—at least when it came to the women in his life—had never been his style. He simply took them as they came—and they came in droves.

But when he'd got back to the lodge the night before, he'd had no interest at all in taking up any of the half-dozen invitations from various women to ''come up and see them sometime.''

The woman he'd met that afternoon was still on his mind. Her flustered freshness intrigued him. Most of the women he knew were jaded sophisticates or naive young girls on their way to becoming jaded sophisticates. Frances Moon was like a breath of clean air in the midst of Times Square.

He found himself opening up the manuscript to discover what else he could learn about her.

Caught immediately by a stubborn, redheaded Irish girl called Molly McGuire—a girl who, it seemed, had more backbone than a whale—he was still engrossed in it when Carter came in at one-thirty.

He stared. ''You're reading?''

Jack nodded, not looking up.

Carter felt his forehead. ''You sick or something?''

Jack scowled and shoved his hand away. ''I'm fine.''

Carter stared at him for a moment, then squinted at the manuscript. "What is it?"

"A book."

"What kind of book?"

"Historical."

Carter's brows lifted. "Oh?" He craned his neck so he could see the pages and began to read aloud, "'Her legs parted for him, sharing with him her secrets, letting his fingers find—'"

"Buzz off."

Carter threw back his head laughing and went to take a shower.

Irritated, Jack went back to the story, to the scene Carter had snickered over. He didn't find it funny in the least. He read it again slowly, savoring every sound, every sensation, imagining himself in the scene as Ben Cutter with Molly McGuire played by Frances Moon. It was hard to believe that the skittish young woman who blushed almost every time he looked at her could be responsible for a scene that made his blood run hot. Avidly he read on.

He wasn't pleased when Carter reappeared, said, "Morning run at nine, okay?" and flipped off the light.

Scant moments later the room was filled with the soft whuffles of Carter snoring.

Jack lay wide awake in the dark, annoyed and aroused. Annoyed at Carter. Aroused by Frances Moon.

Irritated, he rolled over and punched his pillow into shape for sleeping, but the scene he'd just read still haunted him. He closed his eyes and saw an old-fashioned, pine-paneled room, like Frances's living room. In it he saw a four-poster bed, and in the middle of the bed, a freckled temptress with long wavy hair smiling at him.

His eyes flicked open. He flipped over.

Carter snored on.

Jack shut his eyes. The woman was back, teasing, beck-oning. "Damn," he muttered. He flopped onto his back again, tormented, eyes wide open.

Was Frances Moon as feisty as Molly McGuire? he won-dered. He imagined she could be. Was she as stubborn? Probably. As temptingly attractive? For sure.

Would she be as good in bed?

An interesting question. And not entirely an academic one, either. He smiled. It was an anticipatory smile. A wolfish smile. A determined smile.

"Tomorrow," he decided aloud, he would find out.

"Mmmph?" Carter shifted in the other bed. "Wha' say?"

"Nothing. Never mind. Go to sleep."

Carter whuffled.

Jack rolled over again and, decision made, let his imagi-nation have free rein.

It was one of his better fantasies, owing as it did, so much to Frances's own literary inspiration. He wondered if she would be apprehensive the way Molly had been with Ben? Would she be innocent, her green eyes wary, yet hopeful, trusting? And then—his smile grew—when at last he came to her, would she become as enthusiastic as Molly had been with Ben?

He couldn't sleep; he was too restless. He got up finally, grabbed the manuscript and took it into the bathroom where he could turn on the light without bothering Carter. There, at four in the morning, he finished it, undisturbed.

No, that wasn't true. He was disturbed, all right. Aroused. Still.

Inside the shy, somewhat prickly exterior that Frances Moon had shown him yesterday afternoon was a very warm, very sexy woman. Warm and sexy, hell; the woman was volcanic. The things she wrote sent steam out his ears.

He was up, dressed and raring to go when Carter opened his eyes at eight.

"Ah." Carter yawned and stretched. "Knee better? Ready for a run?"

Jack shook his head. "Nope. I'm off," he said. "See you tonight." And he left Carter staring after him.

He didn't exactly expect Frances to meet him with open arms. It would've been nice—saved time and all that. But he had hoped for something a bit more enthusiastic than the look of frank disbelief and determined indifference that he got when she opened the front door to find him standing there once more.

He felt suddenly awkward and unsure. He held out the manuscript and cleared his throat. "Hi."

"Hello," Frances said. "Again."

Jack flashed her a quick grin. "Couldn't stay away. I'm impressed. It was terrific. I-I'm flattered to be Ben," he went on rapidly in the face of what appeared to be stony skepticism. "He's a fighter. A very gutsy man. Stubborn. Determined. And vulnerable," he added, because it was only the truth.

Frances looked skeptical. "Really?"

"Really. And Molly was worth it. Though," he tacked on, to be fair, "there were times I had my doubts, especially when she had the hots for that jerk who ran the general store."

"You *did* read it!"

Jack was affronted. "I told you I would."

She was still shaking her head. "But that was only yesterday."

"Yeah, well, what else did I have to do? I still can't ski because of my knee." Not precisely true, but he wasn't telling her that.

"I would have thought you'd find plenty to do." The way she looked at him made him squirm.

"Nothing I wanted to do," he said flatly. He smiled at her. "You've become my favorite author."

She rolled her eyes.

"Truly." Jack gave her one of his very best grins, willing her to respond, thanking God when at last she did. A reluctant and fleeting grin flickered across her face.

It was enough. Pressing his advantage, a bit more confident now, he went on, "Have breakfast with me."

She shook her head. "I've already had breakfast."

"Then have lunch."

She laughed. "It's only ten in the morning."

"So we'll wait."

"I don't always eat lunch."

Jack gave her body a thorough and assessing glance. "Lunch won't hurt you a bit."

She made a face at him. "I don't not eat to be thin," she said. "I don't eat because I get fascinated with something and I forget."

"And what fascinating thing are you doing today?"

She hesitated. "I'm correcting page proofs."

"Fascinating," he agreed gravely and watched her blush.

He could almost see the wheels spinning in her head, the excuses bubbling to the surface. A minute more and she'd turn him down flat.

And then what would he do? Turn tail and head back to Killington, defeated?

Like hell. If Ben Cutter could sweep 'em off their feet, so could he.

"Are you afraid of me, Frances Moon?" he challenged.

She bristled. "Of course not!"

"Well, then . . ." He paused, letting the silence grow just as her discomfort did.

At last green fire flashed in her eyes. "Well, then what?"

He grinned. "Prove it."

So SHE DID. At least she tried to. She certainly wasn't going to cower in her house and give Jack Neillands the idea that handsome, successful men made her quake in her boots— even if they did. Frances lifted her head and stuck out her chin the way she always had when her sister, Martha, said, "You can't do that. You're too little."

She met Jack's gaze squarely. "You're on."

She directed him to Bacon's Inn in Gaithersburg—because it was nicer, she said, than Beany's, the local eatery in Boone's Corners.

She didn't say it was because she didn't want to run into anyone she knew. Frances didn't even know that was a reason until they walked into the dining room and there by the windows she spotted Aaron Leggett deep in conversation with three other men. Then she groaned.

"Drat." Quickly she looked away, edging behind Jack so that if Aaron happened to look her way, he wouldn't see her.

A futile hope. The hostess, beaming and batting her eyelashes at Jack, led them to "the nicest table in the house," which happened to be only two away from Aaron's.

There was no possibility he wouldn't see her. When he did, a look of puzzlement crossed his face. Frances was sure a look of guilty consternation crossed hers.

She wished she'd rung Aaron last night as she'd planned, but she'd been too astonished, too bemused to do more than stare at her galleys about Ben and Molly while Ben's alter ego played havoc with her good sense.

She had wallowed in the memory of Jack Neillands's astonishing appearance, had hugged it to herself, replayed it over and over. She'd wanted to call Annabel at once and tell her about it. She hadn't because she was almost convinced that, if she did, the experience would lose its magic.

For magic was surely what it had been. It had been an interlude, an astonishing moment in time—a fantasy. Something far too fragile to be exposed to the critical eye with which she usually picked apart the experiences of her life.

She certainly hadn't expected to see him again today. Even less had she expected him to have read her book. He must've sat up all night!

And why?

Because he thought she was a good writer?

Why else?

He couldn't be attracted to her. The thought appeared out of the blue and was immediately squelched.

Don't be a flaming idiot, she told herself. Jack Neillands is not for the likes of you. If she ever decided to take another fling at an enduring relationship, it would be with a man like Aaron.

Jerked back to the present, she gave Aaron a fleeting smile.

He scowled at her.

"Friend of yours?" Jack asked.

Frances nodded. "Yes."

His jaw tightened and he gave Aaron a long, assessing glower.

Aaron glowered back.

Frances goggled at them both. That Jack Neillands might act as if he owned her—untrue as it might be—didn't entirely surprise her. He was that sort of man. But that Aaron Leggett, the mellowest of men, should presume to behave like a Doberman restrained was astonishing.

She gave serious thought to sinking through the floor.

Jack glanced at the menu. "What's good?"

Frances looked at him, surprised. Stephen had always made it a practice to order for both of them. "I, er, the house specialty," she said after a moment. "Venison chili."

Jack's mouth quirked at one corner. "Is that going to be the next food fad in the city? Do the latest crazes play in Vermont before they hit the big time?"

Frances laughed. "Could be."

"Two venison chilies," Jack said to the waitress. "And a beer for me." He looked at Frances.

"Me, too," she said recklessly.

The waitress brought the beers, which they drank while they waited. And when the chili arrived, piping hot and spicy, she brought two more.

Frances knew she should decline, but she didn't. Aaron had left moments before, giving her a dark scowl but no comment. It annoyed her so much she took a deep draught of the second bottle.

Take that, Aaron, she thought. He stomped out the door, and the moment he did, it was as if the little dark cloud hanging over her life had floated away.

She smiled and took another sip of her beer. Even Jack studying her with those fathomless blue eyes of his didn't unnerve her now. She was only having lunch with him, after all, not selling her soul. She could handle this.

"So," he said to her, "aren't you glad you came?"

"Actually," she said, "I am. The chili's very good."

"And the company?" Jack prompted.

"And the company."

"You sound surprised."

"I am, I guess."

Jack gave her a wry look. "Thanks."

"Sorry. I just never expected to be—" she waved her hand to encompass Jack and the dining room "—here," she finished. "Like this, I mean. With you."

"You come with that other guy?"

Frances was startled at the grimness in his tone. "Aaron?"

"If that's his name." Jack speared a piece of venison and chewed it with a vengeance.

"Certainly more likely him than you," she admitted. "Poor Aaron."

Jack bristled. "What's poor about him?"

"He's annoyed at me."

He fixed her with a steady blue gaze. "Does he have a right to be?"

He thought he did, apparently. "No." Frances shook her head firmly, adamantly. "Oh, no."

Jack gave her one of his cover-boy smiles. "That's all right then." He signaled the waitress for another round of beers.

It was the beer's fault, Frances decided somewhat muzzily after all was said and done.

It made her giddy, irresponsible. Else why would she have behaved that way—sitting there eating her chili, laughing and smiling, telling Jack about her childhood on the farm, about her no-nonsense older sister, Martha, and her cat named Pru?

"Martha named her," she told him gravely. "She named her Prudence. It's a virtue."

"Is it?" Jack sounded doubtful.

She giggled at the look on his face, knowing it would shock Martha, suspecting it should shock her. "Oh, yes. But she wasn't a particularly prudent cat. I told Martha we should've called her Pro for Promiscuous. But she was a nice cat. I even named a heroine after her. My first."

"How old were you?"

"Twelve."

He lifted a brow. "You wrote clear back then?"

"I was always writing, telling stories in my head. You have to when you live on a farm. It's so boring."

"If it's boring, why are you doing it now?"

"Because it's where I belong," she said, even the beer not muddying her certainty about that. She'd tried living out her fantasies with Stephen. Now she knew better.

"And," she added, "it isn't the only thing I do. What about you? Tell me about you."

She didn't know where she'd thought New York models sprang from—probably she hadn't—but she was suddenly curious.

Jack assuaged her curiosity. He told her about his parents—a mother who taught seventh grade English and a father who was an attorney specializing in maritime law—two brothers and a sister, three nieces and four nephews. He told her how he'd broken his arm in fifth grade playing football, his collarbone in college riding a bike on Telegraph Avenue, and his nose last year in Greece on a shoot when one of the women models rowing a boat accidentally whacked him in the face with an oar.

"I've still got a bump on it," he told her, rubbing his nose.

On another man it would have been a detriment. Frances thought it simply added a certain roguish element to Jack's appeal.

She found it fascinating to watch the play of expressions across his face as he talked, the quirky grin, the grooved cheeks, the ready smile, the full-throated laugh that made her laugh, too. He was just like Ben Cutter. But real.

It was eerie almost. He wasn't perfect, of course. He was cocky. Even slightly sloshed, she could tell that.

He flirted with the young waitress when she served them and with the hostess when he paid the bill. He took both the teenager's blushes and the middle-aged woman's stammering as his due.

But he didn't call Frances's attention to it as some men might've, the ones who wanted her aware of their appeal. He seemed oblivious to it.

Not surprising, Frances thought almost rationally as they walked to the car. He probably experienced it so often that he really was unconscious of it.

Still, she couldn't hold it against him. It fit somehow.

And, she thought muzzily, if she ever wrote the glitzy contemporary book that her editor was always urging her to do, she'd have to remember to make sure her character behaved like Jack.

Settling herself in the car, she even bent down and reached into her purse for a pen so she could make a note of it.

"What're you doing?" Jack asked.

She sucked on the tip of her pen, then scribbled a few words on her omnipresent notepad before answering. "Just . . . making a note."

He leaned against the open car door looking down at her. "A note? About what?"

She smiled up at him. "You."

His mouth lifted at one corner. "Do I want to know what sort of note?"

Frances frowned myopically at the words she had written, holding the notepad so she could get a better angle.

"Unconscious charm," she read. "Oblivious to appeal."

A smug groove appeared in his cheek. "I'm charming, am I? And appealing?"

Frances tilted her head up and tried to peer down her nose at him. Instead she hiccuped.

Jack laughed and held out a hand, hauling her back out of the car. "Come on, Francesca Luna. I think we should talk about this."

"I—"

"We don't have to leave yet, do we?"

His eyes—Ben Cutter's eyes—mesmerized her, trapped her like a rabbit caught by the headlights of a car. When she got her tongue untangled, all she could do was mumble, "No."

It was the beer and Ben Cutter conspiring against her better judgment that made her forget her good sense and agree. It was the beer and Ben Cutter that made her acquiesce when Jack took her hand in his as they walked up the path behind Bacon's Inn, and it was certainly the beer and Ben Cutter that kept her from objecting when he slipped an arm across her shoulders as, two hours later, they drove slowly back along the winding road through Boone's Corners to Frances's hillside home.

But Ben Cutter and all the beer in the world couldn't undermine her sufficiently to lead him to her bedroom when they got there. She dredged up the sense from somewhere to take her stand on the front porch.

"Thank you," she said firmly, "for the lunch."

Jack paused, his hand on the doorknob. "This is as far as we go?"

"Yes."

She met his gaze steadily—at least as steadily as she could manage with knees like marshmallows, with a brain like shredded wheat.

Jack gave her a rueful look, then a wry grimace. "Well, we know what you *don't* do on a first date. Do you kiss?"

Did she?

She didn't think she ever had. In her vast experience—primarily Stephen, secondarily Hobie Mills who had taken her to the senior prom, and lastly, of course, Aaron—it had rarely come up.

She hesitated.

For Jack, that was enough. He smiled, took a step forward and bent his head.

Frances considered herself somewhat of an expert on kisses—literary ones, at least. She knew passionate, she knew hungry, she knew desperate, she knew sweet. But she'd never known a kiss like this.

When Ben had kissed Molly, he'd been eager, demanding, starved for her taste, and Frances had thought she'd known the depth of Molly's response.

But when Jack kissed her she knew she had a few things left to learn.

His lips covered hers in a kiss that was more than a demand; it was a searching, a questing. It asked for a response, but it didn't insist on it the way Frances had expected. It spoke of tenderness and yearning and hunger all mixed together. It was indeed more than a demand, it was a devastation.

And Frances was no proof against it. It touched a chord in her, unleashed an aching, a longing. Needs long buried

stirred to life within. The warmth of Jack's arms around her
sent a shudder right through her, and before she knew it she
was kissing him back.

The need grew, surged, swamped her, panicked her. Oh,
God, no, she thought desperately and pulled away. Her
breathing came in great labored gasps. She couldn't look at
Jack, couldn't lift her eyes, wouldn't have if he hadn't laid
his fingers beneath her chin and raised it so that she had to.

He didn't say a word, just looked at her, his blue eyes
clouded and serious. Then he touched her cheek, caressing
it lightly with his fingertips. Frances trembled at his touch,
but he made no move to kiss her again.

Then he smiled just slightly. "Remember that."

HOW ON EARTH was she supposed to forget it?

God willing, she would've if she could. By nine o'clock
that night the beer had worn off, reality had set in, and
Frances felt extraordinarily sober and decidedly dumb.

Whatever had possessed her, she asked herself as she wore
a circle in the braided rug on her living-room floor, to go off
with Jack Neillands like that? To smile and fall under his
spell like that? To go to lunch with him?

To let him kiss her like that!

Worse, to kiss him back?

"It didn't mean anything," she told herself. Certainly not
to him. He probably did it with every woman he met.

And to her? No, it didn't mean anything to her, either.
She wouldn't let it.

Still her fingers crept up to touch her lips, to trace the line
of them. The same lips she'd had this morning. But more
sensitive somehow, tingling even yet.

Because you keep touching them, dope. But she couldn't
help it.

She didn't remember them feeling this way after she'd
been kissed by Stephen whom once she'd loved or Aaron
whom she didn't. The closest she'd ever come, in fact, was

when she'd sat at her computer and had imagined Molly being kissed by Ben.

"Fantasy," she reminded herself curtly.

And so was Jack.

At least as far as she was concerned he was. For all that she might "remember" him, that was all there would be—a memory.

Ben Cutter was more enduring. He'd at least have a place on her shelf.

Well, she certainly didn't want Jack Neillands on her shelf. He was far too distracting. He made her think about things better confined to the pages of books. He made her remember the girl she had been, the one with the fantasies, the hopes, the dreams.

He made her remember how she'd sat on the fence overlooking the feedlot and dreamily told her sister, Martha, how she was going to grow up and go away from all this.

"It's not enough," she'd said, hating the confines, the humdrum gritty reality of farm life. "I want more. I'm going to an Ivy League school, teach, meet the man of my dreams, marry him and live happily ever after," she'd said with the clear confidence of a fifteen-year-old whose goals knew no bounds.

"Dreamer," Martha had scoffed.

But Frances hadn't been deterred. She'd done her best, convinced that she could make her dreams come true.

She'd worked like a demon all through high school and had received her coveted scholarship. She'd worked like a demon all through college. She'd got her degree, her teaching certificate, a job. She'd met Stephen, fallen in love, married him. But she hadn't made it work.

She hadn't been the woman Stephen needed. That had become increasingly clear as time went on. Stephen needed a woman he could mold into a law partner's wife. He needed a woman who knew instinctively which fork to use, which labels were in, which restaurants served the latest fad.

Frances fell short. Far short. She'd chafed under the strain of trying, had realized finally that she didn't want to try, that trying was too painful when there was no hope for success. She had, for the first time in her life, said, "I can't."

Stephen had found someone who could, and Frances had gone to Vermont. It suited her. The people were kind. They gave her space. They supported, but didn't smother. They gave her the confidence to believe in herself as a farmer, as a writer, as a friend. She had her fantasies, but they never got out of control now. She had been here for five years and she was satisfied.

It was limited, yes. But Frances knew her limits now.

She didn't want a man like Jack Neillands coming into her life and reminding her of what she couldn't have.

"WHO WAS THAT MAN?" asked Aaron Leggett in a 7:00 *a.m.* phone call the next morning.

"Who was that man?" asked Ebenezer Toot when she walked into his general store at ten.

"Who was that man?" chorused Sisters Ernestine and Bertha, coming in after her, their eyes making them look more like owls than penguins in their black-and-white habits and veils.

"Who was that man?" asked ten-year-old Leif as she came up the steps to his house late that afternoon.

Frances, determined not to let the memory of Jack disrupt the calm of her well-ordered life, faced each of them with bland innocence. "What man?"

"The one you were eating lunch with," said Aaron.

"The one I saw you walking up the mountain with," Eb said.

"The one we saw you driving through town with," said Ernie and Bert.

All of them she fobbed off with vague generalities.

Leif just looked at her as she came into the kitchen. "What man?" he echoed incredulously. "The one I saw kissing you on your porch."

"A man kissed Frances?" Leif's mother, Annabel, stopped squinting at the patchouli she was adding to her potpourri and squinted instead at Frances. "Which man?"

Frances would've liked to discuss Jack Neillands with Annabel. That was why she'd come. Annabel was wise and well-grounded, a voice of realism and sanity, a sensible woman Frances trusted with her deepest secrets. She would say just the right thing to make Frances forget her foolishness and put Jack into perspective where he belonged.

But before she could begin to figure out how to get rid of Leif and talk with his mother, another voice entered the fray.

"It was the Rear of the Year, that's who!"

"What!" cried Frances, Annabel and Leif all at once.

Leif's fifteen-year-old sister bounded down the stairs, tossing her waist-length black hair and grinning smugly. "The guy she was with. That's what we call him at least," Libby said.

"The rear of the—"

"I'll show you." Libby vanished up the stairs to her bedroom to return moments later with a framed poster. "See!"

Frances stared. All around the edges of the poster were action shots—Jack, clad in only a pair of jeans, jumping, climbing, running, stretching, striding this way and that. Eighteen separate Jacks—grinning, scowling, panting, smirking, flirting.

And in the middle, fifteen by fifteen and framed, a close up on the back of Jack. Not all the back of Jack, either. Only the seat of his jeans.

Leif gulped. Annabel swallowed. Frances started to laugh.

"It was him," Libby insisted. "Wasn't it him? We saw you coming out of Bacon's."

Who hadn't seen them? Frances wondered, nodding her head.

"I knew it! I knew it!"

Annabel forgot her potpourri to stare at Frances. "*That's* the man who was kissing you on the porch?"

Frances shrugged awkwardly. "I'd had three beers."

"Oh, of course." But Annabel didn't look convinced. She was looking at Frances as if she'd never seen her before. Frances flushed.

"Where'd you meet him? He's gorgeous. Who is he? Is he in love with you?" Libby came to peer directly up into Frances's face.

"No, my dear Liberty, I assure you he is not."

"Don't call me that!"

"Sorry," Frances repented, knowing Libby hated it. "But don't ask silly questions, Lib."

"Well, why was he kissing you, then? You *saw* them?" Libby asked her brother enviously.

Leif nodded, basking in the glory of his serendipitous observation. "From the goat barn. I was checkin' on Amy."

"How is Amy?" Frances grasped desperately at any change of subject.

But Libby would not be deterred. "Forget your old goat for once. I want to know more about the Rear of the Year. Who is he, anyway?"

Frances sighed. So much for distractions. "Jack," she said. "His name is Jack."

"Jack." Libby rolled the name around in her mouth like a Godiva chocolate, savoring each letter. "Jack." She sang it this time, then twirled around the room so that she ended on her knees, crooning to the poster of Jack's rear end. "Jack. Jack. Jack. Ah, Jack!"

"A good dose of catnip and she'll fall asleep," Annabel suggested, setting down the potpourri jar and filling the kettle.

"Not a bad idea," Frances said.

"As long as I dreamed of Jack, I wouldn't care," Libby fluted. She got to her feet again and once more confronted Frances. "So...?"

"So?" Frances contrived to look blank.

Libby was having none of it. "Come on, tell all."

Frances shrugged. "There's not much to tell."

"The Rear of the Year is kissing you on your doorstep and there's not much to tell?" Libby rolled her eyes. "Where'd you meet him?"

"On my doorstep."

"And?"

Frances sighed. "He's on the cover of my next book. That's all."

"That's *all*?"

"It's no big deal. He was just curious." She went on to chronicle briefly her two encounters with Jack, trivializing them as best she could. She was well acquainted with Libby's tendency to aggrandize as the situation warranted. If things were going to come out anywhere close to the truth, she had to minimize everything as much as possible in the telling.

"So he just 'dropped by' to meet you?" Libby sounded skeptical.

"He was up here skiing and he stopped in—" Frances had been going to say "to thank me," but that would have required further explanation—one she had no desire to give. She'd never said she'd picked Jack out of a crowd of gorgeous men. She wasn't saying so now.

"So when's he coming back?"

"He's not."

"Why not?"

"Why would he?"

Libby did a plié. "Because he's fallen madly in love with you."

Frances looked at Annabel. "Do you have any potions that will increase common sense?"

Annabel laughed. "Liberty, go feed the chickens. Leif, too."

Both children opened their mouths to protest, but met a steely maternal gaze.

Leif shrugged philosophically, but Libby sighed eloquently as she began to put on her boots. "For a person who writes about love," she chided Frances on her way out the door, "you don't have an ounce of romance in your soul."

When the door had closed behind them, Annabel looked up. "You do, though, don't you?"

Frances sloshed tea into her saucer. "Do what?"

"Have an ounce of romance. That's why you're stalking around my kitchen like a cat with its fur ruffled."

"Don't be ridiculous," Frances said, but she stopped pacing.

"You mean you haven't had the occasional stray thought about what might happen if—" Annabel grinned wickedly "—the 'Rear of the Year' does come back?"

"Of course not!"

The look Annabel gave her was as unblinking as Harry the cat's. "Right," she said. Liar, she meant.

Frances sighed. "I thought you, of all people, would understand. Who's always telling me that the things I write about don't happen in real life?"

"They don't," Annabel said. "To me. You I'm not so sure about."

"No." Frances was adamant.

"Doth the lady protest too much?" Annabel suggested lightly.

"No, she dothn't. There is nothing to this. I wouldn't want him even if there were. Jack Neillands is just another Stephen."

"Then what's he doing in Boone's Corner, Vermont?"

"Slumming, I expect."

Annabel considered her friend carefully. "Do you really think so?"

Frances drummed her fingernails on the countertop. "Of course. He was up here skiing, that's all. And he knew I lived nearby. It was a lark."

"Then what brought him back the second day?"

"To return my manuscript." She gave a little laugh. "He was probably too cheap to mail it."

"He read it?"

"Yes," Frances admitted.

"In one day? Good Lord." Annabel looked at Frances closely. "Are you sure Libby isn't right? Maybe he is madly in love with you."

"Be serious."

Annabel shrugged and went back to mixing her potpourri. "He doesn't sound so bad to me."

Frances made a face. "If you like the type."

"You don't?"

"I told you. He's like Stephen."

"You'd rather have a man like Aaron?"

"No," Frances corrected and said again what she'd been saying ever since Stephen had left her, saying again the mantra that had protected her from hurt for the past five years. "I don't want any man at all."

JACK WANTED HER—a fact not in and of itself astonishing. In his thirty-two years Jack Neillands had wanted quite a lot of women. There had been years, in fact, when any moderately pretty girl would have set off all his hormonal urges. He liked to think he'd become more discriminating with age.

He certainly seemed to have in this case. By his reckoning there were probably a million or so eligible women in the city of New York, at least a reasonable percentage of whom wouldn't have been averse to going out with and even to bed with Jack Neillands.

But for the moment at least he didn't want any of them.

All he could think about was Frances Moon.

Her name no longer conjured up a sweet, plump lady in her sixties. It brought with it visions of laughter, freckles, starchiness, refreshing candor, prickly pride. A woman who wrote romance and raised goats. A woman who was almost prim one minute and who kissed like a wanton the next.

What a contradiction. It was perverse. *She* was perverse. Not his sort at all.

Yet he couldn't stop thinking about her, about kissing her. He'd given her a kiss that would have raised the dead—something to remember him by, he'd thought smugly as he had done it.

But he was the one with the memories. That kiss—and her response—was burned on his brain.

He walked through the next three days in a daze.

"What're you mooning around about?" Carter had asked as they drove back to New York from Vermont on Saturday morning.

"What're you smiling about?" his downstairs neighbor, Julie, had asked when he met her while picking up his mail Saturday afternoon.

"Are you listening to me?" asked his lawyer sister, Georgia, when he met her for supper during her layover at JFK on her way back from a conference in Switzerland Sunday night.

And, "Are you deaf, Jack?"

The words shattered his daydream now, splintering the thousandth replay of the quintessential kiss. Mick Halloran glared over the camera at him.

"Huh?"

"Wake up. I said, grab her. Let's see a little passion, a little lust, for crying out loud."

"Oh, er, yeah." Passion. Lust. "No problem."

Jack lowered his lids, put his arms back around the blonde who was doing the cover shoot with him. Her name, he thought, began with a *T*. Tessa? Teresa?

He didn't know; didn't care. He moved his lips within millimeters of hers, and thought instead of kissing Frances Moon.

Once hadn't been enough. Not deep enough, not long enough. He wanted to touch Frances's lips again, to move his mouth over hers, to taste, to feel.... He licked his lips.

He could see her now in his mind's eye. She'd looked wary, apprehensive, innocent. And then their lips had touched and he had felt her initial resistance, had gradually overcome it, coaxed a response, *needed* a response. And he'd got—

"That's better. That's good. That's very, *very* good!"

Jack was sweating. Mick was beaming, camera clicking and flashing. "Swell. Great job. That's dynamite. Pure sizzle. Take a break while I change rolls."

Jolted, Jack opened his eyes. Mick gave him a grinning thumbs-up.

The ditzy blonde he'd been smoldering over stood staring up at him, a speculative smile on her face. "You really get into it, don't you?"

Jack blinked at her, still dazed.

"I'll bet you're 'very good' for real, too," she went on, her forefinger tracing an idle line up and down his bare arm.

Jack swallowed.

She winked at him. "How 'bout we go back to my place after and try it for real?"

It certainly wasn't the first time Jack Neillands had been propositioned. And, unless the world ended tomorrow, he had the cockiness to doubt that it would be the last.

But it was the first time in recorded history that he hadn't had to think twice about the answer.

"I don't think so. No. Thanks."

Chapter Three

"You said no?" Carter flung himself backward on Jack's sofa and stared.

Jack shrugged irritably and went on buckling the gravity boots. "I've said no before."

Carter grinned. "Not often. And certainly not to the hottest gal to come back from France this season."

He plucked another potato chip from the bowl balanced on his stomach and watched with distaste as Jack grabbed hold of the chinning bar in the doorway to the bedroom and swung his feet up to clamp on to the bar.

"So maybe she didn't appeal," he muttered, scowling upside down. He might've known that Carter would think he'd lost his mind.

"Maybe you're becoming gay in your old age," Carter said between crunches.

Jack's whole body went stiff—and not from the pull of gravity, either.

Carter laughed, grinning like a jack-o'-lantern. "So maybe you're not. But, good grief, man, who says no to Therese LaBoobs—or whatever she's called—of all people?"

"Me."

"The more fool you. I'd snap her up in a minute."

"I'd introduce you, but I'm afraid you might actually call her that to her face."

"I'd call her Your Highness, Princess Therese to her face," Carter vowed, "but I don't think an introduction from you would carry much weight at the moment."

Jack did and upside-down shrug. "She's probably forgotten already. She was just curious."

"And you weren't?"

"I . . . had a dentist's appointment."

Carter's eyes did a slow roll. "Now I've heard everything. Swear to God, Jack, since we got back from Vermont, you've been loony. You work out twice as hard, you jog four times around the reservoir instead of two. You turn down beautiful women. You sure all this hanging upside down isn't getting to your head? Next thing I know you'll be taking a vow of celibacy or marrying some chick."

Jack choked. "Let's don't go overboard."

"Damn right." Carter lifted his beer bottle in a toast. "To long nights and lovely women to enjoy them with."

"Hear, hear."

Maybe Carter was right. It did seem crazy not to take advantage of what was so freely offered. But somehow he still couldn't get excited about LaBoobs, free or not.

Perhaps it was because she was so young, not more than twenty. Or maybe it was because, in the few minutes they'd talked before Mick had started shooting, she'd sounded like the average ninth grader. But he suspected it was mostly that, although Therese had eyes, lips and cheekbones to die for, life hadn't yet left its mark on her.

Unlike Frances Moon.

One look had been enough to tell him there was so much more to her than to the flawless Therese. Frances had maturity, intelligence, knowledge and, yet, a sort of fundamental innocence underscoring it all.

She was also sexy as hell.

Jack didn't know which of her many attributes disturbed him the most.

Probably, he reflected with a wisdom that rarely came to him except when he was hanging upside down, what disturbed him the most was that she wasn't his type.

He was used to worldly women, glib gals who wore their hearts under chain mail, girls to whom a roll between the sheets meant no more than a lap around the reservoir.

With Frances, for all she knew about rolls between the sheets and in the hay and on the horse-hair sofa in the parlor—all of which she seemed equally conversant about in her books—it would be more than that. It would matter.

She was so untouched, so guileless she unnerved him, made him feel awkward and unsure.

He was a man of a million lines, most of which could get him into any woman's bedroom. He didn't know one that would get him beyond Frances Moon's front porch.

"Aren't you about done with your bat act?" Carter shook the last crumbs out of the bag and stuffed them into his mouth, then started in on a package of Twinkies.

Jack spread his arms, then crossed them slowly once, then again. "Almost."

He usually hung until the world according to Jack Neillands had straightened itself out. But as long as visions of a honey-haired woman lurked behind his eyelids every time he shut his eyes, that wasn't going to happen. He sighed.

Carter shook his head. "Foolishness."

Jack disagreed. "It's good for me. Straightens the spine. Relieves stress. Takes pressure off my feet."

"And puts it on your brain where you least need it."

Jack grinned wryly. "Maybe if you'd hang upside down it would improve your chances with the LaBoobs of the world."

"Think it would make me look like Redford, do you?"

"Worth a try."

Carter shook his head, crumpled the bag and made a hook shot into the wastebasket. "No, thanks. I'll leave the unnatural acts up to you. You can see what it gets you, though. All that skiing wrecked your knee. And for what? You were too gimpy even to take advantage of all those women around the lodge. Margie and Paula wanted to know where you'd gone."

Margie and Paula were part of the legion of reasons he'd left. "I drove around," Jack said. "I was restless, wanted to see the countryside. Dropped in on a . . . friend of an artist I know."

He still hadn't mentioned Frances by name.

He'd brushed off Carter's questions in Vermont and he'd brush them off now, too. Jack Neillands didn't kiss and tell, he thought righteously.

Especially when there was nothing to say.

Carter popped the top on another beer and started in on the second Twinkie. "Sounds pretty boring to me. And if it sounds boring to me, it must've been a bummer for you." He yawned and stretched. "You wanta go down to Atlantic City this weekend to make up for it?"

Jack arched upward and caught on to the chinning bar, eased the boots off it and swung down. "I'll see," he said vaguely, no more interested in Atlantic City than he had been in LaBoobs.

He was only interested in Frances, damn it. He'd gone to Vermont for a little exercise, a fresh perspective, a challenge. He'd expected to come back refreshed, rejuvenated. Not frustrated within an inch of his life.

"Or," Carter went on dreamily, "we could fly down to Florida." He smiled. "Get a place on the beach, pick up a few women . . ."

"We'll see." Jack padded into the kitchen, turned on the tap and stuck his head under it, letting the cold water drum on his skull, wishing he could wash Frances out of it.

"You all right, Jack?" Carter sounded concerned.

Jack straightened up. No luck. She was still there. "What? Oh, yeah. Fine." He toweled his hair.

"You look lousy."

"Thanks."

"Don't mention it."

"Maybe you're right," Jack said finally. "Maybe Florida."

Florida sounded good. Distant. Distracting. There had to be plenty of women in Florida more suitable than Frances Moon. Plenty.

Carter slapped him on the back. "That's cool. I'll look into it." He glanced at his watch. "Oops, gotta run. Got in a shipment of soy milk and tofu this afternoon and I haven't done the paperwork yet. Catch you tomorrow."

"Yeah," Jack said absently. "Hey, Carter."

His friend turned around.

"You going back to the store now?" Jack Sprat's Health and Wellness Store, he meant.

"Yeah."

"Better wipe the Twinkie crumbs off your mouth."

ELSEWHERE IN THE WORLD Jack Neillands would've been a nine day's wonder.

In Boone's Corner, because Vermonters have less patience with glitz and frivolity than most people, it only took five.

By Wednesday the tongues had stopped wagging, the gossips had stopped speculating, and "a return to normality," to correct a phrase, had swept down the mountain.

Frances finished her galleys, assisted at a lambing, finished rerouting Ernie and Bert's kitchen plumbing, plunged back into her current first draft, and followed Ebenezer Toot from tree to tree all over her property hanging sugaring buckets in the hope that before long they would need them.

She chopped wood, made bread, spun wool, and when she couldn't think of anything else to keep herself occupied, allowed herself to be pressed into grating nutmegs for Annabel.

And if, now and then, Jack Neillands's cocky grin or slumberous blue eyes crept into her mind, she ruthlessly evicted them and grated on.

"Is this enough?" She held up the bowl of grated nutmegs for Annabel to inspect.

"Enough? I could pave roads with it, for heaven's sake."

Frances grimaced. "You didn't say how many. I was only trying to help."

"I know. You have helped. You've been Little Ms. Helpful all week—chopping wood, baking bread, grating nutmegs, spinning wool. What's got into you?"

"Nothing. I enjoy it. I like helping out, you know that. You people are my family."

Annabel smiled at her. "I do know it, and we love you, too. But—" she shook her head "—you really ought to take some time for yourself."

Frances shrugged. "And do what?"

"Enjoy yourself. Go away for a day or two. See the world."

"I've seen the world. It's highly overrated. Besides, I am enjoying myself. There's no place other than Boone's Corner I'd rather be."

Annabel considered her, her warm brown eyes knowing. "You've scarcely left it in five years."

"Why should I? It has everything I want."

"But not everything you need."

Frances looked at her sharply. "What's that supposed to mean?"

"Just what I said. You need more than me and the kids, more than Ernie and Bert and Eb. You have us and you have your sheep. You need someone who appreciates you, cares about you. Loves you."

"A man, you mean?" Frances said flatly.

"Yes."

"I don't believe you're saying this. Is this really Annabel Archer, a woman of the nineties, happily unmarried mother of two? The woman who once told me men were the dregs of the universe, that I was better off without them?"

"Him," Annabel corrected. "You were—you are—better off without him, without Stephen Cabot. Now there's a man who's a dreg. He used you and he left you. He certainly never appreciated you."

She shouldn't have expected Annabel to pull her punches. She never had. "He appreciated the money I brought in," Frances said quietly.

"Too right. And the moment he got his degree, even that appreciation stopped."

Frances sighed. "If I'd been able to change...if I'd learned to want the same things he did..."

"A Porsche and a yacht at Marblehead, you mean?" Annabel's tone was dry. "Oh, come on."

"He'd never had any of those things," Frances excused.

"Neither had you."

"I never wanted them. I still don't. But Stephen did. That's why he worked so hard to get into Harvard." It was a truth Frances had learned the hard way. She'd believed that she and Stephen had everything in common, from their solid, no-frills, middle-class backgrounds to their fundamental values. She'd come for a love of learning, for the challenge to her intellect. Stephen, she discovered as time went on, had come for the ticket to the life-style he desired.

"Just what I said, a dreg."

Frances smiled wistfully, wishing it were that simple. "I don't know. I think it was just that the more he saw of power and wealth, the more he felt we were missing out. He wanted it for me, too."

"Did he?" Annabel said. "I wonder."

Sometimes Frances wondered, too, even though she didn't want to. For if he hadn't, then Stephen hadn't loved her. Not really. And if Stephen hadn't loved her...

"You're better off without him," Annabel said again stoutly.

Frances stared out the window at the softly falling snow, thought about how pure and clean it looked, how undefiled. She turned back and gave Annabel a wistful smile. "I know."

"But that doesn't mean you're better off without any man at all."

"You've survived," Frances pointed out.

"I've come to terms. There's a difference."

"Well, I've come to terms, too."

"Have you? Can you honestly say you didn't entertain a few fantasies about Jack Neillands last weekend?"

Frances managed a laugh. "Of course I did. That's how I met him in the first place. And I love my fantasies. But I'm not fool enough to believe in them coming true. Fantasy and reality don't mix."

"They might."

"No. Oh, no." Frances was sure about that.

If they did, she thought later when she left Annabel's and walked home through the snow, she would have written herself a happy ending long before this.

She would have given herself a man who liked the same things she did—home and hearth, children, animals, cold nights and warm fires. She would have given herself a man who valued commitment, fidelity, tenderness, love. She would have given herself a man like the one Annabel talked about—a man who loved her for all of herself, not just the bits that were useful to him at the moment.

Those were the sorts of men she wrote about.

She wouldn't care if he was heart-stoppingly handsome like Jack Neillands was. She wouldn't care if his hair was razor cut and his clothes had high-class labels. And she certainly wouldn't care if he drove a fast car.

Those things, as she'd tried to tell Stephen, didn't matter.

But eventually she'd had to face the inevitable—to Stephen they had.

"Forget Stephen," she told herself. "That was a long time ago."

But seeing Jack Neillands—who was everything Stephen wanted to be: wealthy, successful, sure of himself—brought it all back to her.

And kissing Jack Neillands had done something else. It had unnerved her, reminded her of dreams set aside, of hopes tarnished and almost forgotten.

She'd thought herself immune to the temptations of those dreams. She was wrong.

But she wasn't a fool.

"Forget Jack Neillands, too," she told herself.

Because there was no doubt in her mind that by now he had forgotten her.

By Saturday afternoon, Frances had more wool than she'd have lifetimes to knit into sweaters, more loaves of bread than the Russian Army could consume in a winter, and enough wood to heat most of central Vermont. She was a chapter ahead of her schedule on her rough draft, and the weather was still too cold for the sap to run.

It was a good thing she had another ewe in labor, else she might've considered taking up posthole digging to fill up her hours.

She wished the high-school girls she invited out every summer from Boston were here now. They were always wonderful distractions. But it would be months before Maeve and Carleen arrived.

She couldn't just sit and think, couldn't spin fantasies the way she'd always been wont to do. Not now. Because, even

though she'd determined to forget him, all her fantasies re-
volved around Jack.

It was horrible. Her imagination had always been her
refuge, her strength. No longer.

It had gone over to the enemy now.

She didn't tell Annabel that. She didn't tell anyone. Jack
Neillands was dying a natural death in the minds and hearts
of Boone's Corner's inhabitants, and Frances had no intention of resurrecting him. What, after all, would be the
point?

She would forget, too. It would simply take a little more
time until it happened to her.

All the same, she was grateful for poor old Lolita, the ewe
who had been muttering and grunting restlessly around the
yard all morning. Lolita had lambed successfully the past
three years, but she'd never been as big as she was this time
or as uncomfortable.

Frances had been watching her carefully for several days,
hoping that when the time came, if there was trouble, it
would occur on a weekday during vet's hours.

Trust Lolita to begin labor on Saturday morning.

It began spitting snow not long after lunch and Frances
urged Lolita into the small barn. If she had to help with the
birth, she preferred to do it with some shelter. Now, the
ewe's water having broken two hours before and with still
nothing to show for it, she was glad she had.

Lolita began straining in earnest as the wind picked up
outside. Gusts of snow blew in the open door. A soft *baa* of
encouragement sounded behind her, and Frances looked up
to see Carlota, who had lambed three days before, peering
over the top of the pen. Carlota's delivery had been a breeze.
This one was taking forever. She called the vet.

"Sorry, dear. He's in Boston at a conference. Won't be
back till Monday," the receptionist said. "You could ring
Dr. Dean over at Gaithersburg. He's on call."

But Dr. Dean was already out delivering someone else's lambs, and Aaron, who, as the county ag agent, might have been of some help, had driven down to Worcester to see his brother.

"Ask Dr. Dean to come by if he gets back soon," Frances said. If he didn't, she was on her own.

She went back to the barn and crouched beside the ewe, scratching her behind the ear. "Just you and me, Lolly," she said softly. Lolita, who usually liked being scratched, jerked her head away and grunted and strained again, shifting irritably between contractions.

"Poor Lol'," Frances commiserated. She pulled out her book on sheep raising and opened it to the appropriate chapter.

She'd helped deliver lambs before, but it was like doing taxes. Every time she did it, it was different, and she didn't do it often enough that she felt confident.

Lolita needed her confidence, though, because she looked sorely lacking in her own. She looked tired, worn down. Her efforts were beginning to flag.

A cursory examination showed Frances the trouble. Instead of the presentation of the nose and front feet, she found a tangle of legs and feet. Twins. At least.

Her job was clear. Crooning soothingly to the ewe, Frances settled into the straw, washed her hands and arms in a bucket of tepid water and set to work.

It was freezing outside, not much better in the barn, but it didn't take long for Frances to begin to sweat. The exertion of fighting against the contractions, trying to sort the lambs' legs began to tell on her.

Finally she found two that belonged to the same lamb and succeeded in tying them together. "Hang on, my lovely."

Her jeans and shirt, clean this morning, were covered with muck and blood. She had grime under her short, clipped nails, smears of nameless goo on her face. But they were almost there.

"Not long now, sweetheart," she crooned.

She wiped a weary hand across her forehead and shoved back her tangled hair, wishing she'd thought to put it in a braid. But there was no time to stop now. She felt the beginning of the next contraction and got ready to pull.

"One more time, girl, one more time," she sang softly, her fingers knotting on the string, ready. And as the contraction built, straining and grunting—Lolita pushing and Frances pulling—the first little lamb slid into the world.

It twitched, then quivered, and Frances felt her throat tighten as she stared, dazed and delighted at this slippery miracle of new life.

But there was no time to stop and appreciate it now. Another contraction had already begun. Swiftly she scooped up the newborn lamp, wiping off the mucus and setting it by Lolita's nose. Then she went back to help with the delivery of the second lamb.

A shadow fell across the doorway.

"Trust a vet to show up when the crisis is over," Frances said without looking around. "I did all the work, but you can deliver the second one if you want."

There was a pause, then, "No, thanks."

Frances's head jerked around. Her eyes bugged.

He stood, thumbs hooked in his belt loops, jacket splayed open, just inside the door of the barn. Tall, sexy, masculine. Clean. Jack.

Frances's heart slammed against the wall of her chest. She stared, openmouthed, then shut her eyes, dismayed, disbelieving.

When she opened them again he was—heaven help her—still there.

Not fair, she thought. *Not fair.* How was she going to forget him if every time she turned around, he was standing there? "What did I ever do to you?" she asked God in a mutter only He could hear.

God chose not to answer. But just then Lolita grunted, another contraction overtaking her. She had stopped trying to clean the newborn lamb, and lay panting on her side.

She'd been in labor too long, and Frances knew it. She had to help deliver the second lamb—and fast.

"Help me," she said, thrusting a roll of paper towels at Jack. "Dry the lamb, will you? Then put him back by his mother."

She didn't have time to look and see if he did it. Lolita's feet kicked out pitifully.

"Hang on, sweetie," she murmured. "Just a little longer."

It took two more contractions to deliver the second, larger lamb, and when she did, it wasn't breathing. It lay limp and lifeless in the straw.

"Is it—?"

"Damn it. No, it isn't! It can't!"

She couldn't let it die. Not now. Not after all this. Frances swiped the mucus away from its mouth and nose. "Breathe, damn you," she urged the tiny lamb. "Come on. You can't quit now. Breathe."

She scooped the lamb into her arms and bent her head, breathing into its mouth, willing it to live. "Come on," she begged, heart in her throat, as she massaged the small animal. "Come on."

Snow blew in the doorway. The wind glued her shirt to her sweat-soaked back. Frances didn't notice, breathing, exhorting, breathing again. There was no response.

Then, long after she'd given up hope, right when her tears were beginning to well, a foreleg twitched, the throat worked and the lamb gave a jerky gasp.

"Oh!"

"By God, you did it," she heard a murmur behind her, and suddenly she remembered Jack.

He looked amazed, astonished, awestruck. Thrilled. Triumphant. He was smiling all over his face. And Frances, just as thrilled, just as triumphant, smiled back. The lamb struggled in her arms, bumping her nose with his own. She chuckled, she laughed. And the tears came anyway, streaming down her face.

"Oh, damn," she muttered, humiliated.

Snatching the paper towels away, she swabbed at her cheeks, making a bigger mess.

"Here. Let me." Jack took them back and caught her face in his hand, daubing at it gently. His own face was scant inches away, his dark eyes warm and intent, and Frances stood mesmerized. His lips touched hers, warm and gentle, persuasive. And Frances, struck by the joy of the moment, didn't resist. Not then. Not until the lamb struggled between them, kicking against her breasts. And then she realized, recollected, and retreated for all she was worth. She remembered the way he'd kissed her last time. She remembered the way she'd felt.

She jerked back, batting his hand away. "Please! I—I'll get blood all over you. Don't."

He looked at her oddly. "Did I hurt you?"

She shook her head, flustered. "No, of course not. But I'm covered with muck and you're... clean, and—" She ducked her head, bending industriously over the second lamb, cleaning it off with a thoroughness all out of proportion to what was required.

"I don't mind," Jack assured her easily.

But Frances did. "No," she said, and prayed he wouldn't press the issue.

He didn't. He simply watched as the first lamb nuzzled against Lolita and began to suckle noisily. And when Frances set it down, the second lamb wobbled to its feet and butted in. Lolita sighed and closed her eyes.

Jack chuckled. Frances slanted a glance at him. He was sitting on his haunches next to them, watching the lambs, his fists full of wet, bloody paper towels, a look of awe still on his face. It made him warm and human and all too appealing.

His eyes shifted slowly as he sensed her looking at him. They came to rest on her face.

"Beautiful," he said.

He meant the lambs, of course. He certainly couldn't mean her, though the way he was looking at her made her blood simmer. And the way he'd kissed her...!

Why? she asked God again. Why was He doing this to her? She'd learned her lesson with Stephen. He didn't need to teach it to her again.

"What are you doing here?" she asked, and was surprised to see the color rise in Jack's cheeks.

He looked, for a moment, as awkward as she felt. "I...came back."

"Skiing?"

"No." There was a pause. "To see you."

Oh, heavens. "Me? Why?"

"Why do you think?"

"I can't imagine," she said quickly, trying to defuse the situation. "Unless," she added brightly, "you're taking up writing and want advice."

"No, thanks."

"Then?"

"I met you. I liked you. I wanted to know you better. How's that?" Jack's tone was almost belligerent.

"There must be a million more suitable women for you to want to know better."

"I told myself the same thing."

And even though it was undoubtedly true and exactly what she wished for, she found that nettled. She opened her mouth to say something when he went on.

"But it wasn't true," he said, contradicting her thoughts, his deep blue eyes meeting her own unwaveringly. "Not true at all."

When she was a girl she would have believed it. She would have hugged it to herself, then embroidered on it to her heart's content. She would have had them married with a half a dozen children in the blink of an eye.

Now she got to her feet hastily, swiping at her jeans, trying in vain to brush them off, trying to put as much distance between herself and her fantasy-come-to-life as possible.

Jack got to his feet, too. Unfair, she thought. She was tall, but he was taller, also more powerful, also undeniably more attractive, even with his hair mussed, his jeans dusty and a streak of dirt on his cheek.

Only a man like Jack Neillands, she thought irritably, could look sexy after being on the business end of a ewe in a lambing pen. Damn.

And there was that quirky grin again. She looked away. "You're not making sense," she said querulously.

"I know."

Disconcerted, Frances stared at him. He stared right back. She looked away first, bothered by the warm light of appreciation in his eyes.

There was only one thing that a look like that could mean, and one didn't need any imagination at all to figure it out.

He was back and he meant to have her. He might not be saying so in so many words, but Frances knew. She was a writer. She was an expert at reading between the lines.

Was this the week to seduce the country bumpkin? she wondered irritably. Had he gone through all the women in New York? It seemed possible. If she let him, he'd make short work of her, too, and she knew it.

A nervous shiver coursed down her spine. A remembrance of her eager response to his kiss taunted her. *Go away,* she pleaded silently. *Just go away.*

But it was obvious Jack was staying right where he was.

HE'D LIED TO CARTER. He'd mumbled something vague about a reshoot this weekend, a last-minute deal. Go to Florida without me, he'd said. Enjoy yourself. Have a ball. Don't worry about me.

And then, bright and early Saturday morning, he'd taken off for Vermont.

By Thursday night he'd realized that his preoccupation with Frances Moon was not going to fade away. In fact with every passing day he thought of her more.

He'd gone down to Mick's for cover shoots five more times that week, and only during the one in which he'd worn camouflage and carried an M-16, had he managed to convey the proper expressions without invoking Frances Moon in his mind.

Friday, in one last-ditch attempt to shake the aberration, he went out with one of the hottest new models in town, a young woman with even more pizzazz than LaBoobs.

He took her to a cozy French provincial restaurant just off Third Avenue where the sauces were subtle and the Chardonnay smooth. She batted her outrageously long eyelashes at him, pouted her extraordinarily full lips at him, and, as they were leaving the restaurant, swished her nonexistent hips at him.

She talked about Boise and basketball, cheerleading and chili dogs. She lamented not going to college one minute and blathered about which were the best casinos in Monte Carlo the next. She spent a half an hour worrying about whether by Monday's shoot in the Hamptons she'd get zits.

He had her home by ten-thirty and didn't regret it a bit.

He needed to get to bed early, he told her. He had a long drive ahead of him in the morning. Oh, she said, where was he going?

Vermont, he said.

That was when he first realized that he was, in fact, going back to Boone's Corner.

He called Carter and begged off. He had to see Frances. Far from forgetting her, not seeing her all week had only made his obsession worse.

What was she doing?

Was she writing? Feeding the goats? Reading by the fire? Spending time with someone else? With Aaron-the-jerk?

That last thought was curiously irritating. *He* wanted to be the one to spend time with her, talk to her, laugh with her... make love with her.

If he'd gone to bed with her last weekend, he probably would've forgotten her by now. He hadn't. She was an itch that he still wanted to scratch.

And Jack Neillands was used to doing what he wanted to do, getting what he wanted to get.

In this case that meant Frances.

He stood now, looking at the dirty, disheveled woman standing in the straw in front of him and wondered what he thought he was doing.

Driving up here he'd only thought he wanted to bed her, to exorcise the effect she had on him. Seeing her again, he knew suddenly there was more to it than that.

Maybe it was the lamb that had done it. Maybe it was seeing her fighting for its life with a concentration, a fierce tenderness that he never encountered in his day-to-day existence that had made him take a long look.

He didn't know. He only knew he wanted to know her, understand her, figure out what made her tick.

Something had made her warm and loving, fierce and caring. Something had made her prickly and distant.

He was going to get to the bottom of it—to the bottom of Frances Moon. Starting now.

He opened his mouth when another voice broke the silence.

"*Fran*-ces! *Fran*-cesss! Where are you?" Footsteps thudded across the yard and through the door. A towheaded boy of about ten skidded to a halt.

His jaw sagged at the sight of Jack. Then his gaze swiveled to Frances, his eyes wide and astonished. "It's him! It's the R—"

"Lief," Frances cut in, "I'd like you to meet Jack Neillands. Jack, this is my friend and neighbor, Leif Campbell." She moved closer to the door, putting the boy between herself and Jack.

"Hi." Jack regarded him without enthusiasm. Another distraction. Just what he didn't need.

"Lolita had twins, Leif. Look." Frances pointed toward the pen.

But Leif didn't notice. He turned back to Jack. "Is that your car down the end of the road? It's cool! How fast can it go?"

Jack smiled. If he couldn't have privacy, he hoped at least for an ally. "It's pretty fast. Want to take a look at it?"

"You bet!"

Frances scowled at them both. "Go right ahead," she said shortly. "I'm going to get cleaned up."

Jack fell into step beside her. "A better idea."

She sighed. "I suppose you'd like a shower, too."

He grinned. "Is that an invitation?"

She blushed. "No, it is not." She took off, practically running toward the house.

Jack followed, enjoying the view.

Chapter Four

He was coming to dinner. With her.

Not at her invitation, of course. Not that it mattered. Leif had taken things into his own hands at once. He'd been sent to see if Frances was coming to the potluck. In a spirit of voluble neighborliness he saw to it that Jack was coming, too.

"Sure you can come. The more the merrier Ma always says," he told Jack.

And when Frances said, "I don't think . . ." Leif finished the sentence, saying, ". . . she'd let me in the door if she knew you were here and I didn't bring you."

Jack looked at Frances. "You're going?"

She nodded.

"Then I am, too."

And that, Frances knew, was that.

"Great! I'll tell Ma." Leif headed toward the door. Then he stopped and turned back to Jack. "D'you s'pose I could just call her and we could ride over in your car?"

"Don't see why not."

Frances, feeling she was fast losing her grip, shook her head. "I'll walk."

Jack frowned. "Then I will, too."

"No," she said quickly. "Really. You drive Leif. He'd love it. And I...I just want a breath of fresh air." A chance to get her bearings, to put a perspective on things.

Jack looked at her worriedly. "Are you all right? You're not too tired? All that business with the lambs didn't..."

She shook her head. "No, of course not. I'm fine. Please," she said, flashing him a brief smile. "Please. For Leif. He'd enjoy it."

Jack nodded. But when Leif was out of earshot, he turned back to her. "The question is, Frances Moon, what would you enjoy?"

And Frances, who was afraid to think about that, fled.

SHE HOPED he would hate it, hoped he would turn up his yuppie nose at Annabel's old frame house, at her motley collection of friends, at the baked beans, corn bread, pot roast and salads they shared.

She hoped they'd hate him, look down their disdainful Vermont noses at this Flatland yuppie in their midst. She hoped they'd indicate in no uncertain terms that this man, like Stephen, was better left alone.

She should have known better.

Libby didn't giggle, she cooed. Staunch, no-nonsense Annabel simpered and smiled. Ebenezer looked down his long narrow nose and proclaimed Jack "a right smart young feller." And, given enough time, Frances suspected he could've charmed the habits right off Ernie and Bert.

"Such a honey," Sister Ernestine whispered to Frances after supper as they watched Jack wiping dishes with Bert. "I like a man who cleans his plate. Isn't he dear?"

"Ooooh, what a smile," Sister Bertha raved later as Jack obligingly, although surprisingly red faced, autographed Libby's poster. "And he's on the cover of your new book, Fran? Why, sales will go right through the roof."

"If they do," Frances said tightly, "it will be because it's so well written."

Bert's blue eyes twinkled innocently. "But of course, love. What did you think I meant?"

Frances ground her teeth. She looked over at Jack. He was bending over a fat volume of herbal remedies, listening intently as Annabel explained something to him. Before dinner he'd expressed fascination with her herbal products, organic compounds and folklore. Grinning, he'd told her he knew just the man for her.

Instead of rising up in righteous anger at the thought of anyone presuming to suggest she needed a man in her life—which she had done on every other occasion as long as Frances had known her—Annabel simply smiled, batted her eyelashes and said, "Bring him on."

Frances was stunned.

But Annabel's reaction was typical. The Congenitally Unimpressed Of Boone's Corner, Vermont, were eating out of Jack Neillands's hand.

And, far from being put off by Annabel's Earth Mother guise, Ebenezer's taciturnity and occasional oracular pronouncements, and Ernie and Bert's Save-the-World ethic, Jack appeared equally charmed by them.

He expressed fascination with Eb's talent for whittling, and Frances was astonished to hear the old man offer to teach him. She'd expressed her interest often enough, and Eb had never mentioned teaching her.

She clutched her coffee mug and scowled at Eb who, as usual, remained impervious to it. So she looked for support from Ernie and Bert only to overhear Bert telling Jack about their rattletrap convent just over the hill.

"Wants us to retire to Boston, the Mother Superior does," Bert told him. "Too old to be hanging on by our lonesomes out here, she says. But I say we're too old to change our ways. Can't see me and Ernie in a city, can you? Heavens, we'd be run over by a bus."

Jack smiled sympathetically. "You'd rather be here, anyway," he guessed.

"Oh, my, yes," Bert said. Then she sighed. "But the house is a drain on the order, and it's too big for just us."

"You ought to turn it into a bed and breakfast."

Bert nodded. "But we'd have to advertise. Fix it up first. Refurbish. Spend money," she concluded gloomily. "Which is just what we haven't got. Peace and quiet we've got. And that's it."

Jack grimaced. "I see what you mean." The two of them looked at each other in perfect understanding.

Then Ernie sighed. "The Lord will provide."

Jack nodded. "I hope so."

"After all, He provided us with Frances," Bert chipped in.

Frances stiffened at the mention of her name. She looked suspiciously at the small woman perched on the sofa.

Bert didn't look at her. She went right on, "We can't do all the work, though we try. But what we can't do, Frances can. She's a savior, that girl. Just this past week she was trying to teach me how to install the new plumbing and ended up doing it herself."

"She did, did she?" Jack grinned.

Frances frowned. Drat Bert anyway. As if being able to do her own plumbing would impress him. Not that she wanted to impress him. But, really, the women he knew probably never got their fingernails broken.

Bert, oblivious, beamed and went on. "Oh, my, yes. If our Frances can't do it, it can't be done. She and Aaron— you know Aaron—?" She waited for Jack's infinitesimal nod. "The two of them put on a new roof for us last year."

"No kidding," Jack murmured.

Frances groaned.

"She can cook, too. And sew. And crochet," Bert said.

"And I have all my own teeth," Frances said finally in despair. "For heaven's sake, Bert, he's not buying me at an auction."

Bert tittered. "No, of course not. But he has a right to know."

"He does? Why?"

Bert looked at her aghast. "Why, I expect he's come to woo you."

"Woo?" Frances sputtered into her coffee, her cheeks burning. "Oh, good heavens."

"I know an attentive young man when I see one," Bert said huffily. "I wasn't a nun all my life, you know."

"You may not be one much longer, either," Frances warned her while Jack sat back and laughed at her discomfort.

"Jack!" It was Leif, halfway down the stairs from the loft. "You wanta see my posters? I got a Lamborghini, two Porsches, and a Ferrari F40."

Jack looked as if he'd rather stay where he was for more exciting revelations. But he shrugged. "Sure. Why not?" He got up easily and started across the room. "Don't go 'way," he said to Frances and winked at her.

She wished she dared. She was the one who felt like the discomfitted outsider tonight. Jack seemed to be one of the gang.

"Didn't believe you for a minute, I didn't," Bert said once Jack had gone up the stairs. She pleated her habit as she spoke and looked at Frances with knowing eyes.

"What are you talking about?"

"You said we'd seen the end of him. I thought he'd be back, first time I saw him. Said to Ernie then, he's the man for Fran, I did. I think so more now. You just watch, I said."

"Nonsense," Frances said firmly. "He's just passing through."

Bert smiled. "You said that last week, too."

Frances picked at a bit of lint on her cords, her chin jutting stubbornly. "So? He passed back through."

"Piffle. He came to see you."

Seeing wasn't what he had in mind, Frances wanted to say. He might be after her, but it wasn't to woo. She wouldn't fit into his life-style any more than she had into Stephen's. And she was sure Jack knew it. He was after what he could get. He'd probably decided to see if she made love as well as she wrote about it. But she didn't say so because for all her pretended worldliness, Sister Bertha Comiskey was shockable.

Still, she couldn't sit here and let Bert spin further fantasies. It wouldn't do either of them any good. She glanced at her watch and got to her feet. "I need to go."

Bert looked up dismayed. "Goodness, dear, it's early yet."

"I have work to do, and I need to check on Lolita and the lambs."

She turned to Annabel who had cornered Jack as he came back downstairs. "I'm off now," she announced. "Don't feel you need to come with me," she said to Jack as she plucked up her jacket and headed for the door. "Stay and enjoy yourself. See you tomorrow, Eb. Bye, all."

And she was out the door without looking back.

The blessed cold was welcome after the stifling heat and closeness of Annabel's living room. The solitude was welcome after all those speculative eyes. Frances knew what they'd been thinking. Exactly what Bert had been thinking.

But it wasn't true, couldn't be true. And there was no use pretending it was. It was better this way. They could enjoy this genial stranger in their midst. And if she was gone, with her chin in the air and a smile on her face, they wouldn't worry about her.

She sucked in a deep breath and began to walk swiftly down the hill.

She'd got scarcely fifty yards when she heard an engine start up. Moments later headlights picked her out. She kept walking. The car coasted up silently alongside her and Jack rolled down the window.

"Get in."

She stayed where she was. "You didn't have to leave."

"You left."

"But that didn't mean you had to. You were having a good time."

"You weren't."

"Of course I was. I was just getting tired. I wanted to check on the lambs. And then I have some work to do."

"So I'll come with you. Get in."

"Why are you doing this?"

He grinned. "Wooing you, you mean?"

She grimaced. "Don't pay any attention to Bert. She has some strange ideas."

"They seem like pretty good ideas to me."

"She doesn't know what you really want."

"And you do?" His voice was soft but definitely challenging.

"I won't go to bed with you, you know."

A corner of Jack's mouth twitched. "Have I asked?"

Frances's face flamed. Thank God for nighttime. There was no way, she hoped, he could see the crimson color of her cheeks.

"What are you afraid of, Francesca Luna?" His voice was oddly gentle.

"Nothing. I'm not afraid of anything."

"You always run from men like this?"

"I'm not running. I just don't see any point in—in you and—and me."

"But I do."

The simple certainty of those words unnerved her. "We're poles apart."

He shook his head. "Not really."

"Of course we are. You're a big-city boy, I'm a country girl. You drive in the fast lane. My lane has wagon wheel ruts in it. You have this incredibly glitzy job and I . . . I sit at home and spin fantasies. They can't compare."

"They can. They do. We're remarkably similar, in fact. We both deal with the imagination. You weave yours with words. I do mine in print or on the screen. But we do the same thing, we cater to people's fantasies."

Frances paused, struck by the notion, then shook her head, afraid of where it could lead. "That's just it. They're fantasies, not reality," she protested.

"We make reality," Jack said softly. "And I think we could make a pretty wonderful reality, Francesca Luna."

But Frances shook her head. No, they couldn't. *She* couldn't. She'd tried. And failed. She hugged her arms across her chest.

A car approached from behind, headlights gleamed off the snow. It slowed, waiting. Jack didn't move, just looked at Frances, waiting, too.

She knew he'd sit there forever. It was the sort of man he was. He smiled. Frances sighed. She jerked open the door and clambered in. "Satisfied?"

Jack grinned and pressed down on the accelerator. "It's a start."

Chapter Five

He was driving her nuts.

One minute he was coming on like gangbusters, the next he was delivering her to her doorstep and striding off into the dark.

His persistence all day long, his following her when she left Annabel's, his determination to drive her home, his hungry gaze and smoldering smile had made her certain she knew what to expect.

But just when they reached the front porch and she turned to take a stand, he slipped the house key from her nerveless fingers, unlocked the door for her, touched her cheek for just a moment, then said, "Good night, Francesca Luna," and left.

Just *left*! As if...as if... Hell, she didn't even know as if what!

He truly was driving her nuts.

Frances stripped off her clothes, tugged on her night-gown and sought refuge under her fluffy down comforter, pulling it over her head as if total darkness might drive out the image of his handsome face.

Why? Why was he doing this to her?

She, who made her living writing books about romance, about relationships, about women and men, certainly didn't have a clue about this man.

"Is that such a big surprise?" she asked herself. She'd obviously never had a clue about Stephen, either. If she had, she would have seen how different their values were right from the start. She wouldn't have fallen in love with him. She wouldn't know the pain of love and loss, of inadequacy and failure the way she knew it now. The way she never wanted to know it again.

"Men," she muttered and flopped over onto her back, shifting restlessly about under the comforter. Harry landed on the bed with an *oof* and planted himself in the middle of her stomach, kneading it to requisite softness before he curled up and settled in.

Frances's hand stole out and scratched his ears. Good old Harry. Warm, furry Harry. He was the only bedmate she wanted.

And the only man she wanted in her life was a man like Ben Cutter. A man who existed between the covers of a book, who was predictable, controllable. A man who couldn't hurt her.

Not a man like Jack Neillands.

She couldn't handle him and she knew it.

She hadn't lied when she'd told Annabel that she didn't want a real live man at all.

As USUAL, what she wanted didn't matter a whit. Jack was back shortly after seven. He appeared when she was in the barn checking on the new lambs and feeding the goats.

One moment she was alone, and the next she felt the brush of something soft and slightly moist against the nape of her neck. Frances almost jumped a foot.

"Morning," Jack said almost into her ear.

Had those been his lips that had just touched her neck, for goodness sake? Frances's fingers surreptitiously rubbed at the spot.

"M-morning."

He looked disgustingly well rested and more than usually handsome, standing there in his faded jeans and soft green V-neck sweater. He grinned at her and leaned against the post of the lambing pen. "Sleep well?"

"Fine, thank you," Frances lied, busying herself arranging the hay in the rack as if it were a table setting she was fussing with. In fact she'd tossed and turned all night. She'd even got up and tried writing. But her hero, a blond giant of a Scandinavian this time, seemed to take on all the characteristics of Jack. Finally she'd erased the whole mess from the disk and crawled back into bed.

"Did you?" she asked politely now.

"Never better. Bacon's has good beds."

So that was where he'd been. She hadn't asked. If she had, she knew he'd say something about staying with her, not meaning it, she knew that now. He'd do it just to tease her. Her sister, Martha, was right, she was abominably easy to tease.

"So," he asked after a moment, "what'll we do today?"

"I have to work." The scene she'd tried yesterday and again last night showed no signs of working. Jess was fading from her mind to be replaced by Ben Cutter's alter ego. *I wonder why?* Frances thought wryly as that very same alter ego fell into step beside her.

"I'll help," he offered.

"I'm writing."

"I could help you there, too." He grinned. "Give you inspiration. And if you wanted to rehearse, try things out a little..."

"Right," Frances said dryly. "As if I'd get anything done with you there."

"Oh, we'd get a lot done," Jack said. "I promise."

She rolled her eyes, but she couldn't help smiling at his audacity. "I can't."

He shrugged equably. "Ah, well, no problem. I'll find something to do. I can read your books."

Frances blinked.

"I can, you know—read. I thought I'd proved that."

"Of course." There was no way she could've forgotten that. But the very thought sent waves of panic through her. "You don't want to bother with my books."

"Why not? Aren't they any good?"

That made her bristle. "Of course they're good." They were solid, well-written novels, soundly researched and carefully plotted. She was quite proud of them. She put a lot of herself in them—and that was exactly the problem.

She didn't mind at all writing straight from the heart for hundreds of thousands of people who would never lay eyes on her.

Writing for the eyes of Jack Neillands was another story altogether.

He saw quite a lot with those gorgeous blue eyes of his as she'd discovered when he'd read *Cutter's Promise*.

And what he would see in *Lone Star*, *The Forever Trap* or *Once a Butterfly* was something she didn't want to contemplate. Even less did she want to think about what he would make of the woman who wrote them.

But what was she going to say? No?

She supposed she could hope he would get bored and not delve deeply. But she found, perversely, that she didn't hope that at all.

If he tried to read one and chucked it away unread, she would be hurt and she knew it. She wanted his interest and approval. Only in her books, of course, she thought hastily.

"We'll see," she said.

"Have you eaten?" he asked as they walked into the house.

"Tea and toast. It's all I ever have."

"Even on Sunday?"

"Even on Sunday," she said firmly, guessing what he had in mind: the same thing Stephen usually had in mind on Sundays—going out for brunch at some trendy restaurant.

"Not enough to keep a grown woman alive. I'll fix you breakfast."

In the act of slipping off her boots, Frances paused and stared at him. Not "I'll take you out to breakfast," but "I'll fix you breakfast."

"Or are the cupboards bare?"

"No, of course not. But—"

But he had already disappeared into the kitchen. She heard him opening cupboards, and followed him to find him peering into the fridge, then nodding his head. "You've got enough. I can handle it."

Frances stared at him, bemused. "And what am I supposed to do while you're cooking breakfast?"

"You said you had lots of work to do. Go do it."

"You're serious?"

"I don't say what I don't mean, Francesca Luna," he drawled. The deep blue eyes bored into hers. The devastating grin mocked her.

Frances steeled herself against both. She hesitated fleetingly, then shrugged. "If you want to," she said and fled.

FRANCES COULD WORK in the silence of a tomb or rush hour at Grand Central Station. When she was in her own private world, the real world faded away. Her powers of concentration were awesome, legendary among her neighbors and friends.

"Don't mind Frances," they often said as they wandered in and out, banging doors and talking among themselves. "She doesn't even know we're here."

You couldn't have proved it that day.

Determinedly she switched on her computer, called up the file she was working on and sat down to the same scene in the cow barn she'd tried to work on in the middle of the night between Maggie and Jess. Downstairs she heard the refrigerator open and the egg carton slide out.

She tried to imagine the rustle of the cows eating hay, the soft murmur of Maggie's voice. She heard each bang of the cupboards, each rattle of the mixing bowls, the clatter of the utensils when Jack scavenged through her top drawer in search of heaven knew what.

She strained to hear the steady thrum of Jess's heart. She heard eggs crack, bacon sizzle, the whisk of a spoon in a bowl. She tried to imagine Jess's rough baritone. Her ears picked out Jack's soft, slightly off-key humming above the mechanical hum of her computer.

She wrote in twenty-seven minutes a grand total of four words.

She was trying gamely, albeit futilely, for the fifth when she heard his footsteps on the stairs.

A head appeared around the corner of the door of her study. "Come and get it."

Frances did. The table was set with a bowl of sliced fruit, stacks of buckwheat pancakes and maple syrup, crisply fried bacon, organic grape juice, and a pot of freshly brewed coffee. Frances's stomach growled just looking at it.

Jack grinned. "My mother always told me the way to a woman's heart was through her stomach."

"Somehow I didn't think it was my heart you wanted," Frances said.

Jack grinned. "Well, not only that."

She shook her head, trying to suppress a smile. "You're incorrigible."

"I try."

And he succeeded admirably. Handsome, charming, and he could cook, too. She should be flattered, Frances told herself. She *was* flattered. But she wasn't a fool. She couldn't think he was really interested in her. She was doubtless no more than the current challenge. But she bet plenty of women were interested in him.

He set a plate of pancakes and bacon in front of her. "Dig in."

She did. It was delicious, but more than delicious, it was a refuge. If she kept her mouth busy eating, she didn't have to try to find things to say.

"How's it going? You looked so intent."

Frances looked up, startled. Was her incompetence so obvious then? She guessed it must be. Stephen certainly seemed to have thought so.

"You were just staring at the screen, absolutely mesmerized."

"Oh!" He meant her writing. A wave of giddy relief washed over her. "Well," she hedged. "I do get wrapped up in it." Please, God, he would never know what—who—she was really thinking about.

"Tell me."

"Why?"

"I'm curious. I want to know."

She didn't speak for a moment, surprised at the request. No one, not even Annabel, voluntarily listened to her talk about her books. Annabel tried, but she didn't have the patience.

"I just can't," she'd said finally. "It's too abstract. How can you spend hours trying to understand the actions of people who don't even exist?"

"They exist in my mind," Frances had told her.

"But not in mine," Annabel had said and shrugged. "Sorry. I have enough trouble understanding my kids. I don't need to manufacture more people."

Frances didn't think of it as manufacturing. She sometimes thought of herself as the medium through which disembodied people found life on the pages of her books. But she hadn't ever said that to anyone. She didn't say it now.

But Jack was still waiting for her to say something, so hesitantly she began to describe her current book.

She described her hero Jess and heroine Maggie, her setting, the conflict. And Jack, unlike Annabel and everyone else, listened.

Frances warmed to her subject. The more she talked, the more relaxed she felt. For the first time since she'd felt his lips on her neck this morning, she felt as if she were in control.

"He's an outlaw then, this Jess?" Jack said. "I thought he was a hero."

Frances shrugged. "He is. And an outlaw. Provides all sorts of possibilities. And a little confusion. The heroine has to wonder if he's a good guy or a bad guy."

"Uh-huh." Jack nodded, looking at her speculatively.

Frances, suddenly aware of his scrutiny, flushed. She got up quickly and carried her dishes to the sink.

"It's a tricky business all the way around," she said quickly. "And if you'll excuse me . . . I've got to start making some progress." She said the last in a hurried mumble and vanished up the stairs.

JACK WAS ALL FOR PROGRESS—but he didn't think he'd made much. Not the sort he was used to at least, but then Frances wasn't the sort of woman he was used to, either. It was rather like being in a maze with a porcupine. You never knew when you were going to run into a wall or get stuck in the eye.

She was such an enigma. Distant, prickly, distracted, she seemed far more interested in the meal than the man who cooked it. She could give a lesser man an inferiority complex. But she wasn't giving him one—not as long as he remembered the way she responded when he'd kissed her.

Had it been a fluke? he wondered.

He'd love to try it again and find out. The kiss he'd managed yesterday after the lambing hadn't been evidence enough. He wanted more.

She wrote a good love scene, that was certain. But she didn't show many signs of wanting to let fiction become reality. Unless perhaps it was just him.

Humbling thought. Did Algernon or Aaron or whatever his name was have what it took to light her fire?

Jack ground his teeth. Someone had, that was certain. She wouldn't know all those things she wrote about if she were wholly innocent and unaware.

She sure as hell got sparkly eyed when she talked about her outlaw. In fact, the only sure-fire way past the marvelous Moon defenses seemed to be getting her talking about her books. Only then did she begin to unbend.

When she talked about her novels she lost her shyness, her face became animated, her gestures freer, her voice more vibrant.

He saw in her Molly McGuire. The same energy, the same enthusiasm.

When Molly had been with Ben, she'd been more alive. Whenever she'd looked at him, she'd sparkled. When Frances spoke of Jess the outlaw, she had done the same.

Jack's jaw clenched. He wanted Frances to look like that when she looked at him.

She rarely looked at him at all.

Damn Jess, Jack thought, staring up the stairs after her. Damn Ben Cutter. Damn all Frances Moon's clever, strong, brave and witty heroes.

What did they have that he didn't?

Physically he *was* Ben Cutter. And there was nothing on earth Ben Cutter—or any other of Frances Moon's heroes—could do that Jack Neillands couldn't do better.

He was damned if he was going to come in second to some paperback hero.

Frances was already sitting at her computer when he strode into the room. She looked up, startled.

"Don't mind me," Jack said, scanning the bookshelves. "I'll read."

"But—"

"Just work," he said gruffly. "That's what you wanted, isn't it?"

"Well, yes, but—"

He spotted a spine with Francesca Luna written on it in flowing script and snatched it down. Carrying it across to the armchair in the corner, he settled in, opened it up and began to read.

He read fast, absorbing all he could, getting to know the men in Frances Moon's life. First he met Gabe McPherson, the hero of Frances's *Forever Trap.* For three hours he lived with McPherson, a lighthouse keeper on the coast of Maine. McPherson was a strong, solitary, no-nonsense sort of man. The sort of man who knew what he wanted and went after it. A man who didn't take no for an answer. Not from corrupt salvagers, not from opinionated townspeople, not from his one true love, Jessica Trehearne.

A man like me, Jack thought and set his sights on Frances Moon.

She was hunched over her computer, staring at the screen, but her mind, he suspected was a hundred years and a thousand miles away. He wondered what she'd think if he told her he could be the Gabe McPherson in her life. He could make a pretty good guess.

He got up to put that book back and pick out another one. Frances banged away at the computer, not noticing him. He scowled at her. What did these men have, for God's sake?

This time he read about Garrett Hunter, Denis Ward's alter ego in *Lone Star.*

Garrett was strong, too. A know-it-all Texas ranger, exactly like Frances had said. He strode into Amelia's life and took it over. Jack liked the idea. He read. And read.

And the longer he read, the more frustrated he became. All Frances Moon's heroes were good men. Strong men,

determined men. But none of them wa[s]
he was.

He sat in the armchair and glared
wanting to grab her the way Gabe McP[h]
sica, wanting to whisk her away to a dese[rt]
Garrett Hunter did Amelia, wanting to
hall and make love to her in that wide sof[a]
the way he remembered Ben loving Mol[ly]

And why the hell not?

He had the same needs, the same desir[es]
McPherson, Garrett Hunter and every [othe]
ro had.

Plus, he was real.

He set the book aside and got purpo[se]
Frances was sitting unmoving at her c[omputer]
seeing he knew not what.

He knew what he saw—exactly wh[at]
seen—the most enticing, enigmatic, de[sirable]
ever met.

He slipped up behind her exactly the [way]
slipped up behind Molly. His arms went around her. Her
head snapped back and caught him square on the nose.

"Damnation!" Frances jumped to her feet, spinning
around, staring at him, her eyes wide and astonished.

Jack, hand to nose to stem the blood, shook his head.
"Wha' th' hell ja do tha' for?"

"Me? You!"

"I was only—" Jack began to wave an arm.

"You're dripping on the desk."

He was. Bright red spots of blood. Head still spinning, he
glared back at her. "Wha' ya 'spect?"

Frances rolled her eyes and reached for his hand. "Come
on." It would've been too much to hope that she'd understood his intentions and was leading him to the bedroom.

He followed her into the bathroom, where she soaked a washcloth and dabbed his nose with it. He winced, then pulled back as she dabbed it again. "Cripes."

"Serves you right. What on earth was that all about?"

"I was reading your books."

She stared at him.

He shrugged. "Ben Cutter did it."

"You're *not* Ben Cutter." Her tone was suddenly fierce.

Their gazes locked, Jack's still slightly befuddled, Frances's more irritated than he'd ever seen it.

He grimaced, wanting sympathy, a little understanding, maybe even a kiss. He gave her a hard look. "And you're sure as hell not Molly McGuire, either!"

Frances flinched. Her lips pressed into a tight line.

Jack angled his face, the better to see it in the mirror. "I need ice."

"It isn't bleeding now."

"I still need ice."

"It'll be all right."

"I have to have my damn picture taken five million times tomorrow. *I need ice!*"

Stricken, Frances turned and flew out the door. He heard her pounding down the stairs. She was back minutes later with some ice in a plastic bucket.

She thrust it at him. "Here."

Jack scooped some out, wrapped it in the washcloth and pressed it against his nose. "Your head is a lethal weapon."

"It was instinctual. I was hardly expecting to be attacked."

"Attacked?" He stared at her, incredulous. "You thought I was going to rape you?"

"Of course not!"

"Then, what do you mean, attacked?"

Her color heightened even more. She looked away. She dug her toe into the rug. "You know very well what I mean."

"That I wanted to make love with you."

Her fists clenched. "Have sex."

"What?"

"It wouldn't have been making love." She fixed him with a stare as lethal as her head had been. "Love would've had nothing to do with it."

"And love is what you want?"

"From you?" She gave a short laugh. "From you I don't want anything at all."

They glowered at each other then, Jack bristling, angry and surprisingly hurt, Frances looking righteous as all get-out.

Did she think he didn't care, for God's sake?

Did she think he spent entire weekends following around women he hardly knew just so he could sneak up on them and jump their bones?

God knew what she thought; he didn't. She was the most perverse woman he'd ever met. Any other woman and he'd have been making love not war with her now.

Misunderstood, spurned, he tossed her book down and turned toward the door. "Suit yourself," he said gruffly. "I've got to go."

Frances, stony faced, nodded. She followed him downstairs, hovering about while he tied his shoes and put on his jacket. She cleared her throat once, but she never spoke.

Just as well. Jack couldn't imagine what she'd say.

When she did speak, as he was going out the door, it astonished him.

"It was nice of you to drop by." She sounded like a duchess at tea.

He stopped dead and stared at her. "Is that what I did, drop by?"

If Frances was aware of his sarcasm, it didn't show. Her face had a closed expression on it. She just looked at him, then scooped Harry the cat into her arms. She walked out on the porch with him, carrying Harry in front of her as if he were some sort of furry shield.

He was. A very effective one. Jack couldn't have touched her if he'd wanted to. He didn't, unless it might be to wring her neck.

"It's been interesting," Frances said.

Jack, nose still literally out of joint, stared, then shook his head. He thought he knew women, but he didn't know this one. "Hasn't it just?" he said.

So. It had happened, just as she'd thought it would. He was gone, and he wouldn't be back.

Because she wasn't Molly McGuire. Indeed, that said it all.

Molly was a woman who knew how to deal with a man. Who had all the right instincts. She was a woman that a man could cherish above all women, a woman a man would value, esteem, admire. Love.

A woman unlike herself.

Frances closed her eyes and leaned her head against the back of the rocker, drained. All the fight had gone out of her. All the adrenaline had fled.

She'd stood rigid, pulses pounding, watching until Jack was out of sight. Then her knees had scarcely held her up.

Harry leaped into her lap, prodded her knees to requisite softness and settled in. Mechanically she reached out and began to stroke him, seeking the comfort he always gave her.

But the softness of his fur didn't soothe her today. The steady rumble in his chest didn't make her smile.

She felt wretched, miserable, hurt. That was why she liked fiction. Fiction didn't hurt. Fiction you could walk away from. It didn't walk away from you.

But Jack had, and she didn't blame him.

She wished it had been different—wished that she was different—but she wasn't. So he was gone. It was, she told herself, better this way.

Still her throat tightened. Her eyes burned. And she wished—oh, how she wished—that Jack Neillands had stayed between the pages where he belonged.

Chapter Six

She had been on the covers of *Elle*, *Cosmo* and *Vogue* in the past six months, on the covers of *Mademoiselle* three times and *Self* twice in the two years preceding. She had long wavy brown hair, thick well-shaped eyebrows, full pouting lips and deep brown eyes that spelled S-E-X whichever way you looked at them.

Her name was Jennifer Jewell, and she was Jack's wife for a week.

And a good thing, too, Jack thought as he locked up that morning and caught a cab for the airport. He needed a break—a totally different environment. Another woman.

He didn't need Frances Moon.

Prickly, irritating women who jumped if you touched them weren't his cup of tea. He touched his nose gently. Arch was going to have a fit when he saw it. Arch was a perfectionist, shooting roll after roll to get things absolutely right. He'd have to shoot the back of Jack's head to make this one right.

Way to go, Francesca Luna.

He sank back against the seat of the cab and tried to put her out of his mind, to concentrate on the upcoming week—on the sun, the sand, the surf. The beautiful women. But they all seemed plastic, ephemeral, only half-alive when compared to the hardheaded Frances Moon.

Still, Jack was confident it wouldn't last. It never had. Out of sight, out of mind was, on the whole, his way of life. A woman in his arms would certainly be worth one in Vermont. He'd never met a woman before that the propinquity of another couldn't banish.

It was a good bet, he thought, that Frances Moon wouldn't be the first.

There were four of them in the shoot, actually—Jack and Jennifer Jewell and two blond all-American types named Katie Dooley and Peter Smith.

In the eyes of the readers of *Bride-to-Be*, they were two pairs of honeymooners, out to have the best, most romantic experience of their lives.

They were going to do it all, open up the "options of the islands," according to the copy waved around by the production crew.

That meant moving from island to island, shooting here and there, capturing a bit of this, a bit of that, touting places to go and things to see, as well as a wardrobe to take along.

"A whirlwind tour," Arch Wilton called it. "If it's Tuesday, this must be the Abacos—that sort of thing."

So they were honeymooning in Nassau on Paradise Island and Cable Beach for a day. They were honeymooning in Freeport for a morning, Hopetown for an evening. And finally, they were honeymooning on Harbour Island and Spanish Wells for the rest of the week.

"We'll start with the casino shots tonight. I think we'll do blonde on blond, dark on dark. Break down the stereotypes, you know," Arch said to them on the flight down Monday morning. He scowled at Jack. "The hell'd you do to your nose?"

"Misstepped."

Arch lifted a brow. "I'll say. Put you behind a pillar tonight. Or a potted palm tree."

"Or me," Jennifer said.

"Or you," Arch agreed. "Maybe Katie. We might switch around, use whichever combination works."

"Swap," said Peter, grinning and rubbing his hands together.

"That's what you think." Katie punched him in the arm. She and Peter were a couple in real life.

Jack, perforce, got Jennifer.

He could have had worse luck. Ninety percent of the male population would have agreed with him. Jennifer was every man's dream.

He'd done shoots with her before—a watch ad and a sportswear catalog. He'd ravished her on a book cover just last month. But he hadn't said more than a half-dozen words to her the whole time.

He was determined to make up for it now. He couldn't seem to manage it, though.

How ridiculous is that? he thought. In the clear light of day, lying on Cable Beach next to one of the world's most attractive women, he should be living for the moment, chatting her up, making her smile. He knew how it was done, for heaven's sake.

But instead of doing it he was, for the thousandth time, rehashing his ill-fated grab for Frances.

He was willing to bet she wasn't thinking about him. She was probably up to her ears in goat droppings, mooning about some imaginary hero and loving every minute of it.

Disgruntled he flipped over onto his back.

"Do me a favor?" Jennifer said.

"Sure."

She handed him a tube of sunscreen. "Put this on my back."

The favor of the year. He did his best to appreciate it.

Jack got to his knees. He squirted a thin stream of lotion onto his hands and rubbed them together, warming them before he touched her. Then he began with smooth firm strokes across her shoulders, then down across the breadth of her back, sliding under the thin ties that held her top in place.

Jennifer Jewell's back was, by anyone's standards, quite nearly as enticing as her front. It was silky soft and honey tanned, smooth and curving in all the right places.

Jack was, thankfully, no more immune than any other man with all the right impulses.

He edged closer, stroking her skin, watching her arch and shiver delicately as his hands reached the small of her back. She sighed, resting her chin in her fist and staring across the sand. He smiled.

She murmured something that made a small, soft sound deep in her throat.

He bent nearer. "What's that?" A little encouragement wouldn't have come amiss.

"I said, it's spring break."

He blinked. "Huh?"

Jennifer lifted her head and looked over her shoulder at him. She was smiling. "It's spring break."

"So?"

"All those guys playing volleyball over there. I bet they're from colleges."

Jack, who hadn't paid any attention to the volleyball players except to note the envious glances they'd been shooting him, squinted at them now.

They did look about that age, lean and gangly, a few still with spots. He couldn't see the attraction.

"I should've gone to college." Jennifer sounded wistful.

He looked at her narrowly. "You probably wouldn't be in the Bahamas if you had."

"Maybe not. But still..." She sighed. "Did you go to college?"

"Yeah."

"Did you like it?"

"I guess. Never thought much about it, really, at the time. I just did it. I was going to go on to law school, but I—" he shrugged "—did this instead."

"At least you got your degree. That's an accomplishment."

"You've got accomplishments. How many covers have you done?"

"Not me, my face."

"You've got a very beautiful face."

Jennifer scowled, wrinkling her pert nose. "For what it's worth."

"It's worth a lot—millions, and you know it."

"That's not what I mean."

He capped the sunscreen tube and laid it down on the towel, then stretched out again alongside her, desire gone. He sighed. "No, I know it's not. And I know what you mean."

"'Cause you're a pretty face, too?"

He grimaced.

"You are. When I was in high school I used to see you in the Penney's catalog and drool."

"Oh, cripes—" He scooped up some sand and tossed it on her.

"I did!" She giggled, brushing at the sand. "And that poster!"

"It wasn't supposed to be a poster, for God's sake!"

He remembered the horror he'd felt when Libby, giggling, had dragged it out. One look at Frances had been all he'd needed. But what could he do about it? It was done. And it wasn't as if he'd been nude, for heaven's sake. "It was only supposed to be a magazine ad."

Jennifer nodded. "Yeah, well, you know ad people. However it sells—"

"I know. But I'm beginning to regret it." He scowled up the beach, his chin resting on his fist.

Jennifer rolled onto her side and lay with her head on her arm, looking at him. "Somebody doesn't like it?"

Jack's other fist tightened around a handful of sand. "Somebody didn't say." Not in words anyway.

"Ah."

It was one of those all-seeing, all-knowing "ahs" that women specialize in. Jack frowned.

Jennifer smiled at him. "I'm glad you've got a girl-friend. I was...worried about that."

He stiffened. "You thought I was gay?"

She laughed. "Hardly. The grapevine's plenty clear about that. I just thought that on a shoot like this you might...might expect..."

His mouth curved slightly, mockingly. "A little nocturnal exercise?"

She colored and her gaze slipped away. "Yes."

"I don't hit on unwilling women." Or not often anyway, he thought, rubbing his nose.

Jennifer looked relieved. "Well, I didn't think...but since Peter and Katie are, well, you know..."

"Don't worry about it."

Jennifer beamed at him, then leaned forward and kissed him on the cheek. "You're a dear, Jack. Truly a dear."

A DEAR. A *dear*, God help him! Like somebody's spinster aunt, for God's sake!

He wondered if he needed his head examined. The answer was probably yes. Arch Wilton and Peter Smith and the rest of the male population of the Bahamas would certainly have thought so, if they'd known.

They didn't because, to all curious eyes, he and Jennifer Jewell were a twosome. And not a platonic twosome, either.

Jack would have been just as happy to run on the beach, swim, work out and read. But whether Jennifer just felt comfortable with him or sorry for him, he didn't know. All he knew was that wherever he was, there she was, too, smiling, laughing, hanging on his arm.

They ate together, they swam together, they ran together, they worked out together.

They were, in Arch Wilton's words, "perfect together. Fantastic chemistry. Sizzling!"

Arch thought they were the quintessential newlywed couple. And on film, even more than in reality, that's the impression they gave. They honeymooned on the beach, in casinos, on board a forty-foot yacht, on something closely resembling a mail boat, and in a moki-moki chugging along narrow, deeply rutted roads.

"Sensational," Arch said. "The perfect match."

Which just, Jack thought, went to show what Arch knew.

Since that first afternoon when he'd seen Jennifer in the light of her comments about the college boys, she'd become about as sexually appealing to him as his sister, Georgia. And for all that she batted her eyelashes and dimpled at him both on camera and off, her words made it clear he was the brother she'd never had.

She thought he had a girlfriend, and she was delighted. He didn't disillusion her. What was the point, after all? The weather was idyllic, the water warm, the sand pink and the drinks tall.

Jennifer, for all her attentive hanging on Jack's arm and cooing in Jack's ear, had her eye on a tall blond guy who was spending his spring break from Dartmouth at the family villa on Harbour Island.

She'd smiled at him the first day she'd seen him. He'd blushed to the roots of his hair and vanished on a sailboard for the rest of the afternoon.

Jennifer, taking it as rejection, clung even more tightly to Jack.

"Bat your eyelashes at him," Jack suggested. "Simper. Coo."

But Jennifer disdained simpering and cooing. And anything else she did intimidated the Dartmouth man even more. Her being seen in the company of Jack Neillands didn't help matters, either, though Jack doubted that Jennifer realized it. He could hardly say anything, though, without sounding like a conceited jerk.

"He just isn't interested," she complained. "He doesn't know I'm alive—or care."

"Join the club," muttered Jack.

Three days of having Jennifer in his arms hadn't worked. Frances was always on his mind. He'd left with the intention of forgetting her. He could not.

If the first weekend had whetted his appetite, the second, even with its disastrous ending, had only increased it. Seeing her deliver the lamb had been a revelation. It accentuated her strength, her capability, her tenderness. Jack stood around on the beach waiting for Arch, eyes closed against the Caribbean sun, and imagined her with a child. His child.

The thought almost knocked him off his feet.

Unaccustomed as he was to considering the possibility of children, except in terms of being responsible enough to prevent them being born into the wrong situation, the positive notion of having a child astonished him.

And with Frances Moon...

Holy cow.

Still, once the thought occurred, he couldn't entirely forget it.

But what did she really think of him?

She didn't seem to like him much—at least on the surface. The thought made him grimace and prompted a growl from Arch.

"I wanted mafia photos I wouldn'ta come to the Bahamas, Jacko."

Jack tried to look romantic. "Sorry."

But sometimes she'd looked as if she had liked him. And that kiss. He still couldn't forget that kiss.

He wished they could start over, that she would open to him, smile at him, that she wouldn't treat him as if he had the plague. He wasn't the only one to have noticed.

"Don't know what's got into Frances," Ebenezer had confided at supper Saturday night. "Most times she's as friendly as a politician at a prayer meetin'. This bump on a log nonsense ain't her."

Jack was gratified to hear it. Now all he had to figure out was how to get at the real woman.

An apology might help. Telling her he was sorry he'd put the make on her. Trouble was, he wasn't sorry. Not about that. About the outcome, yes. But not about that.

Still, he could talk to her. She couldn't give him the cold shoulder from fifteen hundred miles away, could she?

After they finished shooting, he headed for a phone.

She didn't answer.

She wasn't there the next day, either. Or the one after that.

Patience, Jack told himself. It was probably the vagaries of the Bahamian communications network and not Frances's suddenly blossoming social life.

He'd been told it wasn't always easy to reach the U.S.; he'd been told that whenever he went to make a phone call to take a book. He hadn't thought they meant *War and Peace.*

But for every time the call went through and actually rang on the other end, ten other times it didn't.

Ultimately it made no difference anyway. Frances wasn't there.

Or maybe she was, and she just wasn't answering the phone. Maybe she *knew* who was calling.

How paranoid is that? Jack asked himself. But by Thursday afternoon when he tried the same thing without success, he began to wonder. And when Thursday night and Friday morning brought similar nonresults, he began to feel it might be true.

"You know it's been snowing in New England," Jennifer said to him that afternoon over lunch. "Maybe that's why you can't get through."

"Snowing?" It didn't seem possible, not when he was standing in the midst of a tropical paradise, jasmine on the wind and frangipani in the air.

"A blizzard," Peter chipped in, lazily stirring a mai tai. "Sure am glad I'm here."

"Where'd you hear about that?"

Peter shrugged. "Arch gets the paper. One of the hotels has 'em flown in every morning. *The Times, The Wall Street Journal*, you name it. Me, I'd rather not know."

But Jack was already out of his chair, hollering for Arch.

Peter was right; the papers were calling it a blizzard with high winds and fourteen to eighteen inches of snow.

"The sugar snow to end all sugar snows," one commentator wrote, alluding to snowfalls that came during the cold nights and warmer days of late March and which heralded the advent of the maple sugaring season.

"Some parts of Vermont and New Hampshire will be digging out for days," the paper reported.

Was that what Frances was doing? Digging out? Or had she been stranded somewhere else? Annabel's perhaps.

Heartened, deciding that that was where she'd probably gone, Jack felt a bit better. He debated, then decided he'd call her there. It would mean more speculation from Libby and company, ammunition for Sister Bertha, but he didn't care. And at this point, he didn't care if Frances cared. He just wanted to know she was all right. He scooped up his book and headed for the phone booth.

No one was at Annabel's, either.

The five times the connection actually seemed to go through, the phone rang and rang and rang. Jack let it ring—twenty times. Thirty.

Where the hell was everyone? Were all the phone lines down? He rang his agency in New York just to check and to find out what he had to do Monday. He half hoped no one would answer.

They did on the first ring. "Snowing like hell," his booker told him. "But don't worry. They'll keep the runways clear."

Jack wasn't worried about that. He was worried about Frances. What was going on? Was she all right?

Since they'd come to Harbour Island the four of them and Arch had been staying in a huge cypress and glass contemporary house—a private home overlooking the Atlantic that belonged to somebody who consented to rent it to the magazine for the week. The rest of the crew was at one of the small local inns with restaurant and tennis court attached.

But the private house was far preferable, in Jack's opinion. It was only about a hundred yards up a narrow winding path from an almost deserted pink sand beach, a Garden of Eden sort of place—warm, comfortable, enticing. Far nicer than even the more lavish hotel accommodations he usually got on shoots. It had everything Jack considered necessary for paradise. Except a phone.

They were to finish up shooting Friday evening, then fly to Nassau that night and, if a flight was available, on to New York. Then word came down from New York that some of the first day's shots hadn't turned out.

"We'll reshoot 'em early in the morning then," Arch decreed. "We can take an afternoon flight."

Jennifer put a hand on Jack's arm. "Poor Jack," she sympathized. "Now you'll have to wait until Sunday to drive up."

Jack, who until that moment, hadn't realized he was going to drive up, let out a shaky breath. "Yeah, right."

Unless, of course, he reached Frances first. By 1:00 *a.m.* Saturday he hadn't. Really worried then, he spent a sleepless night.

At six he was staring in the bathroom mirror and trying to figure out how best to eliminate the dark circles under his eyes before Arch saw them.

No luck.

"You party boys make my life hell," Arch groused. "Where the hell were you last night?"

"In a phone booth" hardly seemed a reply that would enhance his reputation. Jack sighed and pulled his sunglasses down.

They were reshooting the beach scenes. Wading and splashing scenes, walking hand in hand scenes, building sand castles scenes, gentle kisses while the waves lapped over their ankles scenes. Mood shots, not close-ups, thank God.

Even at seven-thirty in the morning they attracted some local observers—a few adults, a handful of children, mostly teenage boys.

The boys, especially, watched wide-eyed while Jennifer batted her lashes at Jack, put her hands on his shoulders and lifted her mouth for him to kiss. They swallowed hard when she snuggled against him, molding curve to angle as his arms drew her in. Jack moved by rote, his mind on New England weather.

"Kiss her again, Jack," Arch shouted, moving and clicking, moving and clicking. "And keep your nose out of the way this time."

Dutifully Jack bent his head.

"Again," Arch said. Snap. Click. "And again."

Jack moved. Jack kissed. So did Jennifer.

"Nice work if you can get it." One of the boys nudged another.

"And again," Arch directed. "And again. Now on the towels. Jack, lie down. Yeah, on your back. Jennifer, kneel down and hover over him. That's right. Smile. Good. Okay, now pucker those lips"

Snap. Click. "Super. Move in closer. Yeah. *Yeahhhhh.* Perfect." Snap. Click. "Once more. Uh-huh. All right. Kiss

him now. Again. That's right. Like that. Good, Jenn, good.
Kiss him.''

Jennifer hovered. She batted her lashes, smiled down at
him. Kissed him.

As one, the boys sighed.

Jack closed his eyes, parted his lips, lay back and thought
of Vermont.

IT WAS SNOWING when the plane landed, snowing harder
when Jack hailed a taxi, already piling up in front of the
brownstone when he tipped the taxi driver and lugged his
duffel bag up the steps. It was past seven o'clock.

If he had any sense he'd toss his clothes in the washing
machine, put a steak on the broiler, take off his shoes and
collapse.

He went straight to the phone to try Frances again—got
just what he expected—nothing—and repacked his bag for
Vermont.

The highways, just as the radio announcer claimed, were
one hundred percent snow- and ice-covered.

"Great night to stay by the fire," he went on. "Rising
temperatures, but rising snowdrifts as well. And lots more
to come, ladies and gentlemen. A good twelve more inches
is predicted for the Hudson River Valley and moving
northeast.'' That was exactly where Jack was moving, too.

He followed the plow, squinting through the windshield,
knuckles white, forehead furrowed. If the roads had been
salted, the salt had been buried under the drifts. Last weekend he'd made a trip to Boone's Corner in a bit over five
hours. By the time he reached it now, he'd been driving over
eight.

It was past four in the morning when he slid to a stop at
last in the ditch at the bottom of Frances's lane.

He hoped to God she was there now, because if she wasn't
he was going to be there by himself. There was certainly no
getting back out.

He struggled out of the car, hitched his duffel bag under his arm, and began to hike. The sky had an eerie almost pinkish glow to it. The snow, wet and heavy, squelched under the weight of his boots.

He slipped more than once, felt his teeth begin to chatter more from fatigue than from cold, and wondered not for the first time why he had come at all.

It wasn't as if she was expecting him. It wasn't as if she even wanted him.

But none of that mattered. It only mattered that he hadn't seen her in a week, hadn't talked to her, hadn't the vaguest hint that she was alive and well, and he needed more than a hint right now. He trudged on.

There was a light on in the house.

He clambered up the porch steps, stamping his feet, and rang the bell.

It was almost a minute before he saw something moving inside and a few seconds longer until the porch light flicked on and the curtain that covered the glass in the door was pulled back and Frances squinted out.

She looked perfectly fine, hale and hearty. She jerked open the door, astonishment written on her face.

Jack had fury written on his. "Why the hell didn't you answer your phone?"

"What?" Now she looked as if he'd lost his mind.

"I've been calling for days! I thought you were dead."

"No. You must be frozen." She stepped back, and he stamped into the entryway, shrugging off his jacket and shaking his head, scattering snowflakes over both of them.

"So where were you?" he demanded.

She shook her head dazedly, her eyes still disbelieving. "Sugaring. I was sugaring."

He'd bent to untie his boots and now he stared up at her, his turn to be astonished. "Sugaring?"

"Maple sugaring. Annabel, Eb, Ernie, Bert and the kids and I. We do it every year together. At one another's places." She led him into the kitchen and practically pushed him into the rocking chair beside the wood stove. "Sit down. I'll make you some coffee. I...what on earth are you doing here?"

"I was worried about you."

The baldness of his statement stopped her dead. "Worried?"

"I tried to call you. You never answered."

She put on the kettle. "It's been a day-and-night operation since the snow started. I'm only home now because I need to get a bit more work on the book done. Eb thinks I'm sleeping," she confided.

"You should be."

He still wanted to shake her for terrifying him at the same time he wanted to throw his arms around her and hug the life out of her just to prove to himself she was all right.

He contented himself with subjecting her to an intense scrutiny, running his eyes over her face and form the way his hands itched to do. She looked tired as she moved to set out cups and saucers. But her eyes shone, her skin glowed. She was more beautiful to his eyes than Jennifer Jewell or Katie Dooley or any model in any agency's book in all of New York. She shot him quick, darting looks, as if he might vanish if she didn't check on him.

He leaned back in the chair and drank in the sight of her.

Frances was staring at him, too, shaking her head, smiling, shaking her head again. She shut her eyes, then opened them again. "I can't believe you're here."

"I can't, either." And that was God's own truth. He'd been running on adrenaline so long he couldn't believe he'd finally arrived. He sank back into the chair, blinking in the warm light of the room, weariness seeping in, adrenaline seeping out.

"All because I didn't answer the phone?" she marveled.

"All because you didn't answer the phone."

"I thought you were out of town."

"I was. I was in the Bahamas."

"You were calling me from the Bahamas?"

"Yes, damn it."

"Why?" She sounded totally mystified.

"How the hell should I know?" Jack practically shouted at her.

He didn't need doubt and disbelief at a time like this. He needed hugs and kisses and warm arms wrapped around him. He needed comfort, love. He raked a hand through already uncombed hair, then rubbed his cheek, felt a surprising amount of whiskery stubble and remembered he hadn't even shaved today. "Because I wanted to talk to you, I guess. To apologize. I didn't mean to scare you. I just— Oh hell, this is crazy."

Frances grinned at him suddenly. "Yes."

"It isn't funny!"

"No," she said slowly. "It's not."

They didn't move then, only stared at each other, all their emotions, tangled and confusing as they were, hanging unspoken between them. The clock ticked. The tap dripped. A burning log crackled and tumbled in the fire. Outside the wind threw sleet against the windows.

"Come here," Jack said. But he didn't wait for her. Didn't give her any choice. He reached for her, hauled her into his arms and kissed her.

And Frances, after a moment's resistance, let herself be kissed. It was everything he remembered. Warm and sweet. Satisfying, yet tantalizing. He wanted more. Lots more. And knew he wasn't going to get it, couldn't even manage it. Not tonight.

He pulled back, but didn't let go of her, just held her close, felt her trembling in his arms, her eyes wide and worried as she stared at him.

He rested his forehead against hers. "God, I needed that," he said, and his voice shook. "I'm shot."

For a moment Frances didn't speak. Then she shook her head, her voice slightly wistful as she said, "You—you really do look awful." She flushed. "I mean you look—"

"I look awful," Jack concurred. "I've been up for twenty-four hours. I've been on a Jeep, a boat, two planes, a taxi, and I've just driven eight and a half hours through weather I wouldn't send Santa Claus out in." He gave her a weary grin. He pulled her down into his lap and held her fast until she relaxed against him.

"You really are crazy, you know it," she said. "Completely crazy."

"You may be right."

"Coming up here like this. In this weather. Idiotic." She didn't look at him, only at her fingers.

"Yes." Jack leaned his head back and shut his eyes. He held her against him, savoring the weight of her body through the bulky knit of her sweater. He didn't care. Nothing mattered now except just soaking up the warmth of Frances's body and the soft sounds of her fretting over him. It was heaven. Nirvana.

"What am I going to do with you?" she said.

He smiled. "What do you want to do with me?"

She gave him a look that was supposed to have daggers in it. "Don't ask."

He grinned sleepily. "You know you're glad to see me."

"I am astonished to see you. Shocked to the core."

"Just proves you're too shockable. You should've known."

"How could I know you'd act like an idiot?"

He shrugged. "Shouldn't be any big surprise. I get the feeling you expect it."

"I never know what to expect from you."

He lifted an eyebrow. "No?" He smiled then and closed his eyes again, murmuring, "Good. I must be doin' better'n I thought."

He thought he heard her snort. He wasn't sure. It was a distinctly unladylike sound, but that didn't mean Frances wouldn't make it. Frances Moon was a law unto herself.

He sighed, nestled more deeply into the confines of the rocker, and began to drift.

She stirred against him. "Jack!"

"Mmm?"

"Jack!"

"Wha—"

"Forget the coffee. You don't need coffee now. Come on." She slipped out of his grasp and moved away.

He reached for her in vain, then opened one eye. "What? Come where?" She wasn't standing by the front door, was she?

"You can't sleep there. I'm going back to Eb's and the fire will go out."

He started to struggle up. "I'll go to Eb's, too, then. I—"

"You will not go to Eb's. You'll be no earthly good to anyone at Eb's. You're going to bed."

And before he could say a word, Frances had grabbed him by the arm and was hauling him to his feet.

Jack let her. He had neither the strength nor the desire to do anything else. Obediently he followed her up the steps, down the hall and into a bedroom.

She dropped his duffel on the floor and flicked on a lamp. Jack was too tired to notice anything other than the bed. It was wide and white and welcoming. He sank onto it at once, resting his forearms on his thighs. His head sagged. All the adrenaline that had got him here was gone. He could barely keep his eyes open. The moment he'd sat down, he'd been finished. Now he couldn't move a muscle.

Between his knees he could see Frances's sock-clad feet. One of them was tapping expectantly. He couldn't move.

Finally Frances sighed, bent down and began rooting around in the duffel herself.

"Wha' ya lookin' for?" he asked after a moment when she had given up trying to be neat and was chucking things right and left.

"Your pajamas."

"Don' wear 'em."

Her head snapped up. "What?"

"Don't wear them," he enunciated.

She scanned the floor, snatched up a pair of sweats and thrust them at him. "Wear these, then."

He shook his head. "Don' need 'em." He smiled at her. "I'm hot-blooded."

"I bet."

Jack laughed and took the sweats from her, staggered to his feet and began to unsnap and unzip his jeans. The pop of the fastener sent Frances toward the door as if she'd been shot from a rifle.

"I'll just put out the fire," she muttered.

Jack grinned sleepily at her as his jeans slid down his legs. "You do that."

Put out the fire? Oh, Frances, you idiot! she chastised as she stood in the middle of the living room, her arms hugging her chest tightly. *What a thing to say! And there he stood with that knowing smile on his face, understanding all too well just what fire you were worried about!*

Damn Jack Neillands, anyway!

It had been the shock of a lifetime to open the door a few minutes ago and find him standing there. She couldn't imagine it. After the way they'd left things last time, she was certain he'd never be back.

But he was. And he'd driven eight hours to get here? *After* flying up from the Bahamas? Because he couldn't reach her on the phone? And he'd been trying all week? To apologize?

Grinning, giddy, expecting any moment to wake up and find she'd hallucinated the whole thing, that that was what happened when you went virtually sleepless for three days running, Frances shook her head.

She heard the creak of the floorboards next to the bed, then the groan of the springs as he sank onto the mattress. Her mattress! Her bed!

But she had nowhere else to put him. It was only a two-bedroom house, and the second bedroom was her office. It had a small couch, but even Frances couldn't stretch out on it. To put Jack there would have been ridiculous. It was her bed or nothing.

Was he warm enough now? she wondered. Did he need another blanket? Something to drink? She started toward the steps.

Her fists clenched and she forced herself to remain right where she was. He was fine, she told herself. He didn't need a thing. She had no reason at all to go back up those steps and peek in on him.

In fact she was much better off *not* doing so.

She had imagined Jack Neillands in her bed often enough. The reality of it would be more than she could take.

Chapter Seven

She peeked after all.

Not then—then she did exactly what she'd told him she was going to do. She trudged the mile and a half to Ebenezer's house and took up her position as mender of the fire while Eb, Annabel, Libby and Leif lugged buckets of sap, and Bert and Ernie kept the evaporating pan full and heated the next can of sap to be added to it.

But her mind wasn't on the sugaring.

"Throw s'more wood on, girl," Ebenezer groused. "Daydreamin' agin," he grumbled as he headed back out with empty buckets. "It's what we get having a writer for a fire mender. Head in the clouds."

But Frances's head wasn't in the clouds at all. It was back home, peeking in at Jack.

"No point you bein' here," Eb complained at last. "Not when I got to redo every dad-blasted thing you do."

"I'm sorry."

"G'wan home with you. It's that cursed book, I'll wager. You didn't sleep, did you?"

"Er, not exactly. I—"

"G'wan home then. And sleep this time." He tried to glower at her, but a smile crept in. "'S almost the end of it anyways. An' you worked harder'n any of us. Longer, too."

"Are you sure?"

Ebenezer drew himself up to his full five feet seven inches and stuck out his grizzled gray-whiskered chin. "I'm tellin' you, ain't I?"

Frances dropped a kiss on his cheek, making him blush a fiery red. "Yes, Eb."

And so she trudged back the mile and a half, fed the goats and sheep so she wouldn't have to do it later, then let herself into the house, shed her boots and jacket and tiptoed upstairs.

It was just gone ten. The snow was still falling. Heavier and faster than ever.

"More to come," Ernie had said just as she was leaving. "That's what the radio men said. Have you got enough food?"

"I'm fine."

"You don't want to be up there alone, you can come down with us," Ernie went on. "We'd be glad of the company. Bit wearing, you know, just Bert and me."

Frances smiled. "I'm fine." She hadn't said she wasn't alone. She knew what Ernie and Bert would make of that.

So now she was tiptoeing down her own hallway and peeking into her own bedroom, feeling as nervous and sweaty palmed as if she were the intruder and not Jack. She peered around the corner of the doorway and stopped.

He lay on his stomach beneath her down comforter, his face turned toward her, his lips slightly parted, a rumpled fall of dark hair fringing his forehead.

Frances had seen Jack Neillands from many angles. She'd seen him scowling and smiling, smirking and flirting. She'd been drawn from the first to the power of those beautiful blue eyes in a photograph.

But she found now that in reality he commanded just as much power sound asleep, oddly vulnerable, eyes shut.

She edged farther into the room and stood over him, her eyes tracing the way his hair curled in, hugging his scalp at the back of his neck, the way it brushed softly against the top of his ear. His lashes were long and dark, delicate half-moons against his cheeks. And those cheeks! Lean and strong, now stubbled, they drew her, made her want to reach out and touch them. Made her want to brush her fingertips against them, rough one way, silky smooth the other.

She stood quite still, the hems of her jeans dripping melted snow onto the braided rug. Then she moved silently to the dresser and slid open a drawer, fishing inside it for a nightgown, her eyes never leaving Jack. She was reminded of how Molly had come in from the milling once and, unsuspecting, had found Ben Cutter asleep in her bed.

Molly's feelings, as Frances recalled them, hadn't been vastly different from her own. But everything else was different, Frances reminded herself. That was fiction, purely the work of her mind. This—*this* was reality. And Jack Neillands was no Ben Cutter, for all that he looked just like him.

She left him sleeping there and went into the bathroom and ran herself a bath. Then she soaked in a tub of hot water, while Harry sat on the counter and played lifeguard, until the water began to cool and Frances began to fall asleep.

Reluctantly she got out, shivering, dried herself off and put the gown on. Then, having brushed out her hair, she wrapped a robe around herself and padded back out into the hallway.

Harry preceded her, walking with stately elegance toward her bedroom where he stopped in the doorway, looked at the bed, then looked back at her, as if wondering, if Frances were standing here, just who the lump was. He meowed curiously.

She put her finger to her lips. Harry's eyes narrowed to slits as she edged past him, heading for the hall closet to get her spare bedding. She would take it into the office and curl up on the couch, determined not to peek at Jack Neillands again.

Harry waited until she'd passed, then lifted his nose and stalked into the bedroom with Jack.

"Harry, come back here."

Harry, being a cat, ignored her.

She dropped the bedding and went after him. Too late. She'd got halfway to the bed when Harry sprang. Sixteen pounds of muscley fur landed in the middle of Jack's back.

"Ooof." Jack's eyes flew open. He rolled half over, then stopped when he saw Frances standing there, wringing her hands. Harry began to knead the comforter covering his back.

"S-sorry about that," Frances babbled. "It's just Harry. I'll get him out of here." She came forward, reaching for the cat. "I'll—"

Jack rolled onto his back. One bare arm snuck out and caught her wrist. A second later Frances landed on the bed as well.

Harry gave her an indignant look, but she didn't move away. She couldn't. Jack's hand imprisoned her arm. His gaze, slumberous and tender, imprisoned her gaze.

She swallowed. "I—I'm sorry he woke you. I'll take him with me. I—"

"Take him where?"

"Into the office."

"You're going to *work*? In your nightgown?"

Frances blushed, and tried, one-handed, to secure her robe more tightly around her. "I'm not going to work. I'm going to sleep, too."

"Sleep here."

Two words and the world seemed to stop midspin. She opened her mouth to speak, but no words came out.

"Sleep here," Jack said again.

Frances's wrist twisted against his hand, which still held it loosely but determinedly. "Sleep here?" To her everlasting chagrin, her voice actually squeaked.

"This is your bed, isn't it?"

"Yes, but—"

"And there isn't one in your office, is there?"

"No, but—"

"So what're you going to do, curl up in your desk chair?"

"There's a sofa."

"Comfortable?"

"Of course."

He smiled. "Liar. You'd opt for a bed of nails instead of this one, wouldn't you?"

"I . . ." She tried to look indifferent. But it wasn't easy. Not when Jack was looking at her with the same sort of warm, gentle persuasiveness that Ben Cutter used to inveigle Molly into doing whatever he wanted.

"Sleep here, Francesca," he said softly, his thumb caressing the soft skin on the inside of her wrist. "Just sleep."

"I don't think—"

"*Don't* think. Sleep." He eased the comforter back an inch and drew her closer. His eyes never left hers.

Harry yawned and settled in, closing his eyes. Frances, in spite of herself, yawned, too.

Jack smiled at her. "Anyway, what can I do," he asked her, "with a chaperon like Harry?"

Frances looked at the sleeping cat. Harry's purring sounded like Rosie the Riveter. He only purred like that when he was extraordinarily pleased.

"He trusts me," Jack continued, his thumb still stroking her wrist. He yawned then, too, and blinked his eyes wearily. They were bloodshot, Frances noticed, and tiny lines of fatigue radiated out from them. She thought again of all he had gone through to get here. She sighed.

"Trust me, Frances."

"Trust you?" she tried to scoff. "After last weekend?"

"I said I was sorry. And anyway—" he smiled "—I learn from my mistakes." He drew her gently, inexorably down beside him, lifted the comforter and pulled her in. His arms went around her, hauling her back against him, her bottom nestled against his thighs, his chin resting on her shoulder. His breath tickled her ear.

Frances swallowed and inched her head away. She should have inched her whole body away, but nothing in her wanted to do it.

She knew how Molly felt now, drawn in by the spell of Ben's compelling eyes. And, yes, it was fiction and she knew it. But it was so comfortable here, so warm and right.

She could do a better job of writing about it next time if she stayed, she thought. Yes, definitely a better job.

She began to relax in spite of herself, cocooned in the warmth of his arms, cradled in the strength of his chest and legs.

Sleep, Jack had said. Just sleep.

And so she would. Just sleep, nothing more.

"USE ALL FIVE SENSES," Frances frequently exhorted beginning writers. "*Hear* the rough baritone of his voice, *see* the gleam in his eyes, *taste* the hunger of his kiss, *smell* the musky scent of his after-shave, *feel* his hair-roughened thighs."

But hair-roughened thighs had never *felt* so real as when she drifted back to consciousness and discovered she wasn't sitting at her computer, composing, after all.

Her hand, splayed against something warm, alive, and definitely rough with springy hair, moved one millimeter, then another, tentative, worried, groping, finding. Realizing.

Her eyes snapped open. Her head jerked up. She looked directly into Jack Neillands's disconcerting eyes.

She tried to pull her hand away from what was obviously his bare leg or—worse—bare something else, but the comforter was snugged around them tightly. She managed to move all of an inch. Jack rolled from his side onto his back and one long arm snaked out and held her fast next to him.

"Good afternoon. Or is it evening?" His voice was husky, his whiskers darker. He smiled.

Frances didn't answer. She was struggling to get up and away without much success. "Where are your sweats?" she demanded.

Jack glanced at the floor. She followed his gaze. If she'd been with it when she'd come in she'd have seen them then, would have realized he wasn't wearing them, would have realized that he was naked under the quilt. Would have run a mile instead of allowing herself to be coaxed into bed with him.

"Relax," Jack said.

"Easy for you to say," Frances grumbled.

"I didn't ravish you, did I?"

She looked away. "Well, no, I guess not."

Jack gave a huff of laughter. "You guess not? There's a compliment. Believe me, Francesca Luna, you'd remember it if I had."

"I'm sure you're very memorable," she said tartly, still trying to ease away. But Jack scissored his legs, effectively trapping hers, still tangled in the gown, between them.

"Damn right I am," he said softly. Then he wrapped his arms around her and hauled her down against him and she heard a sigh rumble through his chest even as she continued to struggle. "Ah, hell, Francesca Luna," he mumbled, "what am I going to do about you?"

"Let me go," she suggested, her breath fanning the hair on his chest. She felt him tense. His heart was thudding loudly under her ear.

She felt rather than saw him smile. "Not a chance." One hand came up and stroked softly through her hair. She tried to lift her head; he pressed it down again.

"I don't—"

"Shh."

"But—"

"Just shhh." His hand kept stroking and threading, playing gently, almost whimsically with the strands of her hair. His chest rose and fell and, with it, went Frances's head. She couldn't believe this was happening, that she was letting it happen. But she was.

His heart beat a steady, eager thrum beneath her ear. Her own heart was butting against her chest like Meg the goat against the dinner pail.

Take notes, she told herself. But she didn't feel literary— or objective—in the least.

Outside the window in the waning winter afternoon she could see the snow still falling. She watched the flakes drifting down, felt the soft stroke and tender tugging of Jack's fingers in her hair, and took a deep shuddering breath, letting it out slowly. Her fists uncurled against his ribs.

"That's better," he said.

"Is it?" Frances asked wryly. She was trying to be detached, trying to store all these sensations away for future reference at the same time she was trying to remain aloof from them and, with the latter at least, she wasn't having an enormous amount of luck. The feel of his fingers in her hair was seducing her. The solid warmth of his body beneath hers tempted her. She didn't want to move, to leave, to do anything except savor the moment.

"Oh, yes. Much better." Jack lifted his head and she felt his breath against the top of her head. "It's the first time you've relaxed since the afternoon you got drunk."

"I wasn't drunk," Frances protested, her fingers curling again, this time to pinch him.

"Ow. All right. Slightly tipsy, then," he amended with a chuckle.

Another pinch.

He batted at her hand. "Pleasantly convivial, how about that?"

"Better," Frances conceded. She smiled.

He must've felt the muscles move in her face. He couldn't have seen, not from the angle he was, but he said, "You smiled," as if it were a great triumph.

"So?"

"Progress. I make damned little. I have to take pleasure in what I can get."

"You got me in bed with you," Frances pointed out and immediately wished she hadn't.

"Fat lot of good it's done me," Jack countered. "We're in bed, I'm naked, and what're we doing? Arguing."

"We're not."

She felt him shrug. "Sounds like it to me. Why don't you like me?"

"I do like you," Frances protested. That was the problem.

"You give everyone you like the revolving-door treatment?"

"I never—"

"You damned well do. Hello, Mr. Neillands. Nice to meet you, Mr. Neillands. Have a cup of coffee on your way out the door, Mr. Neillands," he mocked her.

Frances lifted her head and glowered at him. But she was still smiling. "I wasn't that bad." A pause. "Was I?"

"Worse," Jack said promptly, giving her hair a tug.

"Liar."

He grinned. "You can make it up to me."

Frances looked at him warily, quite able to imagine how he might like her to do that. "I don't think so," she said.

He looked hurt.

"And anyway, I did make it up to you. I took you with me to dinner at Annabel's."

"Leif invited me to dinner at Annabel's."

"But you wouldn't have been invited at all if it hadn't been for me."

"I suppose not."

"Besides, I'm afraid I'm about to 'make it up to you' royally, hospitality wise," she told him, "because, like it or not, I think you're snowed in here."

Jack's hand stopped moving in her hair. He stared at her. She half hoped she'd surprise a look of dismay on his face, half knew she'd regret it if she did. But what she saw was a look of wonder followed by one of smug satisfaction.

"Snowed in?" he echoed. "You and me? Together?"

"Don't get any ideas. I have work to do," Frances told him darkly. "Lots of it. I'll be very busy."

"No problem." He was still smiling.

"Very, very busy."

He nodded, looking like the Cheshire cat. "Sure."

"Jack—"

But he simply put his arms around her and hugged her. "Hallelujah," he muttered. "Let it snow."

IT WASN'T OFTEN Jack got the feeling God was on his side. Most often He seemed an Omnipresent Disinterested Observer at best. But an Almighty Who kept it snowing for a day and a night and a day, Who piled up drifts of four and five feet, Who provided stinging winds and provoked the National Weather Service to issue advisory warnings was clearly a God in Jack's corner.

Jack was grateful—and pleased.

"The weather's great," he told God while he was shaving Saturday evening, having got out of bed at last. "Keep up the good work. How about working on Frances a little, too?"

But God apparently figured He'd done His bit by providing the weather. Getting around Frances Moon was obviously Jack's problem.

It was five in the evening when she'd resisted his latest attempt to keep her in bed with him and had sped out the door, swathed tightly in her robe, calling over her shoulder, "I have to milk the goats."

Jack grimaced. His only solace was knowing that her errand was legitimate. Still, not many women had chosen a herd of goats over a naked Jack Neillands in their beds. At the moment he couldn't think of one.

That was probably why he liked her, he thought ruefully now as he stared into the mirror and scraped the razor down his cheek. She was one of the few women he'd met who didn't kiss up to him, who didn't bat her eyelashes and flirt with him. She was one of the few women he'd met in recent years that he counted as a challenge.

He finished shaving, got dressed and was building up the fire in the living room when she returned from the barn.

She was wearing a pair of faded blue jeans and a royal-blue down jacket. Her cheeks were rosy from the cold and her hair was covered with a silvery sheen of snowflakes. Her eyes were bright and she was smiling. She was beautiful.

She took off her hiking boots, shook her hair, stuffed her feet into a pair of old moosehide moccasins, and carried the milk pails into the kitchen. A few minutes later she reappeared and padded across to the fireplace to warm her hands.

"And how were the goats?" Jack asked.

"Glad to see me. So were the sheep. I'm a little worried, though." She held out her hands toward the flames. "One of the ewes who should be delivering soon isn't anywhere near the barn."

"Maybe you missed her. Maybe you couldn't tell her from the snow."

"Maybe. I hope. I don't relish the idea of going out looking."

"No?"

"No," she said quite seriously, then blinked and looked at him again, saw his smile and smiled back a little foolishly. "You think I'm crazy, don't you?"

"Sometimes."

She laughed at that. "Makes us even, I guess. Anyone who lives in New York City is crazy."

"It helps," Jack agreed. He stood, noted that she took a quick step back from the fire and took one back himself so as not to scare her off. "Why don't you like New York?"

"It's not New York specifically." She turned her back to the fire now. The flames made her hair look like burnished gold. "It's big cities in general."

"Had a lot of experience with them, have you?"

"Enough. I went to college in Boston."

"I didn't know that."

"Mmm." She moved away from the fire. "How about some supper?" She was already heading toward the kitchen.

"Sure. Where?"

"In the kitchen."

"No. I mean, where'd you go to college?"

She was kneeling by one of the cabinets and poked her head in, rooting around. For a few moments he thought she wasn't going to answer. Then finally he heard, muffled, "Radcliffe."

Radcliffe? Frances Moon had gone to Radcliffe and now she raised goats? Curiouser and curiouser.

"Chili or pork and beans?" Her voice echoed from the interior of the cupboard.

"Chili." He was far more interested in talking about Frances than about food. It was the first time she'd talked about her adult life, about what had brought her to Vermont. "What'd you major in? Animal husbandry?" He was still talking to her back.

She handed a can of chili out behind her without looking back. "English. Applesauce or sliced peaches?"

"Applesauce. How come the goats, then?"

She handed back a jar of homemade applesauce. "Not much call for English teachers up here."

"You were a teacher?"

A box of crackers appeared in her hand. He took it without comment. It was followed by a box of rice. He lined everything up on the counter—the chili, the applesauce, the crackers, the rice.

"I taught," Frances said at last. She stood and took out a can opener, opening the chili.

Jack leaned against the counter watching her. "Where?"

She dumped the chili into a pan, then nodded to a mesh bag of onions on the counter. "Chop one, will you?"

He took out an onion and chopped. "Where did you teach in Boston?" he persisted.

"Charlestown."

Another revelation. He knew Charlestown by reputation. It was a tough, insular, blue-collar neighborhood. It wouldn't have been a piece of cake teaching there. He looked at Frances with increased respect.

"For how long?"

"Three years."

"You didn't like it," he guessed. He didn't blame her. He bet lots of people didn't last as long as she had.

"No, I liked it. It was difficult but not unpleasant. At least most of it."

"So why'd you quit?"

"I got a divorce."

He stared at her, stunned. The words echoed in his ears. He didn't know why they shocked him so much, but they did.

Frances married? Frances with a husband? He felt as if he'd been socked in the gut. He couldn't think of what to say next.

A thousand questions crowded his mind. Whom had she married? Why had she divorced him? Whatever had possessed her to marry him in the first place? How had the bastard hurt her?

Because there was no doubt in Jack's mind that he had. It explained a lot.

He didn't ask. She wouldn't have answered, and he knew it.

In fact she said nothing else. She took in the look on his face, assessed it, then turned and checked on the rice, which was bubbling away now on the back of the stove. She stirred the chili on the front burner and dumped the chopped onion in. Then she rummaged in the drawer and got out the silverware.

Jack rubbed a hand around the back of his neck, easing an already loose shirt collar, trying to come to terms with her words, trying to find words of his own that wouldn't scare her off.

At last he said, "So how long have you been here, then?"

"Five years."

"Why Vermont? Why didn't you go back to Iowa?"

"I'm not a child. I solve my own problems, I don't run home with them." Her voice was tight, as if she were deliberately keeping her emotions at bay. He wondered at it. She was such an emotional writer. But in real life she was the opposite.

Or was she? Was it, perhaps, all an act?

She dished up bowls of chili and rice and motioned for him to take his seat opposite her.

"Why didn't you continue to teach? Why sheep? Why goats, for heaven's sake?"

"As I said, there weren't any jobs. And I knew sheep. My father raised them. And for all that I wasn't running home, I saw the value of the life-style. Sheep and goats are very solid, dependable. You know where you are with them. I wanted that. I was sick of urban life and all its 'promises.'"

"What sort of promises?"

She made a face. "Oh, you know. Higher salary. Better car. Bigger apartment. A boat. Membership at the right clubs. All the goodies of the yuppie world."

"You thought you wanted that?"

"I didn't want it. My husband did."

"So you divorced him?"

"No," she said flatly. "He divorced me."

"Oh." He wished he'd never asked.

Frances's head was bent over her bowl. She was chewing methodically. Her shoulders were hunched as if awaiting the next blow.

To pursue that line of questioning, as tantalizing as he might find it, would undoubtedly hurt her.

He backed off. "Do you miss teaching?"

She looked up briefly, as if weighing whether it was a trick question. Deciding it wasn't, she seemed to relax. Her shoulders sagged slightly. She sat for a moment just stirring her chili before she replied.

"No, I guess I don't. I enjoyed it. I enjoyed the kids. Some of them come out and spend a few weeks of the summer with me. But I have Annabel's kids now, too, and—" she shrugged "—they're enough."

"None of your own?"

He'd gone too far.

The fork clattered against her bowl and her eyes blazed. "No, Mr. Neillands. None of my own. Are there any more rude, prying questions you feel you have to ask?"

"Hey, I'm sorry. Really. I don't know why I— It's none of my business."

"No. It isn't."

He reached for her hand across the table. She started to pull away, but he wouldn't let her. "Truly, Frances. I am sorry. It was rude. You're right."

She grimaced, then shrugged. "I'm too touchy. I shouldn't have jumped down your throat."

He thought he heard genuine regret in her voice. But what she was regretting, he wasn't sure. Did she regret getting angry at him? Or was she missing not having kids? Did she wish she'd had a child by her ex-husband? Did she still love the jerk?

They looked at each other warily.

Then, "Eat your chili," Frances said as if to a child.

Jack smiled at her. "Yes, Mother."

He thought he heard her teeth grinding, but it might have been only her fork.

SNOWED IN with Jack Neillands. Astonishing. Unbelievable. Yet one more example of how truth could be stranger than fiction. But stranger even than being snowed in with him was what they did while they were snowed in. And what they didn't do.

They didn't make love.

They didn't even share the same bed again. For all that Jack insisted he would be just as trustworthy as he was that first time, Frances wouldn't.

"Is it me you don't trust or yourself?" Jack challenged her.

Her face flamed as she acknowledged the accuracy of his question. "The situation," she said.

He had to be content with that.

Frances slept in the living room on the couch. It was even less comfortable than the one in the office. But it was also farther away from Jack.

She admitted to herself finally that she enjoyed having him there. He was fun, he was flattering. He teased her, made her laugh. Sometimes he kissed her. But when she pulled away, he let her go. All was well, she thought.

As for what they did do... Frances taught Jack how to milk a goat. Jack taught her how to play backgammon. They had marathon games of Scrabble and Monopoly. She baked cookies. He made chicken soup. They tracked down the missing ewe and, early Monday morning, stood hand in hand watching while the ewe delivered her lamb. Later Frances sewed a missing button on Jack's shirt. Jack fixed the faucet that had leaked for weeks. Together they completed the last four weeks of the Sunday *Times* crossword.

"I've never done one before, let alone four," Frances told him, smiling. "Not completely like that."

Jack grinned. "Me, either. Together we are one complete intelligence. Just shows how suited we are, how perfectly matched."

And if reality were nothing more than being snowed in in Vermont, Frances might've agreed.

But by Monday afternoon the snow had let up. By supper time it had completely stopped. When evening came they heard the plow already chugging along the roads in the valley below.

By Tuesday morning it would have cleared even the secondary roads. All that would be needed then would be to dig Jack's car out. Then the idyll would be over; he would go back to the city and Frances would go back to work.

She said as much Monday night as she played around with the letter tiles she'd been dealt in their latest game of Scrabble.

Jack's eyes narrowed. "You sound pleased."

"You should be, too. All those assignments you missed."

She'd been there when he'd called in the morning. She'd heard him apologizing, placating his booker, promising to be back as soon as he could, ending the conversation with, "Look, if I could sprout wings and fly, Laura, I'd be there this afternoon. Relax. You've got a city full of guys just like me. Send one of them. I'll be in as soon as I can."

Frances had heard Laura still sputtering on the other end of the line when Jack hung up. She knew how Laura felt. A city full of guys like him? Hardly. The more she knew of Jack Neillands, the less she thought there was another quite like him in the whole world.

She'd expected him to get bored with being stuck out in the middle of nowhere. He didn't seem to. She expected him to complain. He never did. She expected him to talk endlessly about the city and its opportunities the way Stephen had. He seemed to want to forget it even existed.

He was willing enough to talk about himself, if she asked. But he didn't seem to be intent on impressing her.

In fact the longer she was in Jack's presence, the more relaxed she felt, but the less she had her preconceptions to protect her.

On the surface at least, Jack Neillands was glitz personified. The last sort of man she needed—or wanted—in her life.

But underneath?

She didn't know. And she didn't know if she wanted to know, dared to find out.

But it was hard to stay negative with a man like Jack.

He still pushed her, yes. But he stopped pushing sometimes, too. And when he stopped pushing she found him almost more frustrating because then she really didn't know what he was up to.

Like right now, for instance. He had gone out with her just an hour ago to milk the goats. And in the barn he had caught her off guard, coming up behind her and kissing her lightly on the nape of the neck. When she'd spun around he'd grinned and backed off. But he'd stolen another brief kiss when she put out the light, and he'd taken her hand in his when they walked back to the house.

Once they'd got inside, however, and she'd expected him to continue his pursuit of stolen kisses, he had helped her pour the milk into containers, then had calmly suggested a game of Scrabble.

Scrabble, of all things! As if she could think of anything but him! Frances sat cross-legged on the braid rug in the living room now and considered the mixed-up letters on her tray.

She was having no better luck making sense of them than she was of the thoughts that scrambled around her brain.

All her thoughts were on Jack. She licked her lips, which still tingled from the hungry touch of his, and was dismayed to feel desire uncurling inside her.

Jack, sprawled on the rug opposite her, concentrating on his tiles, seemed oblivious. "Well?" he prodded. "You've been staring at those letters for hours."

Finally, in desperation, Frances took her *J* and her *M* and spelled the only word she could think of. Laying them on either side of the *A* in Jack's *BAT* she spelled *JAM*.

"That's twenty-three points with the two double-letter scores," she said.

Jack smiled and nodded. He considered the board for a moment, then plucked up his tiles and surrounded her word with a *P* and an *A* in front and an *A* and an *S* in back.

"Pajamas."

"What do you know about pajamas?" Frances asked tartly.

Jack stretched like a cat on a hearth rug. He grinned. "I know how to spell it. And I know when they're not necessary."

The flames within her flickered again. Annoyed with herself, she did the only thing she could with her miserable selection of letters. She added an *I* before the *S* on *PAJAMAS* to make *IS*.

Jack grinned. He added a *K* in front, an *S* behind it. He winked at her and mouthed the word. "Kiss."

Frances gave him a speaking look, then turned back to the board, determined to ignore the innuendo. She drew another tile, considered, then carefully and precisely spelled *X-RAY*.

"Thirty points," she said in her most businesslike tone. "Triple-letter score on *X*."

Jack leaned forward, added an *S* and an *E*, spelling *SEX*. He got ten points and obvious satisfaction. He smiled.

Frances won the game by eighty-seven points. Jack went on to spell *HUNGER*, *LIPS*, *CONDOM* and *BRA*.

Frances knew what they meant now when they talked about winning the battle and losing the war.

Chapter Eight

The lights were off. The fire was low. The snow had long since stopped, and the plow had come through three hours ago. For two hours—after Scrabble and before bedtime—Frances and Jack had dug out his car and got it back on the shoulder.

In the morning, bright and early, he would go.

Frances lay curled on the sofa and tried to face the prospect with equanimity. It was harder to do than she thought.

She would have peace and quiet, she told herself. She would have the single-mindedness to get her work done, the serenity to focus on what was really important in life.

But for all that she knew that was true, she also knew she'd grown used to another face across the table at meal times, another pair of boots in the entry hall, the sound of off-key whistling in the shower.

Of course, she told herself, it wasn't Jack per se whom she would miss. Not at all. But still . . .

She heard a creaking sound just then and rolled over, looking toward the stairs. Jack was standing halfway down them.

She had expected it.

The past two days had been leading up to it. He might have been every bit the gentleman Sunday, but Frances was no fool.

She knew what had been growing between them ever since she'd first met him. She knew exactly what Jack Neillands wanted, and she'd known it would be only a matter of time. Reality was like that. You couldn't freeze the moment the way you could in fiction, holding on to an emotion, living a beautiful instant over and over.

Always, in real life, it had to end.

When she moved, so did he, coming down the stairs slowly and crossing the room until he stood looming above her. She couldn't see his face clearly in the darkness, but she could hear the soft rasp of his breathing and the sound in his throat when he swallowed.

Frances swallowed, too.

She tried for objectivity, for the ability to step back and observe as she had done with life for so long. It shouldn't be that hard, she told herself. What was happening was like a scene right out of *Cutter's Promise* or any of her other books.

She tried desperately to see Jack as Ben Cutter now, to catalog his reactions as she would Ben's, to note the moment and record the sounds and smells and emotions.

But she never got beyond the last. And the emotions she noted weren't his, be he Ben or Jack. They weren't Molly's. They were her own.

And she didn't so much "note" them as live them.

Fear. Yes, there was that, because there was so much she didn't know, and what she did know had taught her to be wary. Desire. Because knowing Jack had taught her that. Need. Because she had been alone so long—too long.

Love?

The word rose unbidden, catching her unaware. It choked her. Oh, God. No, she couldn't. She simply couldn't love Jack Neillands. Please, God, not that.

She turned away, huddling into an even tighter curl.

"Frances?"

She didn't answer, tried to feign sleep. But it was far too late for that.

Jack reached out a hand and touched her cheek. She tried to shake him off, to pull ever more deeply into herself.

Abruptly he sat down on the sofa beside her and took her shoulders in his hands. "Frances, what the hell's the matter?"

"N-nothing." She didn't look at him.

"Yeah, sure." His voice was softly mocking.

"It's nothing. Go away," she whispered.

"No." He didn't move, just sat there, still holding on to her shoulders. Then slowly, inexorably, he moved closer. He gathered her into his arms. His head came down inch by inch until she could feel his breath against her lips.

"No," she whispered again.

But Jack whispered, "Yes," and then he said no more. Or rather he did, but not with words. His lips spoke for him, touching hers lightly at first, then more firmly, cajoling, persuading.

His hands spoke, too. She felt the tension in them as they held her, and when they slid around her back to draw her closer, she felt them tremble. She trembled, too, wanting, needing. Fearing.

She couldn't. If she did, she would lose him, lose him the way she lost Stephen.

"I can't. Please, Jack. No." She turned her head away.

His fingers gripped her tighter. "Why not?" His voice was ragged.

"I don't—I don't want—"

"How can you say that?"

She struggled against him. "I don't."

He shook his head in disbelief, then pulled back and looked down into her face. "Look at me, Frances. Look at me and tell me you don't want me."

She bowed her head, shaking it. "No. I—I can't. I—"

"Because you do."

But Frances wasn't ready to admit that. She couldn't. To do so would be to destroy everything she had built for herself over the past five years. It would be a folly equal to—no, greater than—the one she'd achieved by marrying Stephen. And that, for all its pain, at least had been marriage.

Whatever Jack Neillands wanted, she knew it wasn't that.

She steeled herself against him. "No," she said clearly and with all the force she could muster, looking up to face him squarely as she did so. "I don't."

He stared at her, still shaking his head slightly as if doubting his hearing.

She repeated them. "I don't."

He looked at her steadily. She looked back, mustering every ounce of strength God gave her to meet his gaze with determination. Gradually his grip loosened, then his hands fell away. He stood, his chest heaving.

"So what *do* you want, Frances Moon?" he asked. There was a rawness in his voice that nearly undid her.

She plucked at the comforter covering her. "I—I'd like us to be friends." She said the words so softly that she thought he might not hear them.

But he did. She could tell by the swift intake of his breath, by the scornful snort, by his incredulous tone. "Friends?"

She swallowed, lifted her gaze and met his. "Why not? Or can't you be friends with a woman? I suppose maybe you can't. I suppose we're all only sex objects to you."

"Now look—"

But she went right on. "No, you look," she said, determination growing, speech quickening, the need for self-preservation strong. "I've never said I wanted anything else from you. I never asked you to come here in the first place. I certainly never asked you to come back!"

"You'd rather I hadn't?" His fists clenched against his sides.

"If you're going to expect to go to bed with me just because you did, yes!"

"And you think that's all this is, just expectation?"

"Isn't it?"

He let out a hiss of breath. One hand slapped his thigh. "Damn you, Frances."

"Isn't it?"

He raked fingers through already mussed hair. He muttered. He growled. He shifted from one foot to the other and rubbed a hand against the back of his neck. "Listen, Frances, I...I..."

Her fist tightened on the comforter. "*Don't* say you love me," she warned him. "Because you don't, do you?" The question contained no hope, only challenge.

He glowered at her. "I don't know what I feel, damn it!"

He reminded her of Ben Cutter now. Ben, cornered. Ben, angry. Ben, fighting. Dear, dear Ben.

And if he were Ben, she might have shared a bed with him, might have made love with him. Because if he'd been Ben, she'd have made herself Molly or a woman like her, and she could write them a happy ending.

But he wasn't Ben. He was Jack. Real. Stubborn. Determined. Uncontrollable. And she was Frances. Equally stubborn. Equally determined. Extremely controlled. And inadequate.

The ending that reality would provide wouldn't be happy at all.

"Then I want us to be friends," Frances told him quietly. "Please."

For a moment their gazes locked, his belligerent, hers determined. A log settled in the fireplace with a soft spitting noise. Biff, asleep on the rug, made a soft whuffling sound as he herded sheep in his sleep.

Frances waited, holding her breath. Jack didn't move for an age. Then he seemed slowly to draw himself together. He got up and tucked one hand in his jeans pocket and looked down at her. He gave a negligent shrug.

"Sure, Francesca," he said quietly. "Whatever you say."

FRIENDS? She only wanted to be friends? Oh, Lord, had she really said that? It sounded like a line out of a Grade B movie. If she'd written it in a book, she'd have cut it out.

But life wasn't a book. There were no rewrites. And Frances knew that was indeed what she had told Jack Neillands.

And Jack apparently took her at her word.

He certainly never reappeared that night. He went straight up the stairs to bed. And if he tossed and turned the way Frances did, she didn't hear him.

In the morning he was somewhat distant, but unfailingly polite. Friendly, she told herself. Exactly what she'd asked for. Exactly what she wanted.

So why did she feel so bereft when he slung his duffel bag over his shoulder and gave her only a casual wave of the hand as he walked out the door?

"If you're ever in New York, drop in and see me," he said easily, as though it might someday come to pass.

Frances followed him all the way down the lane to his car, waiting, wistful, but he didn't once take her hand. He stowed his duffel in the back, then slid in the front.

There was no kiss. No touch. Just a friendly smile. He said, "See you," and he was gone.

Frances stood in the lane until she felt frozen. The only warmth she felt were the tears stinging behind her lids.

JACK LOVED PARIS in the springtime. He loved the Place de Saint-Sulpice most of all. He worked like a fiend on shoots all over the city and all along the south coast of France every day that the sun shone, grateful for the work that kept him busy and distracted. But he was also grateful for the weekends and the rainy days that belonged to him alone.

He got up early on Sunday mornings and walked from the small Left Bank apartment he'd sublet to the café that faced the old Sulpician church. There he and a host of other regulars sat eating crepes and drinking countless cups of strong coffee laced with milk while they read the newspapers and watched the pigeons and the people in the square.

He'd discovered the square five years before on an early trip to Paris. He'd always loved it. It was cheery, cosmopolitan and comfortable, nice alone, better yet with a lover or a friend.

Jack imagined it with Frances. It wasn't hard.

He wanted Frances. Still.

Frances wanted to be friends. The thought made him grit his teeth. Still.

Friends! *Friends!*

Oh, come on, Francesca Luna, he'd wanted to say to her that cold, blustery Vermont night four weeks earlier. You don't know what it is you're asking.

He didn't say it, because if he'd said anything at all, he wouldn't have stopped with that. He would have blistered her ears with what he thought about her chicken-hearted behavior. He would have seared her with questions he had no doubt she didn't want to answer. And while he was at it, he would have delivered a few home truths she didn't want to hear.

He didn't for two reasons: one, if he walked away and forgot her within the week, it wouldn't matter; two, if he walked away and couldn't get her out of his mind, he wanted the door left open a crack, not bolted against him for good.

He didn't forget.

He walked through the Jardin de Luxembourg and Frances walked with him. He stopped in Montparnasse and she was there. He leaned against the stone parapet on the Pont Neuf and imagined Frances standing next to him. And when he ate his crepes and strawberry conserve on Sunday mornings at the café across from St-Sulpice, whether Frances knew it or not, she shared.

He'd shared the table with blondes, brunettes and redheads, with Parisians, Czechs and Germans over the past four weeks, but none of them was more real to Jack than the woman who wasn't there.

"Every day I see a pigeon who reminds me of you," he wrote to her in a postcard. "She's always giving me dirty looks. Wish you were here."

Another time, on stationery from a posh Monaco hotel and casino, he wrote, "On the way down we passed plenty of farms. I counted thirty-seven goats. Thinking of you. Wish you were here."

On the ubiquitous Eiffel-Tower-at-night card, he wrote, "Boring without you. Have you ever played Scrabble in French? Great words. Wish you were here."

None of the cards said what he was really thinking. On none of them did he dare. But he wrote anyway because Frances had said she wanted to be friends.

And that, Jack determined, was exactly what they'd be. He'd show her!

So he sent her cards from Paris, from Nice, from Cannes. He sent them from the Camargue, from Mallorca and from a brief three-day shoot in Sicily and from a week-long stint on the Italian coast. Chatty cards. Cheerful cards. *Friendly* cards. It was only what she wanted, after all.

And when he got back to New York?

Well, Jack thought grimly, New York had a postal system, too.

HOME FREE, Frances thought when the snows melted, the ides of April came and went, she finished her tax returns and four more chapters on her book and never saw a sign of Jack.

Good riddance, she thought, too, convinced she'd pegged him right. He might've been charming and fun, but all he'd been after was a tumble in bed. When she resisted, he was gone in a flash. She felt hollow and unhappy, but virtuous. She congratulated herself on her wisdom, on her steadfastness, on her good sense.

The postcard of the beady-eyed French pigeon came, therefore, as a total shock.

She stood by the road in the rain staring at the strong spiky handwriting on the other side of the card, read the cryptic message and the astonishing closing, a simple "Your friend, Jack" over and over.

She was scarcely even aware that a pickup barreling past threw mud all over her jeans and shirt until it screeched to a stop, backed up, and a window rolled down so the driver could apologize.

Frances blinked at him, distracted. "I—it's all right."

The driver, a farmer from over near Gaithersburg, looked at her worriedly. "You sure?"

Frances smiled wanly. "Sure." Her knees wobbled. Her face felt hot.

"Didn't mean to scare you," the driver went on.

Frances shook her head. "It's all right. I'm f-fine." And she bolted up her lane, her fingers clenching on the post-card in her hand.

Her palm sweated so much the ink was smeared by the time she reached her house. She dropped the rest of the mail onto the kitchen table, then sank into a chair and stared again at the card in her hand.

It's only a postcard, she reminded herself. *Lots of people send postcards.* Her mother sent her postcards, her aunt Elvira sent them. So did her college roommate, Cleo, and her cousin, Pat.

Not Jack.

She had never *ever* expected to get a postcard from Jack.

She didn't *want* a postcard from Jack. It would just make him that much harder to forget.

For however much she had blasély brushed off Libby's and Bert's and Eb's occasional comments and queries about the man who had spent three days snowed in with her, she remembered far more than she wanted to admit.

She was, in this particular instance at least, blessed with total recall.

She still couldn't sit down for a meal without remembering what it was like to have Jack sitting opposite her. She still couldn't feed the goats without remembering how Amy loved to nuzzle inside Jack's coat. In the afternoon when she was sitting at the computer trying to write herself into turn-of-the-century Montana, she was plagued by the same frissons of awareness that she had felt when Jack had sat on the sofa behind her that Sunday, flipping through her books, chuckling softly, snorting now and then, sighing, clearing his throat. She even remembered his arms going around her, his lips touching hers, his arousal that was, at times, all too obvious.

But all of those recollections paled beside what happened when she went to bed at night.

Her bed was no longer her own.

She shared it with Harry, of course, just as she always had. But she also shared it with a brown-haired, blue-eyed ghost.

She had only to close her eyes to remember what Jack Neillands had looked like lying there asleep. She had only to snuggle beneath the covers to recall with vivid clarity the solid warmth of his body against her own.

"And if you had made love with him, then what?" she asked herself.

And the answer made her grateful that she hadn't, but it didn't make her feel less alone.

Day by day, however, she had learned to live with it, had told herself that the memories were getting fainter because, however much she remembered, it was still all in the past. Over. Finished. Gone.

The steely-eyed Gallic pigeon was not.

And he was just the first of Jack's stream of forget-me-not emissaries. Two days later she got the Eiffel Tower-at-night reminding her of their Scrabble game, and the day after that, a letter from Monaco.

At first she tried to resist. She threw the steely-eyed pigeon into the trash. But it glared up at her, hurt and accusing, and so she fished it back out.

She propped it up above her kitchen sink and stared at it while she washed the dishes, inuring herself to the sight of it, to the memories of him. It didn't work.

Day after day the cards dropped in. From Paris, Cannes, Nice, little places she'd never heard of and big places she had.

And once she got over the shock of seeing his spiky handwriting and knowing things weren't entirely over between them, she found herself keeping an ear open for the mailman's rattly van.

Before, the arrival of the postman had been exciting only when he brought an advance check, a royalty statement, a letter from her parents, a proof of a new cover or copies of foreign editions of her books.

Now she found herself almost eagerly striding down the hill and riffling through the letters looking for that one special one. She wasn't precisely expecting one, but the days she didn't find one, it seemed oddly as if the sun hadn't come out.

It was because they were friends, she told herself and that made her happy because it meant she'd been wrong about him. He hadn't disappeared entirely when he hadn't got what he wanted. He had agreed to become what she wanted—friends.

He said so himself, didn't he, with each and every letter he wrote, signing them all "Your friend, Jack."

"Who're the postcards from?" Annabel asked one afternoon.

There were seven now propped up against the wall behind the kitchen sink. And Frances had long since given up trying to resist. Now she simply enjoyed them and congratulated herself on having insisted on friendship.

He certainly wouldn't be sending her postcards if he'd got his one-night stand, she thought.

"They're from Jack."

Annabel's eyes widened. "The Rear of the Year? That Jack?"

"I wish you wouldn't call him that. He's a very nice man."

"Indeed he is." Annabel gave Frances a broad wink. "Would you like to tell me just how nice?"

Frances rolled her eyes. "We don't have that sort of relationship. We're friends."

"Oh, yes?" There was a wealth of skepticism in those two words.

Frances fetched the cards. "See for yourself."

"Read them, you mean?"

Frances nodded.

Pushing her glasses up on her nose, Annabel did.

"See?"

Annabel was looking at Frances speculatively. "Mmm. Very nice. What'd he mean in that one card about even more goats?"

"He said in a letter he'd seen thirty-seven of them on the way to Monaco."

"He writes letters, too?"

Frances shifted in her chair. "Of course. I told you, we're friends."

Annabel smiled. "Oh, right. Did you get one today?"

"Mail hasn't come yet."

"I passed Lloyd on the way up."

Lloyd was the postman, and if Annabel had passed him, then yes, there was mail waiting. Frances half rose in anticipation, then, seeing Annabel grin, she sank back down.

"No big deal," she said. "It can wait."

Annabel laughed. "I should be going, anyway. You can walk me back down the hill and get your mail at the same time."

"I could, I suppose." Frances fetched a sweater. It was mid-May now, but the days were still cool.

There were two bills, three pieces of junk mail, a manila envelope from her publisher, another smaller one with the same return address and her editor's name typed in the corner, and a thin blue airmail letter with three Italian stamps.

Annabel smiled with smug satisfaction when Frances's fingers closed over the letter.

"One from your 'friend'?"

Frances flushed.

"I'm glad," Annabel said. "You deserve him."

Frances shook her head.

"Don't deny it," Annabel said. "You've needed a man like that for years."

"I don't have a 'man like that,'" Frances protested. "It's not what you think."

"Oh, Frances, grow up and look around you," Annabel said. "The real world is a pretty amazing place. I've got to run. I locked the door and Leif will be coming home from school."

Frances stared after her, disconcerted. Then, when Annabel had disappeared around the bend, she opened Jack's letter.

It was short, recounting a crazy day he'd spent shooting in some little Italian seaport village, a day in which the sun had sulked behind the clouds in the morning, then glared all afternoon, then played peekaboo with the photographer in the early evening hours, finally disappearing altogether behind a huge bank of thunderheads that drenched them all. It was also the day in which one of the women models was chased by an amorous mongrel, another broke out in hives from eating shellfish, and the artistic director stomped around saying he knew they should've gone to Greece.

"We may yet," Jack concluded. "Wish you were here, in spite of it all." And he signed it with the perennial, "Your friend, Jack."

Frances leaned against the maple tree and smiled. He didn't, of course, wish she was there. And she didn't, either. It was just a figure of speech.

But she did think the Italian village sounded interesting with its small fishing fleet, its open-air cafés, and its pastel houses strung out along the terraced hills. She was glad she had Jack to describe it to her.

She was glad they were friends. It wasn't her fault Annabel had stars in her eyes—even for her friends. It would be nice, but . . . it wouldn't be real.

She tucked the letter into the pocket of her shirt and decided to wait until she got back to the house to open the rest.

The bills and junk mail were easily dealt with. The letter from her editor wasn't.

It was not, as she'd expected, another one of the photocopied promotional newsletters that Natalie habitually sent along to keep Frances abreast of what was going on.

Rather Natalie wrote raving about the cover of *Cutter's Promise*, telling Frances how pleased she'd be, and passing on what she was sure Frances would consider great news.

"Marketing has targeted *Cutter's Promise* for a big promotion," Natalie wrote. "They're doing posters of the cover art, have authorized special dumps to be placed in bookstores, and—get this—money has just been allocated for an autographing tour. Lucky, lucky you!"

Frances felt ill.

Promotional tours meant New York, Boston, Chicago, Dallas, Los Angeles. They meant glitz and glamour, spiff and pizzazz. And people. Lots and lots of people expecting things of her. To say that promotional autographings were not her cup of tea was an understatement. Cup of hemlock more like.

And Natalie, drat the woman, knew it.

Frances picked up the phone and dialed New York.

"You aren't going to be out on the road forever, love," Natalie soothed. "Only four weeks."

"Four weeks!"

"No biggie," Natalie assured her. "New York, Chicago, Dallas and L.A. And a few little spots in between. Limos, chauffeurs, four-star hotels. It'll be glamorous as hell."

Exactly what Frances was afraid of.

"I have commitments. Responsibilities. I have sheep! I have goats!"

"You might have a best-seller," Natalie said, "if you play your cards right."

"I don't want a best-seller!"

It was as if she had just screamed a blasphemy in the Vatican, as if she'd just said the editor-in-chief wore no clothes.

There was total silence on the other end of the line.

Frances contemplated wrapping her end around her neck. She seemed to have just done so as far as her career was concerned.

"I mean..." she began, then faded out because what she'd said was exactly what she'd meant. She couldn't do it. She just couldn't.

Natalie, to her everlasting credit, did not hang up. If somewhere someone gave classes for editors in dealing with nutty authors, Natalie had doubtless got an A.

She said, after that interminable silence, "Well, of course you don't. You want to write great books. But you want people to read those books, don't you?"

"Of course," Frances agreed feebly.

"Well, that's what marketing wants, too."

Frances didn't say anything to that, unsure sometimes what marketing's goals were, unconvinced on occasion that anyone in marketing could tell the difference between a book and a pair of panty hose.

"Tours like this help books, Frances," Natalie said into the silence. "They make great books best-sellers. Truly. I wouldn't encourage you if I didn't believe it."

"Um," Frances said after a moment.

"It's a great book, Fran."

Frances thought so, too. But . . . She sucked in a deep breath.

"It is." Natalie's voice was quietly insistent. "I want the very best for it. For you."

Frances chewed the inside of her cheek. "I don't like glitz and stuff," she said lamely.

"Of course you don't. You like goats."

On anyone else's lips those words would have sounded condescending. On Natalie's they simply sounded understanding. Drat the woman. She made Frances feel an even bigger fool.

How many people, after all, were offered such a publicity tour? How many authors had marketing that solidly behind them? How many publishing houses offered such extensive promotion to an author who had a solid but not astonishing track record?

It wasn't as if she were Stephen King, Frances thought. Or Judith Krantz.

Natalie didn't have to say a word, Frances realized. In the silence she was doing all the work herself. She sighed. She tugged at her hair. She chewed her lip.

"I'll . . . think about it."

"Good," Natalie said.

It was another mark of her editorial expertise that she said no more than that. Gushing would have turned Frances off. Hard sell would have sent her running away. Any indication of "I know you'll come to see it our way," and Frances would have balked.

She was ready to balk, she was willing to balk. She *wanted* to balk.

But Natalie didn't give her a chance. "Think it over," she said. "I'll give you a call next week. By the way, did you get the copy of the cover I sent?"

Frances was about to say no when she glanced down at the manila envelope on the coffee table. With nerveless fingers she picked it up and fumbled with the clasp, finally ripping the edge to get it open.

For just a moment she shut her eyes, imagining. She had envisioned it in her mind's eye for months.

But the reality, whatever it might be, was beyond her imagination. She had to open her eyes, to see for herself how the artist had rendered Jack Neillands as Ben Cutter on her book.

She slid the cover out of the envelope.

"Isn't it beautiful?" Natalie's voice said in her ear.

It was. It was everything Frances could have wanted in a cover. And more.

The background was the midnight blue of a moonlit Maine night. In the far distance a silhouetted line of pine trees marched along the crest of the hill. Below them, strung out along the waterfront, were the houses of Frances's fictional Day's Harbor, a ghostly silver in the moonlight.

And in the foreground, standing on the point, their arms around each other, were Molly and Ben.

Frances didn't know who Molly was. She didn't care. Whoever she was, she was just right with her auburn hair and the hint of Irish stubbornness in the line of her jaw.

But it wasn't the stubbornness that one noticed in the way she looked up into the eyes of the man who held her. It was the love.

Frances felt as if she'd been hit in the gut.

There was an airless void, a tight gasping where her lungs used to be. No one else had the right to look at Ben Cutter like that!

"Frances?" Natalie sounded just faintly concerned.

Frances sucked air. "Wh-what?"

"Isn't it beautiful?"

It took a moment before Frances could marshal the letters to make the necessary word. "Yes." She tore her eyes from Molly and looked at Ben.

He was Ben, of course, just as she'd always imagined him. Just the way he'd looked when she'd tacked his picture up over her computer all those months ago. The man she'd struggled through hardship and adventure with, the man she'd created, the man she'd fallen in love with.

He was Ben; and yet he wasn't. There was no mistaking that he was also Jack.

Her Jack.

Her *friend* Jack.

The look on his face was not one she'd imagined the artist would choose. She'd expected passion, hunger, desire—those were the sorts of things that marketing said sold books. And Ben felt all those things; she ought to know.

Jack felt all those things, too.

But if there were hints of passion and desire in the man looking down at Molly McGuire, they were submerged in a feeling far more profound. The artist had chosen to show Jack at a tender moment, his features vulnerable as he looked down into Molly's eyes, his harsh profile softened by emotions Frances could only guess at.

It was an expression she hadn't known Jack was capable of until the day he'd arrived as she was delivering the lambs. She had seen it then only fleetingly as if it were as surprised to be there as she was to see it. She had seen it again the morning they had awakened in bed side by side.

Her face suffused with unaccustomed warmth. She took another deep draught of air.

"Well, really," Natalie complained, "I'd expected a tad more enthusiasm. You picked the man, you remember."

"I remember." Frances's voice was hollow.

"The artist said he wouldn't have chosen him, but to tell you that he was glad you had. He was absolutely perfect. Isn't it nice to be vindicated?"

Frances, still trying to master the intricacies of breathing, managed, "Oh, yes."

"Ah, well, less is more," Natalie groused. "At least that's what they say."

"I'm pleased," Frances assured her. "Truly."

"We try to do our best, you know."

"I know."

"Think about that." And before Frances could reply, Natalie hung up.

Think about it.

Natalie meant, of course, that Frances should think about doing the tour, think about braving the glitz and the crowds, think about leading with her chin, allowing herself the possibility of getting caught up once again in a world she couldn't control.

She did think about it.

She sat there in the living room while the fire burned down, while the sun sank lower and lower into the sky until the last rays of purple and orange disappeared behind the hill.

She sat, thinking, staring at the painting of Jack.

Chapter Nine

When Jack left for Paris the girls on the streets were wearing woolies. When he got back they were in short skirts with see-through blouses, and every time they passed him he caught a hint of perfume in the air.

He hit the city running with back-to-back magazine ads the first day, two book covers, a TV commercial go-see and an afternoon of long-sleeve dress shirts for a catalog the next.

He debated calling Frances, then decided that a bit more of the Chinese postcard torture wouldn't hurt.

He went out to the bookstore around the corner, bought a garish cartoon card of a Big Apple, wrote, "I'm back. Your friend, Jack," on it and sent it off.

Wednesday brought a full day of shooting for a hunting and fishing specialty house, Thursday another book cover, two more go-sees and an afternoon of acting as a prop for a fashion shoot behind some of the most gorgeous women in the world.

Friday at 5:00 a.m. he, Therese LaBoobs and a production crew left in a location van for Cape May where they spent the better part of the day standing around in front of restored Victorian houses for a travel magazine spread.

They got back just in time for Jack to play first base on the agency's softball team in Central Park. He struck out in his first at bat, but redeemed himself in the second by hitting a triple and scoring on a squeeze bunt, then staggering back to the grass where he collapsed, jet lag and a full week's work finally having taken their toll.

"Good job, Jack!" He felt a luscious pair of lips touch his.

His eyes snapped open. Jennifer Jewell knelt next to him in the grass. She was smiling, as fresh as a daisy, and when he grinned back, she bent down again and dropped another kiss on the tip of his nose.

"Welcome home."

"Good to be home."

"Did you see our spread in B-to-B?"

He shook his head.

"It's terrific. Just came out. We make a great couple." She tossed her long dark hair with an unconscious elegance as she moved to sit cross-legged on the grass beside him. "I had a chance to go to Italy two weeks ago. You were a great temptation."

He slanted her a glance. "I was?"

"Oh, yes. You and all that money from *Italian Bazaar*." She grinned. "But I ended up in Malibu doing sun-and-surf reshoots instead."

"You probably had a better time," Jack said, his eyes on the game in progress.

"Didn't you?" She sounded concerned.

"It was all right."

"More bad phone lines?"

He turned his head to look at her. "What?"

She dimpled. "Couldn't you get through to Vermont?"

Jack rubbed a hand against the back of his neck. "Didn't try."

"No?"

He shook his head, eyes on the ground ball hit to short.

Jennifer's voice betrayed her concern. "Is it all over, then?"

Jack made a wry grimace. "How about, it never got started?" For, as much as he didn't want to admit it, he was afraid it was time to face the truth.

All the while he'd been in Europe, it was easy enough to tell himself he was biding his time. It was easy enough to pretend that he was stringing Frances along, not that she had dropped him and he was too stubborn—or stupid—to acknowledge it.

But now that he was back, it was harder to fool himself. For all his nonchalance, for all he'd sent her that wacky Big Apple postcard instead of ringing her up, the truth was that he was stringing himself along, not Frances.

Frances Moon was quite content in the wilds of Vermont with her sheep and her goats and her paperback heroes. She wanted nothing to do with him.

If she had, there'd have been a postcard or a letter waiting for him when he'd got back. There'd have been a call, a message on his answering machine. Something. Anything.

There had been nothing. No response. Zilch. *Nada*.

And personal rejection, unlike the professional rejection he was so inured to, hurt.

"Oh, Jack." Jennifer shook her head, her expression gentle, slightly pitying. Another time it would have nettled his pride. Today he simply accepted it, wallowed in it. A little feminine compassion didn't feel amiss.

His teammate swung and missed for the third out. "Last inning. Come back to my place and have dinner with me," he said, getting to his feet and picking up his glove.

Jennifer looked at him warily.

Jack grinned. "Just dinner," he promised as he headed for first.

IT WAS THE FIRST MEAL he'd eaten at home all week. Not that he'd have had to go home, of course. A bunch of them usually went out after the game. But Jack was tired. He didn't want to have to go out and be cheerful tonight. But he didn't want to go home alone, either. It was a stroke of good luck to have Jennifer turn up.

They stopped at a Korean grocery, and Jack ambled up and down the aisles, picking up some pasta and tomato sauce, salad greens and frozen yogurt.

"Fattening," Jennifer complained as they headed down Columbus.

"We'll run around the reservoir afterward."

"You run around the reservoir. I got up at five this morning. All I want to do is sleep," she said as they turned on 81st.

"We could do that, too."

"Is that a proposition?"

Jack gave her a tired grin and dug into his backpack for his house key. "When I proposition you, kid, you'll know it."

"You won't," Jennifer said confidently, following him up the steps to his apartment.

"No?"

"I'm not your type."

Curious, Jack glanced at her over his shoulder. "What's my type?"

"Someone older, for one thing."

He opened the door and walked into the kitchen. "Thanks."

Jennifer gave him a guileless smile. "It's true. I'm much too young for you."

"Which is a nice way of saying, I'm much too old for you."

She shook her head. "I wouldn't be bored, you would. You need more, Jack."

"You got someone in mind?" He was banging around in the cupboards looking for a pot to cook the pasta in.

"I thought you did. Didn't it really work out?"

"Nope."

"What happened?"

"How the hell do I know? I guess she didn't like me."

"I don't believe it."

Jack didn't reply until he had the water for the pasta boiling and had started the sauce. He handed Jennifer some silverware and pointed her toward the table. Then he sighed.

"She liked me all right," he admitted finally, knowing that much was true at least. "She just didn't trust me."

"Why not?"

"Dunno."

"Did you ask?"

"Cripes, Jennifer, it's not that easy!"

"Why not? If I cared that much about someone, I'd want to know."

"You had a spaz attack about that kid on the sailboard," Jack reminded her ungallantly. "But I didn't see you asking him out."

"True. But I'm a girl."

"What's that got to do with it?"

"It's harder for girls. They can't pursue."

Jack snorted.

"*I* don't pursue," Jennifer qualified, reading his thoughts.

"Well, I did, and it didn't work."

"Poor Jack." Jennifer leaned across the counter and gave him a kiss.

"I'll live," he said gruffly. Then, "Help yourself to a beer or a club soda or something, and stir this now and then. I've got to take a shower."

He had his head under the shower when the phone rang. It didn't matter. The answering machine would take care of it; Jennifer wouldn't have to.

So he was surprised a moment later to hear a tapping on the bathroom door. "You have a phone call."

"I also have an answering machine."

"I wasn't going to answer it. But when I heard the message, I thought you might want to take this one." Jennifer

paused. "She says her name is F-F-Frances from Vermont."

Jack jerked the bathroom door open. "Are you jok-
ing?" He was dripping on the rug, a hand towel strategi-
cally placed, his only attempt at modesty. Modesty was the
last thing on his mind. *Frances Moon was on the phone?*

"I wouldn't joke about this, Jack."

"Oh, God."

He stood rooted to the spot, unable to think, unable to
move. He'd hoped for a letter, a postcard—some sign that
she'd noticed he was still alive. But Frances on the phone?
Good grief.

Don't get your hopes up, he cautioned himself. Probably
she had a perfectly legitimate, indifferent reason for calling
him. Something to do with her books or her cover. Something to do with her sheep, though why she'd call him about
sheep he didn't know.

"She isn't going to wait forever, Jack," Jennifer said finally. "In fact, she might've already hung up. She didn't
want to hang on."

"No." She wouldn't.

"She's probably having second thoughts."

Fifty-third thoughts more like. Jack snagged a towel off
the rack, knotted it around his waist and headed for the
kitchen.

"F—" he cleared his throat "—Frances?"

There was a sound like a gasp at the other end of the line.
"Oh, yes, hi, it's me. I—I know I didn't warn you and I'm
sure you're busy, but you said to call if I was ever in New
York and . . . I'm in New York . . . so I thought I'd call and
s-say hi. Well, hi. Thanks for all the cards. They were nice.
I won't keep you. I just wanted to—"

"Frances!"

"Wh-what?"

"You're in New York?" He couldn't believe it.

"Yes." Her voice seemed suddenly softer, as if all the air had gone right out of her.

"Where? Where are you?" He was rubbing his hair with the hand towel and motioning Jennifer into the bedroom to find him some clothes.

"Some hotel in midtown. My editor put me here. I'm on a . . . publicity tour." She sounded miserable.

He wasn't. He could scarcely tamp down the enthusiasm in his voice. Great, he thought. Terrific. Fantastic. "I'm glad you called."

"Well, you agreed we were friends and . . ."

"And I meant it," Jack assured her fervently. "Let's have dinner."

"Oh, I don't know. I—"

"Is your editor taking you out?"

"No."

"Well, then—"

"It's so last minute. I'm sure you're busy. I don't want to impose. The woman who answered the phone—"

"Is a very good friend who was just leaving."

Jennifer grinned and tossed him a clean pair of jeans, some underwear and a T-shirt.

"Oh, sure." There was, for the first time, a hint of natural asperity in Frances's voice.

Jack grinned. "She was. Weren't you, Jenn?"

"On my way," Jennifer sang out loud enough for Frances to hear. "Have a nice dinner."

"See?"

"I don't think—"

"Look, you called. I asked you to have dinner with me. What's the big deal? We're friends, right?"

"Well . . . right." But she didn't sound too sure.

"So let's have dinner."

"I'm really pretty bushed."

"So we won't go out. I'll pick you up and bring you back to my place."

"But—"

"Tell me where are are, Frances."

There was a moment's silence in which he thought she might refuse, might hang up on him. He waited, not breathing. Then, at last, she told him.

"I'll be there in half an hour."

IT WAS THE SECOND stupidest thing she'd done today, calling Jack Neillands. The stupidest, of course, had been getting on the plane at Rutland and coming to New York in the first place.

That monumental idiocy had been preceded last week by the even bigger one of allowing herself to be talked into the tour to promote *Cutter's Promise* in the first place.

Once she had done that, foolishness after foolishness seemed to follow.

But calling Jack— Even now she couldn't quite believe she'd done it.

She wouldn't have, she was certain, if she hadn't been faced with a full evening and night of preparatory panic. But New York, the promise of hordes of people tomorrow, or— worse—no people at all, had her chewing her fingernails, pacing the floor and calling Annabel for moral support.

"Call Jack," Annabel had said implacably. "You're friends."

"I can't do that," she'd protested. "I wouldn't presume."

"Then suffer in silence," Annabel countered. "I have to pick Libby up at the orthodontist." And she was gone.

It had taken another three hours to convince herself that if she didn't talk to someone she'd be a basket case by the next morning. Natalie, who lived in Larchmont and weekended in the Catskills, wasn't available. Marketing would probably send someone to hold her hand, but marketing didn't need to know what a schiz she was. The only one she could call was Jack.

When she'd heard the answering machine, she'd breathed a sigh of relief. She'd almost swallowed her teeth when her message was cut off midway through with a feminine voice saying, "Hold on. I'll get Jack for you."

Frances had declined. She'd protested. She'd argued. But whoever the girl answering the phone was, she was adamant. And Frances didn't hang up because she knew enough about Jack Neillands now to know that if he wanted to find her—even in a city the size of New York—he'd hunt her down.

He was on his way over here this very moment, and she was going to be greeting him in her slip if she didn't figure out what to wear right now. She had four dresses with her— three more than she'd owned a week ago.

When she'd wailed "I don't have anything to wear" at Natalie as another of her protests, it had only been the truth. Jeans, sweats and no makeup were her uniform in Boone's Corner. But when she said so, Natalie was not amused.

"Then get something," she commanded and had gone so far as to drag Frances to Bloomingdale's straight from the airport.

So she had choices at least—but they were all choices that placed her smack in the middle of yuppiedom, choices that would doubtless put her on Jack Neillands's footing. And she rejected every one. Not that she disliked the dresses; she didn't. She had chosen them, albeit with Natalie's advice and consent.

But she didn't feel like herself with them—*in* them—and to deal with Jack she needed every ounce of ego she could get.

Besides, she told herself as she put on the pair of blue chambray slacks and madras shirt she'd brought with her, if she dressed up, he would think she had lied about not wanting to go out. And she hadn't.

She wanted to treat this meeting casually, an encounter between friends.

She didn't let herself think about his proposed alternative. An evening with Jack Neillands in his apartment didn't sound casual at all.

"You are living dangerously, my dear," she told her reflection in the mirror.

"Nonsense," she just as promptly responded. "I spent three days snowed in with Jack Neillands and nothing happened. Nothing at all."

"Nothing?" Her reflection seemed to mock her.

She scowled. If she wasn't going to lie to Jack, she'd better not start lying to herself.

But it wasn't lying to say they were friends. So she said it again firmly and loudly and, she hoped, convincingly, as a knock sounded and she went to answer the door.

The slacks and blouse didn't work. But none of the four dresses would have worked, either.

She'd have needed a suit of armor to protect her from the feelings that assailed her upon seeing Jack Neillands again.

And the worst of it was, he didn't have to do anything to elicit her response. He had only to stand there and smile.

HE COULDN'T THINK of a thing to say that didn't sound trite, trivial or unutterably foolish. He could only think she was everything he remembered and more.

A part of him had been prepared for the magic to have vanished. He wouldn't have been surprised.

The half-life of Jack's interest in one specific member of the opposite sex had generally been about the same as that of a loaf of bread. It could as easily have happened with Frances.

It hadn't.

His mouth felt dry, his palms damp. His tongue seemed welded to the roof of his mouth. He would've liked to sweep her off her feet. Fortunately what little common sense he could muster dictated otherwise. He smiled.

"Hi."

"H-hi." She smiled back. She was wearing her hair down, pulled back with a navy hair band, which made her look for all the world like his ten-year-old niece. But if the hair band was childlike, the rest of her was all woman. "Ready?"

"I, uh—" She stopped, and for a moment Jack thought she was going to refuse. But then she smiled again, helplessly almost, and nodded her head. "Yes."

He'd ridden down on the subway and walked across town. But he flagged down a taxi going back.

Bundling her in, he gave the driver his address, then sat back and looked over at her. She was sitting hard against the far door. He sighed. Friendship was going to take a lot out of him.

FRANCES KNEW EXACTLY what Jack's apartment would be like. She steeled herself as they went up the steps, prepared for sleek elegance, chrome and glass, all the trappings of yuppiedom to which Stephen had aspired. She stopped and stared at the exposed brick wall, the old oak furniture and the laundry piled on one end of the dining room table.

"Sorry about this. I'm still catching up." He swept the laundry into his arms and disappeared through a door. His bedroom, Frances supposed. She wasn't going to follow him and find out.

Instead she stood right where he left her and looked around. His apartment was comfortable, lived-in, not the expected playboy's dream pad. In the living room a modern dark brown sofa was flanked on one side by an old oak end table stacked with magazines and an equally old Morris chair on the other.

The bookcases that lined one wall were stuffed with everything from British mysteries to college law texts to what looked like the complete works of Garry Trudeau. The door through which Jack had gone had a chinning bar hung close to the top—an indication of his dedication to fitness, she guessed. There was no other exercise gear to be seen, though.

The kitchen, at the front of the apartment, was separated from the dining area by a tiled counter. It was modern and spacious and looked as if it had recently been redone. On the stove something was simmering deliciously. Her stomach growled.

"Hungry?" Jack asked from right behind her.

She jumped, backing away quickly, then wished she hadn't because she felt foolish. She wouldn't have been surprised had Jack rolled his eyes, but all he did was step around her.

"Plates in that cupboard. It should be ready."

Grateful to be given something to do, Frances got the plates. Jack piled them high with spaghetti and a thick, chunky tomato sauce. Then he got a salad out of the refrigerator and set it on the table.

"So," he said, "tell me about this tour. Sounds like a big deal."

"It is a big deal." Frances made a face as she sat down opposite him. "I wish I'd never agreed."

"Why?"

"It's not my thing." She gave him a weak smile. "All those people. Or maybe no people at all. Maybe knowing I'm coming will drive them away."

He laughed. "There will be people."

But Frances found his confidence no comfort at all. She shivered. "I'm going to be a wreck."

"You'll do fine." He reached out and squeezed her hand. It was the first physical contact that they had shared since she'd opened the door to her hotel room. It was one hand wrapped around another, nothing more. And yet Frances felt more electricity shoot through her at that simple touch than she had in her whole three years with Stephen.

He's a friend, Frances, she reminded herself. But her hand didn't seem to know it. It wanted to wrap around his and hang on.

"Really, don't worry. You've got nothing to worry about."

She just looked doubtful.

"It's a great book. And I'm on the cover, right? So what've you got to worry about? It's the best of both of us." He grinned at her.

Frances laughed. "Of me, maybe. I think there's more to you."

Jack's fingers tightened around hers, his eyes caught and held hers. He leaned across the table and kissed her. "Thanks."

Friends, Frances told herself. Just friends. But friendship was becoming pretty heady stuff.

"Thank you," she said. "For the vote of confidence."

"Anytime. I'll come tomorrow."

Her eyes widened. "To the signing, you mean?"

"Sure. For moral support. Where is it?"

She told him. "But really you don't have to. I—"

"I'll bring a fake mustache and three changes of clothes." He grinned. "So you won't have to worry about no one showing up. I can be a whole crowd if I want to be."

Jack could be anything he wanted to be, Frances thought. Anything at all.

"Eat up," he told her. "You won't have the energy to sign books if you don't eat."

"It's not exactly a demanding occupation."

"It is if you feel you have to conjure up each and every person."

"I don't—" she began, then paused and shrugged. "Well, maybe I do."

"Don't sweat it," he told her. "Tell me what's going on at home."

She knew he was only asking to take her mind off tomorrow, but was glad he asked. She took a deep breath and plunged in.

She told him about Annabel and the kids, about the sheep and goats, about Ernie, Bert and Ebenezer. She told him about the girls she used to teach in Charlestown who had come to spend several weeks during the summer with her. They were staying with Annabel while she was away.

And Jack made it easy for her, asking the right questions, leading her on, encouraging her.

She relaxed a bit, sipped the wine he poured her, smiled.

Jack smiled back. The light in his eyes made a tingle of awareness slide down her spine. Not that, she thought. Not tonight.

"Tell me about France and Italy," she said quickly.

Jack sighed, but then he plunged in, regaling her with tales that made her laugh and put her once more at ease.

He told her things he hadn't mentioned in his cards—about the lady he'd met eating breakfast at his favorite café, who'd thought she was the reincarnation of Anne Boleyn and who confided that she carried a knife to protect herself from men named Henry.

He told her about the morning in Porto Valdoni when the photographer had bullied them down to the shore at four in the morning so he could get his sunrise, got them all frolicking in freezing water, prepared to shoot, turned to answer a question from his assistant and knocked the camera into the sea.

While they washed the dishes together, he told her about the old lady in Sicily who had come up to him and told him in broken English that he looked just like her grandson who lived in America and whom she'd never met. Wasn't he Luigi? she'd asked him.

"When I looked at her," he told Frances, "I wished I could've been."

She stopped drying the plate she held and looked at him, captured by the honesty in his gaze. "I know what you mean."

After they finished with the dishes, he led her into the living room and put on a CD. It was lute music, Bach pieces that she recognized from a cassette of her own. Something familiar, lulling.

He settled her on the sofa, then handed her the glass of wine she'd been sipping since they'd left the table and regarded her solemnly over the top of his. For all that they'd been friends very nicely for the past two hours, friendship wasn't what she saw in his eyes. Her own skidded away at once.

"Don't you hit your head when you chin yourself on that?"

He blinked. "What?"

She pointed to the chinning bar in the doorway. "It seems awfully close to the lintel."

"I don't chin myself. I hang upside down."

Frances stared.

"Gravity boots." He reached into the cabinet next to the doorway and held up a pair of odd-looking objects. "You buckle them on and they hook over the bar."

"With you in them?"

Jack nodded. "Sometimes I do exercises. Sometimes I just hang. It relieves stress." He shrugged. "Helps me get my head together, figure things out. A new perspective, that sort of thing."

Frances thought she could use a bit of getting her head together right then. Heaven knew she could use a bit of help in figuring things out. Like what she was doing feeling so mellow in Jack Neillands's apartment.

And what she felt about him.

He was standing clear across the room from her now, but she could still almost feel a pull between them. What the

moon did to the oceans to create tides was what Jack Neillands did to her.

"Like this."

Her attention jerked back to Jack. He was hanging upside down.

"My word!"

Jack grinned at her, arched forward and touched his toes,
then let himself slowly back down. Frances got up and
walked over to him. He had stripped off his shirt baring a
vast expanse of tanned, muscular chest and belly, and, as
she watched, the muscles in that belly flexed as he arched
upward again.

She swallowed as they eased slowly and he lowered his
torso to hang straight down again.

"See?"

She saw.

"Want to try it?"

"Uh, no, thank you." Though the need to get her head
together was increasing by the minute.

Again he arched, those incredible stomach muscles flexing again, then easing, flexing, easing.

Frances watched with the fascination of a doe mesmerized by the visible power of a lion.

And then Jack drew himself all the way up, grabbed on to
the chinning bar, lifted off his feet and swung easily to the
ground to stand flushed and smiling before her.

She took a quick step backward. "I should be going. I
have to get up early tomorrow."

But Jack herded her back to the sofa with the ease of Biff
corralling an obstinate sheep. "You won't sleep a wink all
night. Finish your wine."

"I've had enough. I really ought to leave. It's almost
eleven. And I'm a country girl."

"A quick game of Scrabble." He grinned at her.

She laughed. "Not on your life!"

"Chicken," he said, then shrugged. "All right, finish your wine, then I'll take you back to your hotel."

All the way back downtown Frances planned a graceful exit. She didn't want to seem ungrateful, but she wasn't inviting him in.

Thank you for the dinner, she said to herself over and over as the taxi sped through Central Park and zipped down Fifth Avenue. *It was lovely. Don't bother to see me to my room. I'll be fine.*

But Jack was paying the driver almost before they stopped. He had her out of the cab and was leading her up the steps to the lobby while she was still opening her mouth.

In the doorway, he paused. "It's been great. I'll see you tomorrow."

He was gone before she could say a word.

IN HIS LIFE Jack had done some difficult things, some demanding things. He'd hung off the side of a cliff for hours so some wilderness outfitter's clothing would look good. He'd spent mornings in water of arctic temperatures in the best interests of more swimwear companies than he could count. He'd climbed mountains, swum rivers, perched on parapets and, even once, thanks to some ad man's madness, wrestled an alligator.

But he'd never done anything harder or more demanding than walking away from Frances tonight.

And the only reason he could do it at all was that it was all part of a larger plan.

Frances Moon was not going to be bowled over. Her resistance, if it was going to be overcome at all, was going to have to be surmounted slowly, bit by bloody bit.

And he was the man to do it.

Was it worth it? He asked himself as he caught a cab back uptown.

His mind played back over the evening, over her panic about the signing, about her need for reassurance. It reflected on her enthusiasm for her Charlestown girls, for her eccentric neighbors, for her sheep and goats.

He thought about the way her eyes sparkled when she was amused, about the way she looked at him, wary yet wondering, whenever he spoke. He thought about the way she backed away from him at every opportunity, yet kissed him as if she couldn't get enough.

Was it worth it?

He smiled and leaned his head back against the seat of the cab. Oh, yes.

Chapter Ten

He was lurking behind the cookbooks. Earlier it had been the recent nonfiction and, before that, the occult. Frances had spotted him the moment he'd come in, an anomaly among her adoring fans.

And her fans were there. Mostly they were women, ranging in age from fifteen to eighty-five, from blond hair to blue, from briefcase toters to baby toters, not intimidating in the least. They thought she was wonderful, and it wasn't long until her panic receded and Frances felt the same about them.

Jack, from behind the bookshelves, winked at her.

He stuck out like a sore thumb. Not that he lurked obviously, of course. He was very discreet, hanging around with his nose in a book, a pair of glasses on the end of his nose. But the fact that he didn't go away caused the assistant manager some concern.

Finally after forty-five minutes, she came up to Frances, bent down and whispered warily, "Do you know that man?"

Frances smiled. "He's a . . . fan."

The assistant manager's brows lifted and she craned her neck, trying to get a better look. Jack buried his nose deeper into a book on Chinese cooking.

"He looks rather familiar," she said at last. "Poor fellow. I suppose he'd just too shy to come over and ask for an autograph."

Frances just laughed.

The rest of her readers weren't shy in the least. They were uniformly gracious and open, praising Frances's work and the people who lived on the pages of her books.

She was delighted and amazed to discover that they found the people in her books as real as she did. They identified with her heroines, they told her. They fell in love with her heroes.

"Such men," one of the women said to her, sighing and staring at Jack on the cover of *Cutter's Promise*. "I wish there were a few real ones around."

"God, yes," sighed another, looking at the picture. "Especially him."

Frances, catching Jack's eye over the top of a Julia Child dump, saw him lift his eyebrows. A faint flush of crimson ran high across his cheekbones. She smothered a grin.

"But if there were, what would you say to a man like that?" The woman shook her head despairingly.

A young blonde giggled. "Why waste time talking?"

"Well, don't worry your head about it. There aren't any." The first woman thumped a book down for Frances to sign. "'S'fiction, that's all. An' I know fiction when I see it."

Frances smiled wryly. Once she'd thought she did, too.

No more. Not since fiction had deserted the pages, had leaped out from between the covers of the books she wrote and waded right into her life.

Fiction stood now a scant ten feet from her, wearing faded blue jeans, holey sneakers and a T-shirt with Live Bait written on it. And there was truth in advertising for you, Frances thought.

He was leaning against the bookcase with the air of a man used to waiting, a man with determination, with patience, and with eyes that followed her every move. He looked pretty realistic to her.

The devil in her had been telling her ever since she'd seen Jack again that friends wasn't what she wanted to be with him. The devil in her was distressingly interested in getting to know him far better.

She and the devil had tossed and turned all night.

She'd risen finally at seven, taken a long cold shower—to wake up, she assured herself, not for any other reason. Then she had laid out all her dress choices and tried to decide which to wear for her signing.

Momentous decisions, she told herself, needed time.

But the decision she was debating was not whether to wear the tailored shirtwaist, the power suit, or the demure, but slightly sexy peasant dress. The decision was whether or not to call Jack and tell him firmly and flatly that he shouldn't come today.

The reason the decision was so hard was that in fact there was no question; she wanted him there.

Seeing him again had only reminded her how much she liked having a man in her life—having Jack in her life.

And that was a dangerous notion indeed. It frightened her. She knew the joy and optimism with which she had gone into her marriage with Stephen. She knew the disaster that marriage had become.

Jack's not going to marry you, for heaven's sake, she told herself gruffly.

And that, her other self countered, was precisely the problem.

The thought had stopped her dead. Was she really thinking of marriage in the same sentence with Jack Neillands?

The very notion had sent her reaching for the phone forthwith.

The trouble was she got not Jack, but the ubiquitous answering machine with its gruff "I'm not here. Leave a message. I'll call you back."

She didn't want him to call her back.

She did leave a message. "This is Frances. I'm fine. All butterflies gone. You don't need to come by. Nice to see you. I . . . enjoyed our dinner." And she rang off, dropping the receiver as if it were a grenade about to explode in her ear.

She didn't know whether he didn't get the message or whether he got it and ignored it. But at ten minutes past eleven she looked up from signing a book for a little blue-haired lady to see him standing there.

Every bit of defensive common sense she'd bludgeoned into her head that morning went right out the window.

Her mind might have panicked, but her heart sang. Her toes did a tiny tap dance underneath the table. She hid her mouth behind her hand and smiled.

Jack, leaning against history and military, smiled, too. Then he opened a copy of *Planes of the Luftwaffe* and settled in.

He'd drifted around from subject to subject ever since. He never came directly up to her, but hovered in the background, encouraging, watching, smiling. She'd expected to feel awkward and uncomfortable under his scrutiny, instead she was glad he was there.

When she looked up once during a lull and didn't see him, she felt a shaft of disappointment spear her.

She got up to stretch her legs, peered this way and that, over cookbooks, around mysteries. No Jack.

But what could she expect? she asked herself.

He'd hung around for over an hour. She had to stay another hour more. He couldn't hang around all day. He'd come, hadn't he? He'd seen she didn't need nursemaiding, and he'd left.

Still she sighed. Then she walked around behind humor and ran smack into him.

"Oh!"

His hands caught her upper arms. His handsome, wonderful face smiled down at her. "Miss me?" Before she could reply, he followed the words with a kiss.

Quite without meaning to, she found herself leaning into it, into him, her hands resting against his chest, her fingers curling into the soft cotton of his T-shirt.

His mouth was hard and warm and persuasive, and Frances could only guess how successful his persuasion might have been if just then a voice behind her right ear hadn't exclaimed, "Miss Luna?"

She jerked back. A tiny blue-haired lady was staring at her, book in one hand, pen in the other. Her eyes seemed about to pop out of her head.

"Er," Frances said.

"Miss Luna?"

"Um," she said.

"You are Miss Luna? Francesca Luna?" The little old lady's eyes positively danced.

"Well . . . yes, I am."

"I knew it!" The little lady pumped Frances's hand. "I'm Hilma Fincel. I told Gladys. I told her where there was smoke there was fire." She shook a finger at Frances and Jack. "I knew you were a writer who knew whereof she spoke."

While Frances gulped and went crimson, Hilma Fincel wheeled around and shouted down the aisle. "Gladys! Gladys! Over here! She's over here. And even better in person than in her books!"

"Much better," Jack said.

Hilma Fincel looked him up and down. "You're better in person, too, young man," she told him and tapped him on the chest with the book.

Jack gaped, then grinned. "You better believe I am." He gave her a lecherous wink and vanished down the aisle.

Hilma Fincel's day was made.

It was the last Frances saw of Jack, though, until she finished.

But when she gathered up her things and thanked the assistant manager, he was waiting by the door.

When she walked through it, he fell into step beside her. "Where were we? Oh, yeah, I remember." And he spun her into his arms right there in the middle of the Fifth Avenue sidewalk.

"Jack!"

"This is New York. No one's even noticing."

He kissed her soundly, hungrily, making her heart pound and her pulses flutter. Then as abruptly as it had begun, the kiss ended and he laced his fingers through hers.

"Come on," he said, flagging a cab.

He hustled her into the one that screeched to a halt, told the driver the name of her hotel and they were there before she knew it.

"Come on," he said again and towed her inside.

"I don't think—"

"Don't think," Jack said firmly, propelling her through the lobby. "That's half your problem."

Frances thought her problem was she wasn't thinking nearly enough. "But—"

"Just get changed. We're going to see New York."

Frances stopped dead. It was the worst thing he could have said. Her reaction to New York had been a sore point between Stephen and herself. It was an example, he told her, of how ill equipped she was to enjoy the finer things in life.

"I don't have anything to wear," she hedged.

"No jeans?" Jack looked amazed.

"Jeans?"

"We're not going to Lutèce. Unless you want to."

"No," she said quickly.

"Then come on. What're you going to do otherwise?" he challenged her. "Hole up in your room, hypering yourself into a frenzy until you have to go to the airport on Monday? Sounds pretty stupid to me."

It sounded pretty stupid to Frances, too.

"All right," she said at last. "Give me ten minutes."

Jack waited while she slipped into the bathroom and skinned off her historical author's outfit. Then she doused her face with cold water, stared at herself for a long, wondering moment in the mirror, and donned jeans and a cotton shirt.

She emerged to find him staring out the window at Central Park. She hesitated, and then he turned and grinned at her.

"Much better." He held out a hand. "Let's go."

The New York City Frances saw with Jack was nothing like the one she'd visited with Stephen.

The moment Stephen had had a regular paycheck at Bradley, Fitch, Monroe and Monroe, he'd booked them into the Sherry Netherland, hauled her to Lutèce, to Zenon, to Studio 54.

"We can finally afford to go where the 'in' people go," he'd told her, pleased.

Frances had felt awkward, out of place.

"It's not me," she'd told Stephen.

"It will become you," he'd said.

He'd insisted they see the latest Broadway plays to "improve their cultural understanding," bought her clothes at Saks and Bergdorf Goodman's to "improve her image," and gifted her with perfume from Dior, Frances supposed, to "improve her smell."

Jack's first move was to determine that she was hungry. When she admitted she was he bought her a hot dog from a street-corner vendor and took her to the zoo in Central Park.

"The zoo?"

"You don't like zoos?"

"I love them, if they're kind to animals."

"This one is. It's only been open since last summer."

They wandered happily through the exhibits, laughing at the antics of the monkeys, amazed at the grace of the huge polar bears, delighted by the baby rabbits in a children's exhibit.

"Busman's holiday," Jack chided when Frances hung over the railing and watched avidly as the rabbits hopped about.

Frances laughed and didn't even pull away when, as they left, Jack's fingers laced with hers and for a second his lips brushed against her ear.

After all, she thought, what could happen in the middle of Central Park?

It was midafternoon by then and the summer sun was hot on her shoulders. On the canyonlike streets, where she'd always been with Stephen, it would have been sweltering. In the park it was pleasant.

She found herself smiling at the man who walked next to her. She found herself melting when he smiled back.

He bought her an ice cream at the snack bar by the boat house. And while she was licking it, he rented a rowboat.

"You row?" she asked, skeptical.

He handed her in and shoved off, then settled down opposite her. "No. I thought you did."

She stared, nonplussed, at his blank-faced innocence, then laughed with relief moments later when he fitted the oars neatly into the locks and proceeded to row them out into the lake.

It was magic. It was New York in its absolutely best light—the urban crush held at bay, the harsh geometric skyscrapered horizon softened and mellowed by the lush curves of meadow, lake and trees.

A soft breeze lifted Frances's hair. She smiled, stretching out her legs, closing her eyes and lifting her face to the sun, letting its warmth soothe her nerves, her muscles, her emotions.

"Suit you?"

She opened her eyes and smiled. "Oh, yes."

She was enchanted. And even after their time on the lake was over, the magic remained.

Frances found that a bit surprising since Jack had attempted, not very successfully, to teach her to row.

She wasn't good at it. In fact she was very, very bad.

But unlike Stephen, who expected her to instantly live up to his expectations, Jack didn't seem to care. He just laughed at the water she splashed all over him.

"Cools me off," he said wryly.

"You have the patience of a saint."

"I do," he said gravely. And the look he gave her was so penetrating that she wondered if they were talking about the same thing.

But he said nothing else, just took her hand as they left the lake and followed the path toward the street. And Frances, lulled, rubbed her thumb along the side of his hand as they walked, marveling at how right it felt.

They walked up Central Park West, discussed the possibility of a brief jaunt through the Museum of Natural History and decided against it.

"It's not that I don't like that sort of thing," Frances told Jack. "It's just that I prefer my animals breathing."

"Let's go back to my place, then. I'll get cleaned up and we can go out for dinner."

"I should change, too."

"No problem. You come with me now. Then we can go down to your hotel. It's on the way."

Was she going to say no? Did she want to say no?

No.

She went.

"Help yourself to something cool while I catch a shower." He pointed her toward the refrigerator, then disappeared into his bedroom.

Frances stood looking at that door until she heard the water running in the bathroom, until her mind's eye reminded her what Jack Neillands looked like naked.

Then she went and got herself a long, tall glass of pure ice.

IT WAS THE BEST of times. It was the worst of times. It had nothing to do with Charles Dickens. It had everything to do with having Frances in his life and not in his bed.

He wanted her desperately, more every passing day. And yet every time he considered going to bed with her, Jack found himself backing away.

He wondered if he was losing his mind.

What he was afraid of losing was Frances.

He stood in the shower, letting the cold water beat down on his skull and went over yet again the ramifications of making love with her. For ramifications there were.

Once he took her to bed, once he made love with her, nothing was going to be the same. There was no way either of them was going to be able to take refuge in the notion that they were just "friends." Change was inevitable.

And, Frances's obvious reservation aside, what if he didn't like the change? What if where they went from there wasn't where Jack wanted to go?

Did he even know where he wanted to go?

He was getting inklings. But Jack was in uncharted territory now. He'd known a lot of women, but he'd never known one he wanted to know the way he wanted to know Frances. He'd never cared about anyone the way he cared about her.

It was scary. But if he was scared, she was more so. And that thought made him bristle. He was a lot of women's dream man. It was galling to think he wasn't hers.

Well, he would be. It might take time, but he would manage in the end. Jack Neillands had never met the woman he couldn't woo.

HE TOOK FRANCES to a funky little restaurant-cum-antique store down in SoHo. He knew a hundred places he might've taken her—elegant places, intimate places, upscale, yuppie places, French places, Chinese places, North Carolina bait-shack sorts of places. But he'd decided on this one because he thought it suited her.

It was quiet, unpretentious, yet appealing. The service was good, the food better, the atmosphere warm but not overwhelming. He thought she'd like it.

She did. The uptight, apprehensive Frances who'd paced around his apartment the night before like a claustrophobic cat had disappeared.

Tonight she was the same mellow Frances he'd plied with beer in Vermont, the same starry-eyed Frances who'd delivered the lambs. But she drank only mineral water with her meal and there wasn't an animal in sight.

There was only Jack, smiling at her. And he hoped it wasn't just his imagination that saw her looking at him the same way.

With another woman he'd have had a line, a verbal tease designed to take them one step closer to the bedroom.

With Frances he only said, "I'm really glad you called yesterday," and it was nothing but the truth.

She looked up and met his gaze, her own as bright and happy as he'd ever seen it. "Me, too. You've made New York a lot nicer than I'd anticipated."

He shrugged. "That's what friends are for."

She smiled, then sighed.

"What's wrong?"

She shook her head. "Pity I don't have a friend like you in every city."

"I'm glad you don't."

She laughed. "No fear. There's only one Jack Neillands."

"And thank God for that." Then his grin vanished and he considered her seriously. "You still worried? Anything else I can do? For moral support, I mean?"

She gave a brief shake of her head. "No. You've been marvelous, really."

He'd like to be a whole lot more marvelous, Jack thought. But he knew that if he even suggested it, he'd have the old Frances back again—the one who made a career out of running scared.

Take it slow, Jack, he cautioned himself. *Take it easy.*

So he sucked in a deep breath and said, "I know a little place nearby that has a good jazz combo. You interested?"

She was. They walked there, hand in hand, and sometimes their hips and shoulders brushed. And when they got there, it was so crowded, he thought she'd refuse to go in. But she just pressed closer to him as they moved through the throng. And when they finally found a place to sit, she was almost in his lap. Her hair brushed his lips when she turned her head. He couldn't move his arm without touching her breasts.

It was a refined sort of torture, Jack thought. He didn't see how it could get worse.

Frances showed him.

They were riding back uptown in the cab, just approaching her hotel, and she was sitting snugly beneath the curve of his arm while he breathed in the soft scent of cinnamon and flowers that he'd come to associate with her.

He had his head turned toward her, his lips brushing her ear. He wasn't kissing her yet, though God knew he was going to before he let her go upstairs without him again tonight.

And that was when she sighed. "I hate hotels."

He didn't move. "What?" His voice was a mere whisper. What was she saying? Implying?

She shifted slightly away from him. "I hate hotels, even nice ones like this one," she said softly. "They're so imper-

sonal, like cages. I wish they'd found me a bed and breakfast. A home.''

"I've got one."

She looked at him, her eyes round and worried.

"Stay with me."

"I—"

"We're friends, right?" he rushed on before she could
object. "I stayed with you."

"Yes, but—"

"I won't put the make on you. No pressure. No lines.
Nothing. Bed and breakfast. I swear it.'' He *was* losing his
mind. He wasn't really swearing all these insane things, was
he? But it seemed he was.

Frances brushed her hair away from her face. "Jack, I
don't think—"

He turned her under his arm so that they stared at each
other, their faces only inches apart. "Have you had a good
time or not?"

"Of course, I have."

"Are we friends or not?"

"Yes." Slowly.

"Do you trust me or not?"

"Well, not—"

"Come on, Frances. Do you really want to go back up
there to that cage?"

"It's a pretty elegant cage."

"But do you want to be in it?"

She sighed. A limo passed, followed by three taxis. Jack
waited, wondering what he'd do if she said yes. Wondering
what he'd do if she said no.

"No," she said.

He breathed again. "Then come with me."

"You won't—"

"I won't. I promise." He crossed his heart.

One corner of her mouth lifted. "How do you know *I*
won't?"

He looked her straight in the eye. "You're very welcome to, believe me."

Frances grinned then. "That makes me feel much better. I would've known not to trust you if you'd said you didn't want me to."

Jack groaned.

"All right. I'll come."

PROMISES. Promises. The trouble with promises, Jack thought, was that he kept them. Always had. Always would. It made him a "good guy," he supposed. But it sure as hell made him a frustrated one, too.

So what else was new? He'd been frustrated since March 23, since the day he'd walked into Frances Moon's life. But he could scarcely complain to her about it.

She'd probably look him straight in the eye and tell him there were plenty of other women in the world, what was he waiting for?

He'd said it to himself often enough. He knew the answer now.

He was waiting for Frances.

He spat a mouthful of toothpaste into the sink, rinsed his mouth and opened the door.

In his dreams Frances was always lying in his bed waiting. Her eyes were always wide and expectant, her lips curved into a smile.

In reality she was, naturally, nowhere to be seen.

Jack sighed and followed the sound of the television into the living room.

She was curled into the corner of the sofa, her knees tucked under the elongated T-shirt she wore. Her arms were wrapped around them, and when she looked up at him as he hovered in the doorway, her eyes grew wide, but they were more wary than expectant. Her lips, however, did smile.

Jack sucked in a deep breath. "Good show?"

Frances shrugged. "It was on."

He dropped onto the sofa beside her, not right next to her, but close.

Frances kept her eyes fixed on the television screen. It was an old movie. Spencer Tracy was trying gamely to get the best of Katharine Hepburn—with about as much success, Jack realized, as he had getting the best of Frances Moon.

He edged closer. His bare shoulder brushed her sleeve. His bare knee lurked just inches from her own. His bare toes hovered in the corner of her vision.

Frances stared straight ahead.

Jack sighed and shifted slightly closer to her. Just because he was going to be a good boy this evening she needn't think he intended to sit across the room. At the very least he ought to be able to hold her hand.

But at the moment Frances was holding her own hand and hugging her own knees. He might as well have left her at her hotel room.

"Look!"

His head jerked up. Frances was staring raptly at the television, a wide grin on her face. He looked. And groaned.

Spencer and Katharine had vanished. In their place he saw an upscale New York bar, dark wood, plate glass mirrors, trendy people—and himself. Jack Neillands in living color— a ravishing redhead draped over his shoulder while he hoisted a beer.

Jack groaned.

Eight seconds later he was hoisting himself out of a pool where a buxom blonde offered him a beer. Another eight and he was lying on a sofa before a roaring fire, his arm around a beautiful brunette, a can of the same beer balanced on his chest.

At the last he was sitting on a wide sand beach, looking the camera straight in the eye and winking.

"For those of us who've got what it takes," he said, hoisted the beer, winked again and shrugged.

"Oh, hell," Jack said.

Jack was generally dispassionate whenever he saw himself on the tube. He was indifferent whenever he encountered his face in magazines, newspapers, on billboards. Even the poster, idiotic though it was, never bothered him much. It was a job. He got paid for it. It wasn't him.

The beer commercial wasn't him, either, but try telling Frances that.

Spencer and Katharine reappeared, but Frances didn't seem to notice. She turned to Jack, looking at him as if she were seeing him for the first time.

"It's just bull," he said, wanting her to say of course, it was.

But she didn't say anything, just looked at him.

Jack stared back, seeing three months of painstaking effort going down the drain with thirty seconds of babes and beer. He flicked off the television and hauled her to her feet. "Come on."

"Come on where?"

"We're going to bed."

Chapter Eleven

Atta way to go, Jack.

Such finesse. Such subtlety. You're a real charmer, you are.

He ignored these and all other similar chastisements that reeled through his head as he led Frances into the bedroom. It was too late to listen to them now. Too late to do anything, except...

Except nothing, which was what he'd promised.

He stifled a groan.

Frances was looking at him warily, as if he might at any moment turn into a werewolf.

He hesitated, then let go of her hand just long enough to fold back the thin cotton blanket and the sheet. He'd half a notion that she might bolt.

She didn't. But she stood there looking for all the world like a statue of Our Lady of the Petrified Forest, which didn't do wonders for his morale, either.

"There's never been a woman you couldn't charm," Carter often complained.

Carter had never met Frances.

"Hey," Jack said softly. "Relax." And hoped the advice worked on himself as well. The nervous tension vibrating through him was almost palpable. He felt young, inexperienced, gauche. A novel feeling.

He drew a deep breath and reached over to flick off the lamp. The room dimmed, illumined now only by tiny lights from the tall apartment houses that loomed on Central Park West. He angled the blinds so that their starlike gleam spilled onto the bed. Then he caught Frances's hand again and drew her down beside him.

She came, wooden, but unresisting, so that her head rested in the crook of his shoulder, her hair blanketed his chest. The subtle scent of cinnamon teased his nostrils. The warm weight of woman blew his mind.

He willed himself to lie still. If ever a man could control his body, his emotions, his reactions, Jack could. It came with the job. Usually it was a cinch. It was murder now.

Frances shifted.

He shrugged.

She sniffed.

He squirmed.

She sighed.

And then, at last, there was silence.

No, not silence. There was in the distance the wail of a siren, the insistent blast of a car alarm, the *oo-gah*, *oo-gah* of a horn. There was overhead an airplane and, closer, the spiky heels of his upstairs neighbor moving around.

Closer still, ruffling the hairs on his chest, he heard the soft, nervous sound of Frances breathing.

He felt the solid, seductive warmth of her body pressed against his—the solid, seductive warmth he'd promised to resist.

"Now what?" Frances said in a whisper.

Now what indeed?

"You tell me," Jack said. "I've never done this before."

She pulled back. "I'm sorry. I should leave. I—"

"Stop that," he growled. "I'm fine. I'm not going to expire from frustration, I promise."

"But—"

"Damn it, Frances. Relax." He pressed her head back against his chest and held her there.

"Me, relax?" she said after a moment and he felt her smile. "What about you?" Her hand massaged the tense muscles of his stomach.

Jack grimaced. "I'm trying. Tell me a story or something. You're a writer."

"I always get writer's block when I send people to bed."

He lifted his head and glanced down at her. "Truly? You don't imagine it?"

She hesitated, then smiled. "Oh, yes, I imagine it." The softness of her voice sent a shaft of desire right through him.

"Did you imagine it with . . . Ben?"

She shifted over onto her back and cleared her throat. "A bit."

"Just a bit?"

"Some," she allowed.

He smiled. "Was it good?"

Her fingers dug into his ribs. "What do you think?"

He thought he was going to die of frustration whether he said he would or not. "I think it would be wonderful," he said, and he couldn't help the sigh that escaped his lips.

"You promised."

"The more fool I."

Frances smiled in the silvery darkness of the room. "But I appreciate it."

"Oh, good." His voice was self-mocking.

She looked innocent, virginal lying there beside him. Yet he knew she couldn't be, not having been married. He wondered about the man who had made her the way she was. She certainly hadn't been born this way—edgy and afraid. What had he done to her? What had her marriage been like?

He wished like hell he could ask. He didn't dare.

He lifted a hand and brushed her hair away from her face. Lingering, his fingers tangled in a lock of it, reveling in its softness.

Before he could think better of it, he moved, covering the distance between his lips and hers, and kissed her hungrily.

And for a moment—just that, no more—she was kissing him back. Her lips sought his. Her tongue touched his. And then she pulled away. He heard her draw a shaky breath. He drew a longer, deeper one of his own.

"No writer's block for us," he said unsteadily.

But then, even though everything in him objected, he moved away.

If he was ever going to get past that other man's sins, he wasn't going to do it by pushing. He had to bide his time, wait, learn patience. All those things his mother and countless photographers had always told him. He grimaced wryly and folded his arms behind his head.

Frances shifted slightly away, too, so that her head rested on the pillow now, but she didn't turn her back. Instead she propped herself on one elbow and looked at him. He didn't move.

"You never cease to amaze me, Jack," she said softly.

"I never cease to amaze myself."

"So," she said, a hint of a smile in her voice and less tension than he'd heard from her since she'd agreed to come home with him, "what sort of story do you want to hear?"

THE MIRACLE WAS, it worked.

They lay there for hours with their arms around each other and Frances told Jack about life on the farm when she was growing up.

She told him about her fourth-grade teacher, Mrs. Steffen, who encouraged her writing. She told him about working so hard to get a scholarship to Radcliffe, about confounding everyone's expectations and actually succeeding there. And in his arms she felt a comfort and a joy she hadn't felt in years.

She listened, too, while he told her about his childhood, about being the oldest of four, the one his mother always thought could cope.

" 'Jack can handle it,' she always said," Jack told her.

"And you did," Frances said confidently.

"But it wasn't always easy. You were lucky with your fourth-grade teacher. Mine was a dragon. Mrs. Boswell, her name was. We called her Mrs. Broadswell. She was, well—" he grinned "—ample, you know?"

"You're terrible." Frances giggled.

"She was terrible," Jack said darkly. "She made my life miserable. It's a wonder I survived."

Frances thought Jack could probably survive anything and said so.

"I'm not one of your heroes," he protested.

She shook her head and laid her cheek next to his. "No," she said. "You're better."

And before he could prove her wrong and himself fallible, she turned her head long enough to press a kiss to his lips, then she snuggled into his arms and fell asleep.

Jack thought martyrdom by sexual frustration was a heck of a death.

"Morning." The voice was husky and male and close enough so his breath tickled her cheek.

Frances resisted. Her mind strained to hang on to the dream. It was a marvelous dream, a sexy dream. The sort of dream she counted on to get her through her love scenes. The sort she rarely had and desperately tried to memorize for future reference. She scowled and pushed against the intruder.

It was like pushing against a hard, warm rock.

Frances frowned. She pushed again. Solid. Slightly hairy. Hairy? Perplexed, she opened her eyes a fraction.

The dream vanished into thin air, unnoticed and unmourned. For once reality was better.

Jack lay there, head propped on one hand, smiling at her. She felt incredibly awkward. She'd never mastered the etiquette of waking in a man's bed; she'd never needed to. Until now. She swallowed and licked her lips, then smiled back. "Morning, yourself."

"Sleep well?"

She stretched experimentally. "Mmm. Yes." She felt slightly embarrassed that she had. "Did you?"

"Mmm."

Whether that was an affirmative or a negative, Frances didn't know. But Jack didn't look unhappy or unrested. He looked wonderful—even with his hair mussed, his expression sleepy, and dark stubble shadowing his cheeks and jaw.

Frances's fingers itched to reach out and touch that stubble, to brush her hand down his cheek, savoring its smoothness, then back up, delighting in its sandpapery roughness.

She didn't, of course. She had trusted him. She had slept with him.

But even she knew there were limits to a man's forbearance. Touching Jack Neillands now would be playing with fire.

Yet she couldn't help feeling a sense of wistful longing for what might have been—what should have been—when Jack moved away, sat up, threw back the quilt and bounded out of bed.

He didn't say anything, didn't indicate any regret at all as he tugged on a pair of jeans and pulled a shirt over his head. The regret was hers.

Watching him, she felt an almost desperate loss and a brief flare of anger—not at Jack, but at herself.

Some small insistent part of her kept repeating the old feminist adage, "Is this all there is?" and knew that it wasn't.

She had the humdrum day-to-day barnyard chores, of course. She had the washing, ironing, cooking, sweeping that women all over the world had. She had the mucking out of sheep and goats. She also had, by many standards, a glamorous career. In feminist parlance, she had it all.

Except a man to love.

Her throat tightened. Her eyes shut.

What had happened to her man to love?

When she and Martha had sat up far into cold winter's nights talking about the future, about plans and predictions, hopes and dreams, the man had seemed the easy part.

Martha was settling for Rod Willerts who worked at the feed store.

Frances had wanted more. "He's out there, I know he is," she'd insisted.

Martha had pursed her lips. "Dreamer," she'd scoffed. "You'll be an old maid schoolteacher."

"No. Oh, no." Frances had been certain. "He's there, and I'll know him when I see him."

And when she met Stephen, she thought she had.

Dreamer, she mocked herself now.

But she couldn't help remembering how it had been in the early days of her love for Stephen. She couldn't forget the closeness she'd felt. The warmth.

Until . . .

Until she hadn't measured up.

She watched Jack run a comb through his hair, then grimace at his reflection. She wanted to go to him and put her arms around him, wanted to share the closeness they'd shared in the night, wanted more than that closeness.

She wanted love.

And then what? she asked herself.

But the niggling notion that there ought to be more didn't go away.

It grew.

It grew while they shopped for breakfast goodies. It grew while Jack made waffles and Frances squeezed orange juice. It kept on growing while they sat in the living room swapping sections of the Sunday *Times*.

It would stop, Frances told herself, if they got out of the apartment, had some space, some distraction. So when Jack asked if she'd like to go to the Botanical Gardens, she said yes.

The day was surprisingly cool for June, and still slightly foggy toward the river.

But when Jack said, "Mind if I keep the top down?" Frances said it was fine with her.

In fact she was delighted, and as they sped up the Henry Hudson Parkway the wind whipped through her hair and stung her face. She grinned, licking her lips, tasting the ocean in the foggy air. She glanced over at Jack and found him watching her, a bemused, indulgent smile on his face.

The insistent fire inside her burned stronger.

Nothing that happened for the remainder of the day quenched it.

They ambled hand in hand through the rhododendron valley, along the nature trail, then down the azalea way and up Snuff Mill Road until they stood on the bridge overlooking the Bronx River.

Most of the flowering season was past, but the thick banks of evergreens and laurels, the gracefully arching willows and the elegant dogwoods all wreathed with wisps of fog were enchanting anyway.

She slanted a surreptitious glance at Jack and found he was looking at her as well. The naked hunger in his eyes surprised her. But what surprised her more was that, in response, her shy glances, her wistful longings and vague stirrings seemed to crystallize into a consuming hunger of her own.

She wanted Jack.

And the sheer overwhelming desperation of that desire rocked her.

Her fingers clenched around the bridge railing, her knuckles whitening. She drew a long, steadying breath. But even having drawn it, she didn't feel steady. She felt fuzzy-minded, weak-kneed, a far cry from the woman she thought herself to be.

Shape up, she commanded herself. *Get a grip on your-self.*

But she didn't. All she could think about was how swiftly the day was passing, how in less than twenty-four hours she would be on her way to Chicago, then Dallas, then . . .

But she didn't want to think about that. Didn't want to think about leaving. Didn't want to think of days—and nights—without Jack.

You're going to have a lifetime of them, she reminded herself. But knowing it was true didn't make things easier. If anything, it made her desperation worse.

Life wasn't a book. There weren't rewrites, and there weren't guaranteed happy endings.

She didn't expect there would be. Her marriage had shown her that.

But she did expect that Jack would be a skillful, tender lover.

And, heaven help her, she wanted—just for one night—to know that love.

She wasn't asking for forever. She wasn't asking any-more for the sort of love that only happened in books. She'd tried that once. She knew the pain of it.

But was it so wrong to want a memory? To want one night to hang on to, to take out and cherish, to hold when the hours were long and the nights were cold?

Was it wrong to want just that much of Jack?

"What's the matter?" He was looking at her, a little worried, a little wary, and very, very dear.

She shook her head, looking at him carefully, assessing, wondering and, finally, smiling.

"Nothing. Not a thing." She reached out and this time she took his hand.

He paused for a second as if her action startled him. Then he smiled wryly back at her, gave her hand a squeeze, and they walked on.

HE'D HAVE TO TAKE HER back to her hotel. Soon.

He'd never survive another night like the last one. There was just so much proximity without consummation a man could take.

And this particular man had reached the limit.

He'd thought going to the Botanical Gardens was an inspiration. He'd thought nothing could happen there.

But something was. Maybe it was just because his whole body was sensitized beyond belief. Maybe it was that he wanted so much, had waited so long.

But just the way Frances's thumb caressed the back of his as they walked hand in hand through the forest, and—even more—the way every movement of their entwined fingers brushed his hand against her thigh, was slowly driving him insane.

She didn't know what she was doing to him. She couldn't know. She probably still thought they were "just friends," he thought grimly. He'd said it often enough.

But he wanted to throw her down and make love to her right here in the middle of the *Tsuga canadensis*, and he'd certainly never been so inclined with any of his other friends.

He slanted her a glance, wondering if she had any idea what was going through his head. He was still fascinated with watching her.

Used to women who emoted on cue, he was enchanted by Frances's spontaneity—by her smiles, her frowns, her nervous lip biting, her sudden surprised laughter.

He never knew from one moment to the next how she would look, nor how she would be looking at him.

Usually it was with apprehension. He'd grown used to that. He didn't like it, but he thought it masked liking more than indifference. Sometimes she smiled. Then he smiled back and felt his heart quicken.

But right now the look she was giving him made his heart turn a triple somersault in his chest. She had a warm, slow smile on her face and a come-hither look in her eyes. A look he'd never seen. Not on Frances.

He stopped dead and stared at her, disbelieving, thinking he must be imagining things.

But she didn't look away. She looked right at him, her eyes wide, her cheeks flushed, her lips slightly parted and curved into a smile. A tempting smile. A beckoning smile.

"Don't," he muttered.

"What?" Her voice was soft and slightly sultry. She sounded confused.

He didn't blame her. "Nothing." He opened his eyes, expecting to see the wariness back in her face. But she still looked up at him with shining expectancy. He sucked air.

"...should be going," he mumbled, starting to drag her along the path back toward the museum building. "...getting late."

"Sure." Frances kept pace with him, her thumb still caressing the side of his hand. Warily he looked down at their entwined fingers, looked again at her.

She smiled and gave his hand a squeeze.

Jack tugged her on, loaded her into the car and set a record getting back to Manhattan.

They were driving down Fifth Avenue toward her hotel when she said, "I'll fix dinner for you tonight."

Jack hit the brakes. There was simultaneously a screech behind him, a blaring of horns, a couple of loud earthy epithets. His fingers flexed, then tightened on the steering wheel.

"Unless you have...other plans, I mean," Frances said quickly. "I didn't mean...I don't want to...to impose."

"No," he said, fool that he was. "No other plans. We could...go out. I don't have much in the kitchen."

"Let's go shopping." She actually looked eager.

Baffled, bemused, he shrugged. "Whatever you say."

Jack cut across the park at 66th and stopped at a supermarket on the way up Broadway. It was there that he began to feel that whatever was happening was inevitable, that some higher power than he had definitely taken over, because he found a parking place right out front.

Frances commandeered a shopping cart and trundled through the aisles. Jack followed, curious, as she squinted at the rows of canned goods, conferred with the butcher, prodded the tomatoes, scrutinized the lettuce.

She moved purposefully from aisle to aisle without asking for advice or opinions. Just as well since he didn't have any.

He pulled out his wallet at the checkout, but Frances beat him to it.

"My treat," she said firmly, and gave him another one of those disconcerting smiles. Equally disconcerting was the new sway to her hips as she preceded him out the door. Was it deliberate?

"What can I do?" he asked when they returned and she took over his kitchen.

She handed him a bottle of wine. "Open this."

He poured them each a glass, then stood leaning against the counter watching her tear the lettuce.

With Frances there were none of the flirtingly coy glances and seductive remarks he'd got from the legions of women who'd cooked him dinner over the years.

She was all business as she mixed her Worcestershire sauce and lemon juice, as purposeful as Julia Child confronting a plucked goose.

He must've been hallucinating earlier, imagining the erotic caress of her thumb, the smoldering heat in her glance.

At least that's what he thought until he sat down to the first course. His brows lifted.

"Oysters?"

"You don't like them?" Frances looked both worried and guilty.

Jack grinned. "I like 'em fine. I'm just . . . surprised."

She shifted in her chair. "Er, well, you know how it is." A definite line of color appeared across her cheekbones. "We get so little good fresh seafood in Vermont. I never get to use this recipe anymore and, well, I . . . I couldn't resist."

She looked like a child caught with her hand in the cookie jar. Jack bet that when she was little she'd never got away with anything.

His grin widened. "Of course. Dig in."

He wondered if she'd done it on purpose. The oysters, yes, she couldn't have helped but known the aphrodisiacal qualities they were reputed to have. But the tomatoes with basil? The asparagus? The Caribbean chicken with lime? The chocolate mousse.

Had she chosen them all just because she liked them, or was there a message there?

Because, thanks to those months he'd worked in Carter's health-food store, Jack knew that chicken, tomatoes, asparagus and chocolate had reputations, too.

IT WAS OVERKILL, Frances thought.

She should have gone with the oysters as a declaration of intent and stopped there. But no, she'd charged ahead and grabbed every aphrodisiac Annabel had ever mentioned.

"A dinner should have a theme," she remembered reading in one of those upscale homemaker magazines Stephen kept proffering before he'd given up on her.

Obviously, unbeknownst to both of them, the lesson had stuck.

The question was now—did she dare go through with what the theme suggested?

She hoped so. That was why she'd bought that very expensive bottle of wine. The aphrodisiacs were to let Jack know her feelings; the liquid courage was for her.

She couldn't tell if Jack had got the hint or not. He ate the oysters readily enough. He also helped himself to plenty of salad, asparagus and chicken. But it might be just because he was hungry. It was already past seven o'clock.

Frances took another long swallow of wine. She gave him a nervous smile. She batted her eyelashes. She felt more than a customary amount of sympathy for the heroines she'd sometimes required to seduce her heroes.

But she couldn't muster up as much sympathy for them as she felt right now for herself.

After all, she could control her heroes' reactions. She was at the mercy of Jack's.

She supposed she could simply tell him she'd changed her mind.

But what if he'd changed his?

What if he'd decided that friendship with her was all he wanted? What if he thought she wasn't worth the bother? What if he thought she wouldn't be good in bed?

By Jack's standards she very well might not be. He certainly had plenty of basis for comparison. What if he thought she was a dud?

After a time, Stephen had.

Suddenly she was on her feet and carrying her dishes to the sink.

"Hey! You're not finished, are you? You hardly ate a thing."

"I'm not very hungry." Her voice sounded hollow even to her. She scraped her plate into the sink. Her hands shook, her cheeks burned. Her whole body felt like an inferno. She was such an idiot, such a fool! How could she ever think—

"Frances?"

She started, stiffening, as Jack's hands came to rest lightly on her shoulders, their touch cool and compelling. His breath was warm, though, as it ruffled her hair.

"What?" Her voice cracked.

His lips were next to her ear. "Thank you for the dinner."

She held herself rigid. "It was nothing. I—"

"And for the thought." He turned her in his arms, still keeping hold of her shoulders. Her eyes, downcast, were on a level with his mouth.

Jack Neillands had a beautiful mouth, the lips firm and well molded. But the most beautiful thing about it was that it was lit by a smile that was both tender and tentative, not in the least mocking. Not in the least like Stephen's.

Her gaze flicked up cautiously, but still curious to see what she could read in his eyes.

She saw the same gentle, cautious hope there. He didn't look like a man who expected her to be a dud. He looked like a man who wanted her very much. She swallowed.

"Th-the thought?" she stammered.

"The oysters. And—" he gave a wave of one hand, a corner of his mouth curving slightly "—the chicken, the tomatoes, the chocolate."

She blushed. "You knew?"

"I hoped." A pause. "I'm still hoping."

Frances studied his toes, she studied hers. At last she lifted her gaze and eyed him warily. She licked her lips. "I . . . I don't . . . I'm not . . ."

Her insecurities were strangling her. She brushed a lock of hair off her cheek.

"This is crazy, Jack," she said desperately.

Jack's hands slid down her arms raising goose bumps. He took her hands in his, strong and firm. He met her gaze.

"No," he said with soft assurance, drawing her with him toward the bedroom. "It isn't. Not a bit."

SHE SHOULD HAVE TAKEN NOTES. She should have viewed the whole experience objectively, dispassionately, filing away the sights, the smells, the sounds.

She didn't; she loved.

And she was loved. As thoroughly and completely loved as she had ever been in her life. It was astonishing, really—loving Jack—wholly new and different. Not like Stephen in the least.

Stephen had been, well...studied. She sometimes thought he had become so thoroughly obsessed with attaining a place in the firm that he wouldn't take off his coat and tie, let alone his pants, day or night. And that was the way he'd made love—with one eye on the next morning's appointment and legal precedents running through his head. And afterward, there came the critique.

It was nothing like that with Jack.

Not that she'd been making comparisons at the time. At the time she had been so totally and thoroughly involved that she couldn't think, let alone compare.

The moment Jack had taken her hands and drawn her into his arms, she'd been lost to everything and everyone but him.

Her worries about being a dud had resurfaced for a moment only to be kissed away. And her own need to make this a night to remember had helped her overcome any lingering shyness.

In fact she discovered in herself a boldness she didn't know she possessed. Just as Jack took his time, discovering her secrets, so she learned his. She explored his body, learned his responses, touched him, and ultimately loved him with an eagerness that astonished them both.

And why not?

This was Jack—her hero—the man on whom she was going to depend for memories of love and intimacy for the rest of her life.

She held nothing back.

Nor did Jack.

It was everything she had hoped—and nothing that she had expected.

He had made her feel as if she mattered more to him than anything else in all the world, as if there could never be another woman, as if she were all.

She hadn't expected him to tremble, to murmur, to thrust so deeply into her that she ceased to know where she left off and he began.

She hadn't expected to want to cry.

She had been a fool, but she didn't regret a bit of it.

She'd had her night. She had her memory. And when she gathered up her things, put herself together and stole out to seek a taxi in the hazy New York dawn, she knew that she would carry it with her till the end of her days.

Chapter Twelve

It was like a bad movie. A terrible book. A rotten play.

The trouble was, it was his life.

It was seven when he awoke and reached for her, needing again the warmth and love they'd shared in the night.

And she wasn't there.

Not in the bathroom showering or brushing her teeth. Not in the kitchen making a cup of coffee. Not anywhere.

Gone. Vanished. Fled.

For a moment, sitting there on the edge of the bed with his head in his hands, Jack wondered if he'd imagined the whole thing.

It had never happened to him before, being left without a word.

It was not, in his opinion, a salutary experience.

He didn't even know for sure what it meant. Except he had a pretty good idea that whatever it meant, it wasn't good.

Damn it, what was with the woman? Hadn't she enjoyed it?

He was willing to bet she had. Either that or she was wasted on writing and slopping sheep; she should've been an actress instead. If the passionate response he'd got from her last night was an act, she was an Oscar winner.

He didn't think she was.

So why did she leave?

Guilt? Consternation? Second thoughts?

Possible reasons. Even probable ones. But unfair for all that.

What was he supposed to do? Notch his bedpost and go merrily on his way?

Well, he had news for her. It didn't work like that.

Not this time.

One night with any other woman in the world might be plenty. Not with Frances.

His interest in Frances had started as a curiosity, evolved into a challenge, and now . . . now it was . . . now it was . . .

Now it felt as if she were a part of him.

"Oh, God." Jack rubbed his face with his hands. He took a deep breath. And another. Then he grabbed the phone and punched out the number of her hotel.

It took an age before he got a response. When he did, he said, "Room 722, please."

The desk clerk yawned. "One moment, sir."

The phone rang. And rang. And rang.

"Sorry, sir. I'm afraid there's no one there."

There was someone there, all right. "Let it ring," Jack said.

Five minutes later, the clerk was back. "I'm afraid—"

Jack was, too. "She hasn't checked out, has she?"

"No, sir. Not yet."

Jack reached for his watch on the nightstand. Seven-thirty.

He hung up and grabbed his jeans.

SHE KNEW SHE SHOULD answer the phone. It had been ringing for ages. Importuning. Demanding. Reproaching her.

It could be Natalie or the publicity department or the driver who would be taking her to the airport. It could be

Annabel telling her something horrible had gone wrong at home with the kids.

All of them could be desperate to reach her. All of them would be furious when they couldn't.

But it also might be Jack.

She wouldn't talk to Jack. She *couldn't* talk to Jack.

If she'd been able to talk to Jack she'd have stayed where she was until he awoke. She couldn't. It had been too beautiful. Too perfect. At least it had been to her.

If it hadn't been to Jack, as so often it hadn't to Stephen, well, she didn't want to know.

She slipped her last dress into her garment bag, zipped it up, ran a hair brush through her hair, applied some last-minute lipstick and went to check out.

She felt like a criminal. She looked over her shoulder while she crossed the lobby. She glanced around warily while she signed the bill. And she almost embraced her driver with relief when he arrived before anyone else she knew.

But not until the car pulled away from the curb and slipped into the anonymity of Madison Avenue traffic did she breathe easily again.

Free, she told herself. Free at last.

No, not so. Her body might be free. But Jack Neillands had a hammerlock on her heart.

She didn't know if she'd ever be free of that.

Of course, she would, she told herself briskly. She'd be fine.

She had survived Stephen, she had survived the divorce. She could survive this.

She hadn't counted on pulling up to the American Airlines terminal at LaGuardia and stepping out into his arms.

"Jack!"

He looked grim and forbidding, unshaven, hair barely combed, as if he'd just got out of bed. Probably he had. The million-dollar smile was nowhere to be seen. A million-dollar frown was in its place.

"Why'd you leave?"

She shook her head, mute, panicking. Clearing her throat, she tried again, failed, and again shook her head.

"Was it that bad?"

"Bad?" she croaked.

His mouth twisted. "Why else would you leave?"

"Oh, heavens." Instinctively she reached for his hand. It was cold and hard against her palm. "No, of course not. It wasn't. It wasn't!"

He just stared at her, his expression disbelieving.

A horn honked. A crowd of teenagers brushed past. He didn't move, just looked at her.

The driver tapped Frances on the shoulder. "Hey, lady, you want I should check your bags?"

"Er, please." Frances let go of the door to fumble for her ticket, but before she could hand it to him, Jack took it out of her hand. He peeled off some bills and handed them to the driver as well. "I'll do it."

The man looked at the money, then at Jack. He winked and grinned. "Whatever you say, man." In an instant he was gone.

"So why'd you leave, then?" Jack hadn't moved an inch. The implication was that she wasn't moving, either.

Frances sighed. She twisted a strand of hair and wished she'd left it down instead of pinning it up. It would be so much more satisfying to rake her hands through it.

Jack waited.

"I . . . not because it was bad." How could he even think that? "It was . . . wonderful." The memories of it still had the power to heat her blood, probably would for years to come. She felt her cheeks begin to burn.

"You sure didn't leave me with that impression." His voice was harsh.

"I'm . . . sorry." She looked down for a moment, then sighed and shrugged. "I guess I'm not up on the etiquette of the one-night stand."

Jack said a rude word. He took hold of her arm and hauled her against him, his dark eyes spitting fire. "Is that all it was to you?"

"Me?"

"You said it, I didn't."

"I'm not the one who's in the habit of bed hopping!"

"You sure as hell hopped out of mine!"

"Only because I was afraid to be there when you woke up."

Horns hooted, buses rumbled, a gabble of voices rose and fell around them. But Jack was impervious. He stared at her.

"Why? Why, Fran?"

"I was afraid." She barely whispered them, was sure the words were lost in the roar of traffic, in the rush of jet engines overhead. But Jack must've heard them because he shook his head, his expression baffled.

"Of me?"

Frances shrugged awkwardly. "Of you. Of me. Of...everything."

"Don't," he said. "I won't hurt you."

And how could she tell him it wasn't him? That the hurt would come whether he willed it or not? Numbly she shook her head and looked away.

"Frances?" He touched her cheek. She trembled, looked down. But when his thumb stroked her chin, silently chiding, persisting, she had to look up again.

One corner of his mouth lifted slightly. "Scared me, too," he said.

She blinked. Her mouth formed a silent question.

He shrugged almost sheepishly. "I'm not used to moving heaven and earth." He grinned.

Frances smiled, at first hesitantly, then more widely. He'd felt it, too? She thought a ten-ton boulder had been lifted from her shoulders. She felt as if she'd scored the winning run, been given The Good Housekeeping Seal of Approval.

"Oh, Jack!" She put her arms around him, hugging him tight.

He gave her his million-dollar grin. "Oh, Frances," he mocked her. "So...want to try it again?"

"Jack!" Her face went crimson.

"Do you?"

"I have a plane to catch!"

"I know. In—" he glanced at his watch "—fifty minutes. But you're not going to be on the plane forever. Pretty soon you're going to be back in Vermont."

"And you're going to be in New York."

"I can drive."

"I'm not into long-distance romances," Frances protested, backing toward the terminal, fearing now as much as she hoped.

"What kind are you into?"

"None!"

"I don't believe you. No one who writes about it so convincingly can hate it that much."

"I don't hate it. I—" She crab-walked toward the terminal.

"So give it a try."

"I can't—"

"You can do anything you want to do, Frances. You proved it last night."

Oh, God. "I—" Still backing up.

"Didn't you? Didn't you prove it, Frances?"

She was against the glass wall now, staring into his eyes, seeing in them the fire and the passion she'd seen last night, the gentleness and humor she'd seen yesterday and countless times before. She swallowed hard.

"Frances?" His voice was soft, but determined. One hand came up and touched her cheek, his thumb stroking it gently, then holding it so that his lips came down and met hers.

"Oh, Jack."

"We'll do it again, Frances. Won't we?"

Frances nodded her head.

THEY WOULDN'T, though, she was sure.

Once she had boarded the plane, once Jack's persuasive words and stunning smile were only memories, all her insecurities returned.

And the longer she was away from him, the greater her certainty became. The tour took her over. Marketing ran her life. She was swept up into a whirlwind of posh people and places. She was wined and dined, feted and praised. She saw all the head-turning possibilities of Jack's world, and couldn't believe he could really be that interested in her.

He had been kind. He had been a good friend. He had listened to her panic, had paid attention to her fears, had known she needed distraction, so he had distracted her. And what better way to distract her than to take her to bed, especially since she was willing.

But once she was gone, she was sure that was the end of it.

He came after you, she tried to tell herself. But that, she decided, was ego. Jack hadn't liked being left, so he'd followed her.

Having got her "testimonial," he would be content.

It would be folly to expect more. Idiocy to want more. Foolishness to hope.

But sometimes—in the dead of night, when she forgot what city she was in, forgot what she was going back to, forgot everything but the fulfillment she'd found in his arms—then, yes, sometimes, she wished.

And once hope got the better of her and she took a page from his book and sent him a postcard.

"Trip not as bad as I expected. Nice places to visit but I wouldn't want to live there. Thank you for everything." And because she was who she was, she added a postscript. "Please don't feel obligated." She signed it simply, "Frances."

Then she set about trying to forget.

"RECKONED I'D FIND YOU here," Bert bustled into the goat barn and loomed over Frances, who was almost done milking. "Haven't seen hide nor hair of you since you got back."

"I've been busy," Frances apologized. She'd got back at last on Monday to be faced with an upcoming book deadline, an ailing sheep, a pair of eager teenage girls dying to hear all about her glamorous tour, and a leaky roof. She hadn't had time to do more than touch base with Annabel. The rest of her friends would have to wait.

"Figured you had." Bert plopped down onto the other milking stool and beamed at the younger woman. "Come to thank you. And to say I told you so." Her brown eyes were positively dancing.

Frances cocked her head. "That sounds ominous. Thank me for what? Tell me you told me so about what?"

"Jack."

Just his name made Frances's heart skip a beat. "What about Jack?"

Bert's brows drew together. "You don't know?"

Mystified, Frances shook her head. She hadn't heard a word from Jack. There hadn't even been a postcard waiting when she'd got home. She knew; she'd looked. And his silence fed her insecurities better than even time and distance had.

Bert made a *tsking* sound. "You young folk. Mercy me, I don't know what he's thinking of. You mean he didn't tell you?"

"Bert! Tell me *what*?"

"Why, that he's negotiating to move an entire borough of New York City in with us."

"What?"

Bert's eyes were round and solemn. "Tomorrow. I thought you knew."

Frances shook her head. "Tell me." Faint stirrings of hope, excitement, enthusiasm came to life within her. Mechanically she pulled the goat's teats.

"Called last week, he did. Before you got back. Talked to Ernie about needing a place to come for a catalog shoot," Bert said. "Not just Jack, half of New York from the sound of it. A photographer, his assistants, a hairstylist, a make-up stylist, a clothes stylist, an ad-agency lady, a studio man—the whole works. And they're coming to stay with us."

"Holy Mary, Mother of God."

"That's what Ernie said. I said Mary may have had something to do with it, but I think we owe it all to you."

Frances just stared at her.

Bert gave a satisfied little nod. "I told you he was wooing you."

Frances gulped. Was he? No, he couldn't be. A fling, yes. That made sense. A little, at least. But not wooing, not courtship. Not . . . marriage.

Besides, he'd never even mentioned it to her. She pointed that out.

"You weren't here."

"But he could've written. He didn't."

Bert shrugged. "He's a man. What does he know?"

Frances laughed. "Oh, Bert. Don't be ridiculous."

"'T'isn't ridiculous. I say he's smitten, and I say we're going to have a wedding on our hands."

Frances shook her head. "No, Bert. No weddings. I've been there."

"Been, spin," Bert sputtered. "That's over. Past. Where's your faith in the future, child? Where's your faith in the power of love?"

Wordless, unable to argue, Frances shrugged. She could hardly tell Bert she didn't have any. Not anymore.

Still, he was coming. Her palms felt damp. Her heart raced.

Don't, she cautioned herself. *Don't get your hopes up.*

She tried not to. She squelched the feeling deliberately and made herself concentrate on the business at hand. Collaring the next goat, she turned to milk it. It was Amy's kid.

Bert *tsked*. "You won't get much out of him, love."

SHE CHASED CARLEEN and Maeve, her Boston girls, off with Libby the next morning, knowing full well they'd go watch the shoot.

"Come with us," they pleaded.

But Frances said no. "I've got work to do."

She was in the midst of ripping a scene to shreds when Leif and his friends knocked on the door. "Wanta come with us?" Leif asked.

"Can't," Frances said. "Too much work."

"You got to. What'll Jack say?" Leif asked.

Frances didn't know the answer to that.

If he had called, if he had asked her . . . if she thought he wanted her there . . .

But there'd been nothing. Not a single word. It could be only coincidence. She didn't want to presume.

"Presume? How idiotic can you get?" Annabel said.

But however idiotic it was, Frances didn't go. "I have work to do," she said.

In fact, she made work. She couldn't write. She tried. So before she shredded her whole book, she turned to more mundane tasks. She washed her kitchen floor, ironed her sheets, cleaned her cupboards. And when her shelves were rearranged, she went down to the store and rearranged Eb's.

"Damn fool woman," Eb mumbled. "G'wan. Git outa here. Won't be able to find a thing 'fore spring at this rate. Go find some other feller t'hassle."

On the way out the door she ran into Aaron and took Eb's advice at face value. She accepted Aaron's offer of a date.

It was a mistake. She knew it the moment she got in Aaron's car that evening.

She was poor company, distracted, irritable. Aaron had to say everything twice. And when he asked her if she had gone to the shoot that afternoon, she snapped "No" so loudly he flinched.

"You don't have to bite my head off, Fran." He patted her knee. "You must've had a rough day."

She gave a guilty shrug. "You could say that."

"What'd you do?"

"The usual. Chores. Worked for Eb. Wrote." Or tried to.

"Poor Frances."

Poor Frances indeed. Stupid Frances. Foolish Frances. She stared distractedly at her watch all throughout the movie in Gaithersburg; she pushed her pie around her plate at the coffee shop afterward. She wondered what Jack was doing, if he'd asked about her, looked for her.

"Still having trouble with that ewe?" Aaron asked.

"What?"

"The one with the foot abscess. How is she?"

"She's, uh, fine. Much better."

Aaron stirred his coffee and looked at her quizzically. "Is it the goats, then?"

Frances just looked at him, baffled. "Goats?"

"Thought they might be giving you trouble."

"No."

"Then it must be your book." He spoke with the fatalism of long experience. "'Fraid I can't do anything about that."

Frances shook her head. "No. You can't."

Aaron drained his coffee cup. "Ready to go?"

He took her hand as they walked to the car. Frances let him because he would think it odd if she pulled away.

They rode back to her place in virtual silence.

It reminded Frances of nothing so much as those long rides home in the car after she and Stephen had been out to dinner or a party with the partners in his law firm when Stephen had been silently, but almost visibly emanating disapproval, like a volcano starting to seethe inwardly, gathering strength. And then, right before they would get home, the volcano would erupt, the criticisms would begin pouring out.

Frances waited warily, expecting the same thing here. But when Aaron pulled into her yard, he only sighed.

"I hope you get your book straightened out. Beats me how anyone can get so uptight about making things right for people who don't even exist. Hard enough for those of us who do."

Tell me about it, Frances thought. But she smiled at him, grateful that he was Aaron, not Stephen.

She leaned across the gear shift and kissed his cheek. "I'll try."

He held on to her and angled his mouth so he could get a far better kiss than the one she'd hoped to get away with.

Frances didn't flinch, but she didn't respond, either, just waited him out.

Finally Aaron pulled back. "Don't suppose you want me to come in with you?"

"I'm really tired. And Carleen and Maeve are there. They sleep on cots in the living room."

Aaron rolled his eyes. He paused as she opened the car door and got out. "Get those characters sorted out by the next time I see you, Frannie. And buy a bed for your office. It's hard to court with an audience."

She smiled regretfully. "Good night, Aaron."

She stood in the moonlight and watched as he backed the car around and headed down the lane. A scattering of stars lay sparkling around the full moon overhead. An evening breeze touched her cheek, its touch more welcome than Aaron's.

There was only one man's touch she wanted, she thought as she turned to go up the steps. If only she dared go to him and ask for it.

"'Bout time," said a voice from the shadowy darkness of the front porch.

Frances stopped dead.

Jack stepped forward into the pool of moonlight. He looked irritable, fierce, and absolutely beautiful.

She smiled all over her face.

His scowl deepened. "I've been waiting for hours."

"You didn't call. You never said...I didn't think..." She was grinning, laughing.

Jack was furious. "You don't think! You jump to conclusions. I suppose you thought you were a notch on my bedpost, that you'd never see me again."

"Well, I—" Since it was actually quite close to what she had thought, she didn't finish the sentence. She kissed his cheek. She put her arms around him and hugged his waist.

He held himself rigid for a moment. "You knew I'd come. I said I would."

She shook her head, burrowed against his chest, kissed his neck. "I—"

"Damn it, Frances!" But he couldn't resist her any longer. His lips met hers, warm and hungry, demanding, wiping out Aaron's touch, Aaron's memory. There was nothing, no one left but him.

He pulled back before she'd begun to have enough. "I keep my promises, Frances. Don't I?" His voice was low and hard, his mouth a millimeter from her own. His voice was rough, eager.

"But you talked to Bert, not me. I thought maybe you were just working, that you didn't want to...to bother—"

"Don't be an idiot," he said.

She laughed.

"What's funny?"

"You sound like Annabel. And Eb. And everyone else in Boone's Corner."

"I'm in good company then."

"But why?" she asked him. "Why didn't you call?"

There was a fraction of a minute's pause. Then, "I didn't want to give you a chance to tell me not to."

Frances stared at him, astonished. "You thought I would?"

He stared a moment at his toes, then lifted his head and met her gaze. "Your postcard wasn't exactly encouraging, you know."

Frances flushed guiltily and looked down. "I wasn't . . . I mean, I didn't want you to feel obligated."

Jack groaned. "Do I look obligated? Am I here under duress?"

Frances lifted her eyes to meet his. She smiled. "I don't know. Are you?"

He smiled, and there was such tenderness in that smile that it made her shiver. "What do you think?"

"I think I missed you."

"I missed you, too."

And then she was in his arms again, kissing him hard. And the hunger, the desperate longing that had been her constant companion for the past month melted in the feel of the hard warmth of his embrace, the taste of his lips.

"Let's go inside," he muttered.

Frances groaned. "Maeve and Carleen are there."

"No."

"What do you mean, no? That's where they sleep."

"Not tonight. They're at Annabel's."

"How do you know?"

Jack grinned. "Because Annabel invited them. She arranged it."

Their eyes met, Frances's wide and wondering, Jack's warm and wicked.

"Annabel arranged it? Or you arranged it?" Frances asked knowingly.

"I think it's called a conspiracy. Now can we go inside?"

Bemused, astonished, thinking that a truly resourceful man didn't need her to get a bed for her office at all, Frances took his hand and led him in.

She didn't even turn on the light. She led him right upstairs. She knew if she stopped to think about what she was doing, she'd panic. So she didn't.

But in the moonlit night after the loving, the question came to her anyway.

What was she doing letting Jack Neillands into her life, into her home, into her bed?

What was she getting herself into?

And the answer came to her clearly and frankly when she woke up beside Jack before dawn the next morning.

She was having an affair.

Chapter Thirteen

It was going to be—Frances was determined—an affair to remember. The affair to end all affairs.

At least by her modest standards it was. Because the memories of it were going to have to last her a lifetime.

She only had the fortitude to do this once, and she knew it.

So she was going to give it—and Jack—all she had.

Life was going to hit her in the face sooner or later. She was aware of that. If it had with Stephen, whom she'd always thought was her perfect soul mate, it certainly would with Jack, a man as wrong for her as Stephen has been right. But she was tired of cowering, tired of running.

This time she was leading with her chin. So she threw caution to the wind, buried her circumspection, turned a blind eye to her upbringing.

She opened her arms, her bed, her life to Jack.

She was, however, discreet. She didn't flaunt her relationship with him in front of Maeve and Carleen.

She might never have spent another night with Jack had the girls not come to her and asked if she minded if they went with Libby and Annabel on a foraging trek.

Frances had looked at Annabel doubtfully, but the older woman's expression was perfectly ingenuous. "We go every year and you know it. Eb's staying with Leif," she said. "So it's just Libby and me, and you know Libby—she'd much rather have other kids along.''

That was true, of course. So Frances nodded and gave her permission.

"You won't miss us, will you?" Maeve asked her, and if there was the faintest hint of a smile on the sixteen-year-old's face when Frances assured her she had plenty to keep her busy, Frances didn't want to think about it.

She didn't want to think about anyone or anything but Jack. And most of the time, she got her way.

He had to be up at the crack of dawn for the shoot, and then he had to be back again in the evening when the light once more was favorable.

Frances scheduled her writing so she worked then, too. In between they were inseparable. They cooked together, talked together, walked together, slept together.

"I don't know what I'm going to do when you're gone," Frances confessed on the night before Jack's last day there.

They were lying in bed with only the moon to light the room. It bathed their limbs in a silvery glow that seemed to Frances as beautiful and unreal as the whole week had been.

"Come with me."

She stared at him.

His hand stilled on her hip. "Why not?"

She shook her head. "I—"

"Just for a few days."

"I can't. Carleen and Maeve—"

"Can stay with Libby and Annabel. They did before. They're perfectly happy there and you know it."

Frances did know it. And if this were a book, she'd do it in a minute.

There was nothing she would like more than to throw caution completely to the winds and follow Jack wherever he said. But a headlong disregard of convention might be fine for a week, *was* fine in a book. It was something else as a way of life.

She wasn't that daring. She needed limits. Boundaries. Guidelines she set.

"I have a deadline," she said. "And the goats. And the sheep. And—" she shrugged helplessly "—lots of stuff."

Jack's smile was rueful. He touched her cheek, first with his fingers, then with his lips. "Yeah, I know. Lots of stuff."

His eyes were dark and tender. They were eyes she would like to wake up to every day of her life.

But there was no future for them, and no sense in getting maudlin that there wasn't. She knew they were worlds apart when she went into this. It was an affair, pure and simple. Jack had never even hinted that he wanted more. She wouldn't have believed him if he had.

They couldn't change the rules now.

She smiled then with all the bravado she could muster. "You'll manage fine without me," she told him, but still it was hard to conceal the pain she felt.

"The hell I will. Come here," Jack said and hauled her into his arms.

There was a desperation in him, too, and he did nothing to conceal it at all.

He left shortly after noon the next day, but not before he'd told her, "I'll be back on Saturday."

On Saturday he was.

HE HONKED THE HORN when he turned up her lane, and hearing it, Frances forgot the line she was typing and ran to meet him. She had been waiting all morning. Hoping. Fearing. And now that he had come...

"You're here!" She practically flung herself into his arms the moment he stepped out of the car.

He caught her, kissing her, his lips as hungry as hers. He laughed, shaking his head. "Is this really you, Francesca Luna?" he asked.

It really was. She could hardly believe it herself. She never probed her actions too deeply. She just accepted them. Concentrated on the present. Told herself that was enough.

"How was your drive?"

"Long, tiring." He smiled. "But worth it. What'll we do today?"

Frances shrugged, a light of mischief in her eyes. "I have work to do."

"Oh?" He sounded suddenly wary.

"Oh, yes. I've got some indoor work and some outdoor work. I was sort of hoping you'd help me with both."

"Like what?"

"Chopping wood." She gestured toward the logs near the side of the house. Eb had hauled them up for her the week before.

Jack flexed his shoulders, regarded the logs, then the woman looking so starry-eyed at him. He shrugged. "Why not?"

He stripped off his shirt and set to work. He chopped, and Frances stacked. It was warm work, sweaty work, but enjoyable work nonetheless.

Much more fun with someone than alone. More fun with Jack than with anyone else on earth. He told her about his week, asked her about hers. He listened while she complained about her uncooperative current hero.

"I was much more cooperative," he told her as he finished the last log and began cleaning the blade of the ax.

"You were," she agreed.

"You weren't."

"Me?"

"Most uncooperative woman in the world." He smiled. "Fought me every step of the way."

She flushed. "Sorry."

"You're not fighting me now, though." He looked like a satisfied panther, his dark hair clinging damply to his skull, his bronzed skin coated with a sweaty sheen.

"No," she said, just watching him and smiling.

"So, let's go inside now and not fight anymore."

Frances stood up. "We can go inside. But we still have work to do."

"Work? What kind of work?"

She slipped her fingers through his and started leading him toward the house. "Well, it's like this. I'm working on a love scene, and it's just not the way I want it to be. Too predictable. Boring. I thought I might persuade you to help me . . . with a little research. Innovation."

"Hands on?"

She batted her lashes at him. "What do you think?"

Jack grinned. "I think you're asking for it."

She was.

And she got everything she asked for—and more.

He swept her up the stairs and into the bed and loved her with a thoroughness that left them both shattered. Then, arms wrapped around each other, they slept. In the late afternoon they awoke to love again.

"How's that?" Jack murmured in the aftermath. "Figure you can write it now?"

Frances stretched like a contented cat. "Well, I wasn't taking notes. But—" she dodged his questing fingers "—I'll make an effort."

She wrapped a sheet around her, wandered into her office and sat down at the computer, which sat, still waiting. Jack followed her.

"'He sighed as her hands moved lower,'" Jack read, leaning over her shoulder. "'Yes,' he said. 'Oh, yes. Like that.' Hey—" he scowled "—we didn't try that, Francesca."

Frances turned, smiling, and touched his belly, then, still smiling, she slid her hand lower. "You were saying?"

Jack groaned. "Oh, yes. Like that."

THE AFFAIR LIVED ON. Most weekends found Jack on Frances's doorstep, in her kitchen, in her bed. Every chance he got he made the trip to Vermont. And when he couldn't get away he called or wrote.

"Aren't there any women left in New York City?" Frances teased, though always she was pleased. She felt like a convict on death row given a weekly reprieve.

Jack didn't even smile at her teasing. "Not like you," he said.

He could've meant anything, of course. Not as easy as her? Not as wonderful as her? Not as weak willed as her? But the way he made her feel when he was with her caused all her frustrated musings to fade into insignificance.

She lived for the moment and she was happier than she'd ever been in her life.

He asked her to come to New York to see him, but she wouldn't do it. It was tempting fate, she thought. Asking for more than she dared.

"You come here," she said. "It's good for you. Keeps you honest."

So Jack shrugged and came week after week.

If Frances was delighted to see Jack whenever he came, everyone else in Boone's Corner was, too.

Ernie and Bert were convinced he'd been sent by the Holy Spirit. "Why not?" Bert said, sticking out her little round chin. "He saved us, didn't he?"

And Frances certainly couldn't argue with it because, it seemed, he had.

Word about "the convent on the hill" had traveled like wildfire around New York. And before long it wasn't only Jack who was making the trip north.

Bert and Ernie's rambling, drafty monstrosity was suddenly the "in" place to be. Not so much as a spot for commercial shooting—though it got its share of that, too—but mostly as the ultimate place to get away from it all.

When the crew and the models who'd come with Jack had gone back to the city, they'd raved about the eternal quiet, the stunning scenery, the good fishing, the great food and the two sisters who made it all possible. Reporters and columnists came to check it out.

"The ultimate in R&R for burned-out, high-stressed execs," said one of the New York weeklies.

"Nirvana in Vermont," said another.

"Sheer heaven," said a third.

Ernie and Bert were thrilled.

"I knew he was a good man," Ernie said to Frances one afternoon when she stopped in Eb's to pick up the yarn she'd ordered.

"Yes," Frances said, sorting through the skeins and handing Ernie hers.

"Good for you, too."

"Yes."

"Told you so," said Bert. They both eyed her speculatively as if waiting for an announcement.

But Frances made no announcement because there was none to make. Never would be. But Ernie and Bert couldn't be expected to understand that.

"I'm knitting him a sweater," Ernie announced, waving the yarn in front of Frances's nose. "To match his eyes."

"It'll be lovely," Frances said.

"'T'will," Ernie agreed. "Ought to be you doin' it, lovely."

"I can't knit," Frances said.

"I could teach you."

"Like I'm teachin' Jack to whittle," Eb put in as he came out of the back room.

Amazingly enough, he was. Every weekend when he came, Jack stopped over to see Eb for an hour or so. Whenever he came back, he had a new piece of pine to work on. Then while Frances cooked or puttered about in the kitchen, he'd sit on the porch with his feet up on the railing, whittling away at the chunk of pine he held.

He whistled, he smiled. He looked as if he belonged.

Sometimes Frances would stop what she was doing, caught by the sight of him—at the rightness of him—just sitting there. And she would feel a throbbing behind her eyes and a tightness in her throat.

Like she felt today.

It was already into October. The eighth weekend in a row that Jack had driven up from New York. A weekend on the surface no different from any of the others. They'd laughed, they'd talked, they'd loved. But Frances had sensed a tension in him she'd never felt before. He'd smiled. He'd kissed her, loved her. But he'd been distracted.

She swallowed a taste of fear. Was this it? she wondered. Was this the beginning of the end?

Perhaps he wouldn't ever criticize like Stephen had. After all, he had no need to find fault. They had no marriage to try to save.

Jack could just smile and say goodbye one day, and that would be that. There was nothing at all to stop him walking out of her life.

Frances tried not to think about it, tried to concentrate on the moment at hand.

Annabel was pressing cider from the windfalls Leif and Libby gathered, while she peeled apples for sauce. Jack was sitting on the porch next to her, chair tipped back, knife in hand, his head bent as he concentrated on the piece of wood. He had been sitting there for the better part of an hour without saying a word.

"What are you making?" Frances asked finally.

He shrugged. "Nothing. Just practicing."

"For what?"

"In case I want to make something." There was a tiny edge to his voice, an impatience. He stared intently at the wood, shaving a bit of it off, running his thumb over the spot, shaving some more.

"You'll cut yourself," Frances said lightly.

Jack shrugged. "Maybe."

"Anyway, it doesn't go with your image," she chided.

All four feet of the chair hit the porch floor. Jack looked at her squarely, his expression serious, a lock of dark hair falling across his forehead. "Haven't you got past my image yet?"

Frances shifted awkwardly. "Well, I mean, a fast-lane, glitzy life like yours . . ."

Jack scowled, his fingers tightening on the knife. "What do you know about my life? What do you really know?"

The question startled her. She looked at him. His face was tight, strained.

"Well, I—"

"You never saw me working when the crew was here, did you?"

She hadn't, no. It had seemed too dangerous. The implications were too great.

She hadn't wanted to mix his work and their pleasure. To welcome him with open arms, to create with him their own private fantasy world when he came back to her every afternoon and evening, yes, she'd willingly done that.

But she hadn't gone to the shootings. If this was her real world, that was Jack's. To have deliberately gone and watched would have only emphasized the gulf she knew existed between them.

If she didn't know, she could pretend.

But now Jack straightened up and put down his knife. "I have to go to Newport tomorrow night. We're going to shoot a catalog there starting Monday. Come with me."

"Don't be silly."

"What's silly about it? It's a perfectly straightforward invitation."

Frances shrugged him off, concentrated on peeling the apple in her hand, uncomfortably aware that Annabel, Libby and Leif were all listening attentively.

He'd done it on purpose, she thought, conscious that it would be harder for her to say no in front of them.

Why did he care? Why did he want her there? Why should he want to emphasize the fact that in real life they were leagues apart?

Unless . . . unless he was getting tired of her.

"I know a hell of a lot about the way you live," he said. "You know zilch about my life-style."

"I know enough."

"What?"

"I said, 'I know enough.'" Enough to know she couldn't live it, wouldn't try. Not again. She pressed her lips together and whacked the apple in half on the cutting board.

Jack reached over and caught her chin in his hand, making her face him. "What's that mean?"

Frances's gaze slid away. "Nothing. Never mind." She twisted out of his grasp.

"Come to Newport with me."

"I don't—"

"You do. Come on, Frances. The world is bigger than Boone's Corner, Vermont."

"I know that!"

"And you should see it."

"I've seen it."

"Yeah, Iowa and Boston. And now this."

"If you don't like it, no one's making you come here," she blazed at him.

"I want to come here," he said with a calmness that simply accentuated her overreaction. "I just want you to come somewhere with me."

"Honestly, Jack, I—"

"Annabel will watch the place, won't you?" He turned to her friend.

Annabel didn't hesitate. "Of course."

"And Leif will feed the goats."

Leif nodded.

"And I'll feed Harry and Biff," Libby offered.

"My book—"

"Your book can come. You can work on it there." Jack's tone was implacable. He paused. His tone changed. "Just this once, Frances, come with me. Please."

Frances stared at her hands, at the apple in them, at the peeling paint on the board floor of the porch.

The "please" echoed in her head. It wasn't a command; it wasn't a demand. It was a request.

The others she would have found easy to reject. The wistful "please" haunted her. She lifted her gaze and stared out across the yard at the trees beginning to turn color, at the rough-hewn barn, at the homely herd of sheep picking their way along the side of the hill. She thought of Newport, the embodiment of urban sophistication, of the fast-lane life Jack was asking her briefly to share.

She thought of the wonderful days they'd already shared, of the tiny private world in which the disparities of the life-styles, their goals, their ultimate desires didn't matter.

She would hate to lose that. But she would lose it anyway if she refused.

"Will you?" Jack stepped between her and the hillside she was contemplating.

Frances drew a deep breath and, even though she recognized it for the foolishness it was, "All right," she said. "Yes."

JACK ALWAYS TRUSTED his instincts, knew at once what he wanted and went after it. In the past, though, he'd always known what the goal was from the start.

But not with Frances Moon. At first she'd been a challenge—an intriguing woman he'd wanted to know better, a cheerful woman he'd wanted to spend time with, a tantalizing woman he'd wanted to bed.

But once he had known her, had spent time with her, had made love with her, the desire hadn't vanished. It had, against all odds, increased.

But what he'd wanted with her, he wasn't sure. He felt as if she were leading him on a chase, but it was a chase through uncharted territory, a chase without a discernible end.

He told himself when she'd called him in New York that at last he was getting what he wanted. But his sigh of relief had been premature. He told himself when she'd at last made love with him that finally things were settled. They weren't.

Waking up without her was the single most devastating moment of his life. And the moment he'd put her on the plane to Dallas after he had finally tracked her down wasn't much better.

He'd felt as if he were letting her walk out of his life. He'd wanted desperately to go on board after her and haul her back.

He'd never felt like this about a woman before.

Not surprising. There had never before been a woman like Frances Moon.

So he pursued her, came to Vermont after her, wore her resistance down. And slowly—almost imperceptibly—he sensed her trusting him, opening to him, letting him, bit by tiny bit, into her life.

But she never came back to New York. Never, in fact, ventured beyond Gaithersburg.

And every time he suggested it, she refused. She had too much to do, had her book to write, her goats and sheep to tend, Eb's store to look after, or half a dozen other excuses.

At first Jack hadn't been concerned. He thought he understood. But as time passed and they remained right here, his concern grew.

It was as if Frances would only see him on her terms, in her world. It was as if, however much she might be opening to him, there were still absolute inviolable perimeters for their relationship, and she wouldn't stray beyond them.

He recognized what she was doing. He'd done it himself.

Often enough in the past he'd determined the frequency with which he'd call women he was dating and the time and the space of their dates. He'd never permitted them to get too close, to have too much of a hold on his time, on his life.

It was a way to protect himself, not to let them any further into his life than he wanted them in.

He didn't like having the roles reversed. He didn't like being shut out.

Jack wanted in to Frances Moon's life. All the way in.

He'd waited patiently, but he'd waited as long as he was going to.

He'd come up to Vermont this weekend prepared to argue her into the ground, to kidnap her if necessary to get her to come with him to Newport.

He'd figured it was the perfect place to get her used to his life. Newport was charming, slightly quaint, only overpowering if one aspired and fell short of the extreme wealth and privilege advertised by the palatial summer "shacks" along the shore. To a woman like Frances, one with her feet on the ground, that wouldn't be a problem.

And the catalog shoot wouldn't intimidate her, either. It was for a specialty house, Nor'easter, which dealt in serious sailing gear and action-oriented clothes. That was why they were waiting till October to shoot.

"They won't be canceling for rough weather," the booker had told him. "They want it that way."

It sounded fine to Jack, too. He didn't mind shooting in wind and rain. Not as long as he had Frances to curl up with afterward.

And he had Frances, he thought, shooting a pleased look at the woman in the car beside him. He'd half expected her to come up with an excuse to back out at the last minute. But when he'd said it was time to leave on Sunday, she'd got her suitcase and come with him.

She was quiet, yes. But Frances often was quiet. That was one of the things he liked about her. She didn't feel the need to chatter on and impress him all the time.

He deliberately quelled the need to impress her.

Seeing him at work would impress her enough, he'd decided.

There would be glitzy bits—part of this catalog shoot would doubtless focus on the glamorous places these clothes could go.

But it wouldn't be all high-class restaurants, trendy bars and drinks at the yacht club. There would be long hours on the open sea, plenty of time and experience to convince her that he was serious and hardworking. And all of it would bring her into his world, proving to her that their universes could overlap.

It would also give them time together—time without Annabel and the kids, both animal and otherwise, time without Ernie and Bert, Eb and Aaron. He was already thinking about all the ways he could show her how he loved her.

And nothing, absolutely nothing would go wrong. He was sure of it.

HE GOT SEASICK.

Not just mildly queasy, not just a tiny bit dizzy and nauseated. No, not at all.

He got gut-wrenching, white-lipped, sweat-drenched seasick. Frances was the least of his worries. He hardly thought about her at all. He lay on the deck of the yacht between shots and moaned.

The only thoughts he had focused on the relief of dying, on the joys of Christian burial, on the happiness of life everlasting. But no matter how appealing he thought death might be, it didn't happen.

He only wished it would.

Everyone was sympathetic. There were others who found the sway and chop made them vaguely ill. Others still who said that once upon a time they had.

But nobody was turning pea green the way he was, no one had parted company with their breakfast long since, no one else said they never wanted to see a meal again for as long as they lived.

Just Jack.

With Frances watching.

He might not think about it much, but he couldn't help but be aware. Whenever he did manage to string two coherent thoughts together, and one of them wasn't how fast he could get to the head, he remembered how determinedly he'd insisted that she be there.

Monday she'd seen the glitzy bits. She'd sat on a stool out of the way and watched the eight of them—four guys and four girls, one of them Jennifer Jewell—do the posh shots.

They shot at the outdoor bar up at the Inn at Castle Hill overlooking Narragansett Bay, then later in a posh colonial restaurant downtown and, finally, at the Marina Pub on Goat Island, all settings that were supposed to prove that Nor'easter clothes were appropriate anywhere.

It had been a long and tiring day, but Jack had gone through the motions expertly, flawlessly, always aware of Frances in the background.

She had watched wordlessly. He caught her eye occasionally and smiled at her, and she smiled back. But it didn't look as if the smile reached her eyes, and she hadn't said much afterward, either.

It made him nervous. He felt her almost imperceptibly drawing away from him. And even that night when they made love, he felt as if she wasn't really with him, as if he had even less of her than he'd had in Vermont.

But he'd told himself that tomorrow would make it all right. Tomorrow she'd see that it wasn't all fun and games.

"I don't think I'll go today," she'd told him when the alarm went off at five-thirty.

"You have to," he told her. "Ben says rough seas this morning. This is where you find out what it's really like. The nitty-gritty, as it were."

Truer words were never spoken.

"Ten minutes, Jack." Jennifer Jewell bent over him, a hint of sympathy in her voice. "They want you in the yellow slicker, the green turtleneck and jeans next."

Jack groaned and rolled onto his side. It wasn't supposed to be as gritty as this.

THE SEASICKNESS was her undoing. Not her own. She never felt a bit. But as Frances sat in the stern of *The Gladiator*, out of the way of the cables, the baffles, the makeup and camera gear, watching Jack go greener and greener, her resistance waned.

She tried to remain detached, to smile at the proper intervals, to speak at the proper times, and yet to hold herself aloof. So she could let go easily. So when the end came, she wouldn't get hurt.

It was surprisingly easy on Monday. Seeing all those gorgeous women Jack worked with did wonders. If he had them around all the time, she reasoned, he certainly couldn't be serious about her.

She was just a fling to him—exactly the same thing he was to her. She was a novelty, just the way she'd always thought.

And when she watched him go through the motions in front of the camera, turning on and off his smile, flashing his charm as he went through practiced moves, focusing on

Jennifer Jewell with just the same intensity that he had last spring focused on her, Frances thought again and again how easy it must be for him to convince any woman in the world that she was his one and only.

"You always suspected it," she reminded herself. But seeing it in action, first with this woman and then with that one, particularly with the obviously chummy Jennifer, didn't make her feel any happier.

And when the shoot was over, and Jack turned that exact same smile on her, she felt the icy finger of Fate raise the hairs on the back of her neck.

Which was why it was perverse to feel so wretched for him when they got out on the yacht Tuesday morning and, as the wind blew out from the north and the tide came up the bay from the south, he got sicker and sicker before her eyes.

She didn't want to care, but she did.

At first she did her best not to notice him lying on the deck, his face pale, his cheeks sunken while the yacht heaved and swayed against almost square waves. It seemed to be the way he wanted it; he shut his eyes the moment he saw her looking at him, as if, when he couldn't see her, she wasn't there. But the third time he disappeared below, she began to worry.

Before she could make a move to see how he was doing, however, he reappeared, paler than ever, thin lipped and sweating.

The makeup woman, *tsking*, dusted his face with a bit of powder. The photographer motioned him into position by the winch and the assistant tossed him a line.

"Hang tough," Frances heard her say over the rising wind. It whipped through his hair and threw salt spray against the yellow Nor'easter slicker he wore. Jack grimaced at her.

"Perfect!" the photographer shouted. "Brace yourself now. That's right. Make it look like work."

The yacht pitched and yawed. The wind howled. Jack braced, his jaw tensed. Frances saw him swallow, saw him grit his teeth. It did indeed look like work.

The camera clicked again and again. The photographer moved, angled, crouched. "Lookin' good. More profile. Turn into the wind. Yeah, that's it. Yeah."

Jack squinted. His Adam's apple worked up and down in his throat. He chewed on the inside of his cheek. He bit his lip in concentration.

"Terrific!" the photographer yelled. "One more time." More clicks. "That's it."

Jack hung over the side.

"NOT MY FINEST HOUR."

Frances, wiping his still-clammy brow with a towel, kissed him gently. "You were very brave."

"Oh, sure." Jack rolled his eyes, then groaned. The slightest movement and—even though they'd been back in the bedroom at the inn for two hours—he still felt as if he were adrift on a stormy sea. He felt like an idiot. He felt like the biggest wimp in the world.

"You were brave. It must've been awful."

It was. But this wasn't. This was the stuff of which dreams were made—Frances warm and comforting, Frances gentle and loving, Frances kissing him. He thought he must be imagining it. His head still spun.

She kissed him again. "Shhh. Just rest."

He rested. He couldn't do anything else.

He certainly couldn't understand what was going on in Frances's mind. He'd expected she'd be hightailing it for Vermont as fast as she could the moment the yacht hit the harbor. If what she'd witnessed yesterday had had her pulling back from him, what she saw today should have had her in the next state.

Instead, once the photographer had freed him, she'd hurried over, hanging over the side next to him, mopping his face, holding his head. And when he'd finally staggered back to collapse on one of the lockers, she'd plopped down next to him, making soothing noises and cradling his head in her lap for the rest of the trip.

He tried to make sense of it then and now, couldn't, gave up, and closed his eyes.

Gentle lips brushed across his forehead. He raised his arms slowly and carefully, as if the wrong move might still pitch him overboard. Then he wrapped them around her, hanging on the way a drowning man hangs on to a life preserver.

He felt her body slide down and mold itself to his, warm and comforting. He felt the tight coil of tension loosen and ease inside him. He felt her breath on his cheek . . . and then he felt no more.

SHE WAS SLEEPING, the afternoon sun angling across her body through the sheer lace curtains. The light accentuated the scattering of freckles across her shoulders, the ivory smoothness of her breasts. Jack eased himself away, seeing it the way a photographer would—light and shadow, line and angle, curve and hollow. And it was beautiful—*she* was beautiful, all of her.

But it wasn't the juncture of light and shadow or curve and angle that was her primary beauty. Her beauty was in her person, in the woman that Frances was. In her warmth, her caring, her enthusiasm. It was in the way she gave of herself for others—for Eb, for Ernie and Bert, for Annabel and the kids, for Maeve and Carleen and countless others. For himself.

He had come to her out of curiosity, he had stayed out of enchantment.

He wanted a future with her because of love.

As long as she had insisted on remaining in Boone's Corner, as long as she had set limits on their relationship, he'd wondered if the feelings had just been his. It was possible, he'd conceded. Love wasn't something he knew a lot about.

Sex, yes; lust, yes. But love hadn't been as easy to pin down.

Now he knew.

Yesterday and today the barriers had fallen. Frances had seen the glitz, the glamour, the girls. She had seen the boredom, the dreariness, the work. She had—today—seen him at his worst.

And she had loved him anyway.

Jack smiled and began to love her.

She shifted under the soft stroking of his hands; she stretched, her neck arched, she smiled. Her eyes opened.

"Marry me," he said softly.

Her body went still beneath him. She looked stricken, terrified, a doe staring into the barrel of a gun.

"Frances?"

She shoved him off and scrambled out of the bed, shaking her head, backing toward the bathroom, grabbing for her clothes as she went.

"No," she said, as if her body language hadn't said it for her. "Oh, no."

Chapter Fourteen

"No?"

But by this time she was in the bathroom and he could hear the door locking. He sprang out of bed, then caught on to the four-poster frame as a wave of returning seasickness swamped him.

"No?" he croaked again, torn between disbelief and anger.

He could hear her stumbling around in the bathroom, presumably dressing. "That's what I said," he heard her mutter.

He hadn't thought he'd got it wrong. Even so, it didn't make sense. He banged on the door. "What do you mean, no?"

Frances opened the door, shirt haphazardly tucked into her jeans, one deck shoe on, the other in her hand.

"Just . . . no." Pause. "Thank you." She met his gaze for one split second, then her eyes skidded away and she tried to slip past him.

He caught her arm. "You love me."

She didn't answer, just pulled away, making his head reel, and grabbed her suitcase, flinging it open on the bed.

"Frances?" His knuckles were white on the bedstead.

She pulled her dress off the hanger and tossed it on top of the sweater and shirts already packed. Her movements were controlled, precise, but there was an underlying wildness he didn't understand.

"Frances!"

She whirled past him to grab her jacket. Jack felt as if he'd unleashed a gale right there in the room. Anchored, he strove for calm, for sanity, for common sense. "What are you doing, Frances?"

"Leaving."

"Why?"

"I can hardly stay now, can I? Not after I've just said no."

He shook his head, hoping to clear it, not succeeding. It spun abominably. "Why'd you say no?" Reeling or not, it didn't make sense.

She didn't reply.

He was getting angry now. "Frances, damn it. You're acting like I've insulted you!"

She fastened the suitcase and shrugged into her jacket, then lugged the case to the door. In a second she was going to walk out on him, leave him standing there.

He knew it as well as he knew if there was any way humanly possible, he was going to stop her.

He sucked in a deep breath and lunged. The room spun, the world shifted, he wrapped his arms around her, falling, and together they hit the floor.

"S-sorry."

She didn't say a word, just lay there, rigid and resisting, her eyes desperate, shocked.

"Are you all right?"

"I'm fine." She started to pull away.

"Damn it, Frances. We have to talk."

She shook her head, struggling against him. He let her sit up, but he kept a hand on her.

"I won't let you go until we do."

"There's nothing to say."

"There damned well is! You can tell me why you're turning me down, for one thing, why you're acting like an idiot, for another." God, he felt sick. He wanted to lie there and die, not fight for his life.

"It wouldn't work."

"It wouldn't work?" His tone was halfway between mockery and disbelief. *That* was her explanation. "How do you know that?"

"Experience."

He stared at her. "What experience?"

"I've been married, Jack."

He could see her throat working. She chewed her lip.

He cocked his head, considering, getting a faint glimmer of understanding at last. "This isn't to do with me at all then, is it?" he said after a moment. "It's to do with that jerk you were married to—what's his name."

"Stephen." Her voice was flat.

"Yeah, Stephen. Well, I'm not Stephen."

"I know that."

"Well, then what's the problem?"

But he didn't get an answer, only a look in her eyes he'd never seen before. She looked desolate. He reached out his hand. She drew away.

She wrapped her arms around her knees, pulling inward, shaking her head. "No, Jack. Don't." She trembled. Her whole body seemed to twist with tension.

Jack waited, no less tense himself. "Forget Stephen," he said.

She gave a short harsh laugh. "I wish I could. I wish . . . oh, God, I wish . . ." She lay her head on her arms, then lifted it moments later to meet his eyes. "But it's no good wishing, you must see that."

"I see damned little. One minute I was making love to you and the next you were flying out of bed as if all the devils in hell were after you."

Frances didn't say anything.

"I want to marry you, Frances."

"No."

"Yes."

"Jack, please."

"I'd be happy to please you." He willed her to smile. She didn't.

"You know what I mean."

"I don't."

"Well, I can't be any clearer."

"Try."

"Jack—"

"Tell me you don't love me, then."

"Jack, stop it."

"You can't, because you do love me." His voice was implacable, certain. "Don't you?" he challenged her. She had to.

"Love has nothing to do with it."

"No? That's news to me."

"I don't want to get married, Jack," she said flatly. "Not to you, not to anyone."

He opened his mouth to argue.

She cut in. "It isn't all it's cracked up to be, believe me."

"Frances—"

"No!"

He stared at her. He'd never seen her like this. Not ever. She'd been prickly before. She'd been distant. Irritated. But she'd never been unreachable.

"I don't believe you," he said. "I want the truth."

She glared at him. "That is the truth! What's the matter?" Her voice was hard and cold and bitter, not like Frances at all. "Can't accept rejection?" Her voice mocked him.

"I get rejected all the time. It's part of my job."

"Well, this isn't a job. It's life. And there are some things in life you can't have! Some goals that, no matter how much you want them, you never achieve!"

There was an almost hysterical edge to her voice. She was shaking. He knelt and tried to put his arms around her.

"No! Go away!"

"Frances, damn it, I love you."

"Well, you can't have me!"

"For God's sake—"

"No. Just let me go, Jack. Please." She sucked in a deep breath. "It was fun while it lasted. No, not fun. Wonderful." She tried to smile, but bit her lip instead. "But it couldn't last. We're too different. We don't share the same goals, the same life-style, the same ideals."

"That's not true."

"It is. You're glitz, I'm goats."

He would've rolled his eyes at the simplistic idiocy of that statement except that he knew she was deadly serious. "We can work it out."

"No, we can't."

"This is stupid, Frances—"

"Yes, it is. It was a momentary aberration. Foolishness on both our parts. An affair, that's all."

She couldn't really believe that, could she, after all they'd shared?

"You'll thank me someday for saving you from making an enormous mistake," she told him.

"I will, huh?" He almost snorted his disbelief.

"Yes. You will." The look in her eyes was as desperate as it was determined. Jack didn't understand it, didn't understand her.

They stared at each other. Outside in the hallway he could hear Jennifer's tinkling laugh, the photographer's gruff baritone.

He didn't move, just waited, hanging on for dear life, ready to argue with anything she said.

But Frances was done arguing. The fight went out of her. The light of desperation, of anger, of battle—of life—vanished from her eyes. He saw sadness in her face, weariness and resignation, and a flat, cold indifference that froze him to his toes.

She got to her feet. "This isn't one of my books, it isn't one of your ads. And all the pretending in the world won't make it work. It's life, Jack. It's real. And you have to face it. I have," she said quietly.

"But—"

"There are some things in life—in real life—that, no matter how hard you work for them, no matter how much you want them, you just can't have."

"HOW WAS IT?"

"Fine."

"See lots of hunks?"

"Yes."

"And lots of glamour girls?"

"Them, too."

"But you only had eyes for Jack," Annabel said and laughed knowingly.

Frances kept scrubbing the floor.

"Well, I must say," Annabel complained good-naturedly, "you're being remarkably closedmouthed about the whole trip. You've been back three days and you haven't said boo. Haven't even been answering your phone. You all right?"

"Fine."

There was a pause from Annabel, as if she hoped Frances would fill it. Frances didn't.

"Next time we'll have to send a more forthcoming soul. Ernie, maybe?" Annabel suggested, grinning. "Or Bert."

Frances shrugged her shoulders and scrubbed on. Once every year she got down on her hands and knees and stripped the old oak planks all the way down. This seemed like the very best of times.

"So what was it like?" Annabel persisted, sipping the tea she'd made for herself when Frances hadn't offered.

She wasn't leaving until she got some sort of answer; that was clear. Cornered, Frances groped for words. "Cold. Drafty. Busy. On the way home it rained," she added. Or she thought it had. Perhaps she'd been seeing only her tears.

"But you had a good time."

"Enlightening."

"Jack coming up for the weekend?" It was Friday afternoon already. On an ordinary weekend he'd be walking in about two hours from now.

"He didn't say." That seemed a wiser response than a flat no. A no would have garnered Frances even more questions. She didn't want Annabel prying, but Annabel wouldn't consider it prying. She'd consider it her right to know as it would be everyone's in Boone's Corner.

"If he does, and you want to, come for supper tomorrow night."

"Thanks."

Annabel gave her a long, curious look, but Frances kept on at the floor. Finally, sighing, Annabel got to her feet and put the teacup in the sink. "Tell him hi," she said on her way out.

"Yes."

But life was back to normal now. Fantasy had separated itself from reality. The end had come, although not the way she'd thought it would. She never thought he'd ask her to marry him.

It was as if her dearest hope and her worst nightmare had become one. All she could imagine was his love turning to displeasure, his caring turning to disparagement. If she hadn't been able to live up to Stephen's expectations, she certainly couldn't live up to Jack Neillands's.

"Tell him to stop by if he has time, even if you can't come to supper," Annabel said.

But Frances wouldn't be telling him anything ever again.

"A SALUTARY EXPERIENCE, rejection," Carter said through a mouthful of cheese curls. "Builds character. I know. Happens to me all the time."

Hanging upside down, Jack grunted. He arched his back, then curled forward, his stomach muscles clenching, holding, then releasing one millimeter at a time. Smooth, fluid, controlled.

The only thing he seemed to be able to control these days, his stomach muscles. He wasn't doing so well with his life.

"Takes time," Carter was saying just as he'd been saying for the past month and a half.

Jack curled again, held, released. He was sweating. Sweat ran into his eyes, making them sting. He curled again. And again. It hurt.

Carter got up and wandered over to the bookshelf and considered the photographs. "Neither of your parents looks like an opossum." He turned and looked down at Jack's head. "Or an idiot."

"Perhaps I was adopted," Jack said dryly.

"I'm sure they hope so. I'm sure they also hope you begin to act like a normal person one day soon. We all do."

Jack curled up, grabbed the chinning bar and swung his feet down to the floor. "Is this a polite way of telling me to get my act together?"

"You could say that. You could also say that we care. We don't like to see you...beat." Carter gave an awkward shrug.

Jack didn't like being beat. But he was getting used to it. It was, he supposed, as Carter had said, a salutary experience. It certainly put a different perspective on life.

He was beginning to understand what Frances had been getting at. He was beginning to understand a bit how arrogant he must have seemed.

I want it. I can get it.

It was a pretty simple philosophy of life. It was amazing how long it had worked. It was devastating to find that when it came down to the one thing that really mattered in life—his love for Frances—it didn't work at all.

He felt rueful, humble, and not very happy most of the time. Carter wasn't the only one who noticed.

"You're different," Jennifer told him one evening as they scuffed their way through Central Park.

His mother, flying through on her way to meet his father at a maritime conference in Gibraltar, looked at him over a shared supper and said, "Are you sure you're coping, Jack?"

It was nice of her to have noticed. He wished he took more comfort from the thought.

"You need a distraction," Carter decreed now. He crumpled the cheese-curl bag, aimed it at the wastebasket, missed.

"I'm fine." Jack hooked the bag into the basket, dropped into one of the armchairs and reached for his knife.

Carter who had watched the hook shot with envy, watched with despair as Jack began to whittle. "This is not you, Jack. I look to you for inspiration, for enthusiasm, for joie de vivre. And what do I get? A whittler."

Jack gave him a rueful smile. "Sorry." He couldn't help it. He needed it. It kept him busy, kept him focused, kept him sane.

"Well, you can't keep it up much longer. It's not allowed. Thanksgiving's coming up." Carter rubbed his hands with enthusiasm. "Shall we hit Vermont again?"

"No!"

"Right. Sorry. Aspen, then. Let's go to Aspen."

"I don't want to go to Aspen."

"Winter Park? Vail?"

"No."

"But we always go skiing on Thanksgiving."

Jack concentrated on the wood under his knife. "Maybe we should try something else."

"Florida? The Islands?"

Jack shook his head.

"You want to stay here and eat soybean turkey with my employees?" Carter's voice was worried.

Jack went on whittling, rubbing his thumb over the wood. His head was bent. Shavings were piling up at his feet. "Why not?"

Carter let out a soundless whistle of exasperation. He bounded to his feet. "Right. Stay, then. Feel sorry for yourself. Mope. Sulk. I'm going skiing. When you snap out of this nonsense, give me a call. If you do it in time, you can go with me to Aspen at Christmas.''

THEY WERE MAKING LOVE when the doorbell rang.

Frances, jerked back to reality, cursed the daydream that had afflicted her once again. She got up quickly and strode down the stairs, grateful for the break, grateful for anything real, anything substantial, anything that tore her mind away from memories of Jack.

It must be the snow causing it, she thought.

The first real substantial snow of the season had begun to fall during the night. Ernie and Bert had been wondering aloud just yesterday if they'd have a white Christmas this year.

"Can't remember a year we didn't have snow before December 21st," Bert said.

But the way it was falling there was no doubt now that they would.

Frances was happy for them and for all those who wanted it, all those to whom the memories of snowfalls were happy ones. For herself, she found it still brought pain.

She'd thought she was over it. Heaven knew she'd had the time. Two and a half months to get over him. And most of the time she was fine.

She wrote, she cared for the animals, she worked for Eb, she went to the occasional movie with Aaron, she made bread three times a week for Ernie and Bert's stressed-out guests. She had determined to get her life back to normal as quickly as she could. She had done so. And if she felt hollow and lost at times somewhere within, the feeling rarely immobilized her.

But today, with the snow, the feeling deepened, carving a place for itself deep inside her. And into the hollow it made came memories of Jack, bushels of them.

The ringing came again. Louder. More insistent. She started down the steps.

There was a man at the door. She could see him through the curtain. A tall man, with dark hair and a dusting of snowflakes across the shoulders of his dark brown jacket. A man just like the man who had been there nine long months ago. Frances closed her eyes, her knuckles whitening against the banister.

He rang the bell again. Short, sharp, demanding.

She swallowed, bit her lip and descended the stairs. Then, drawing a deep breath, she opened the door.

He grinned and thrust a package at her. "Line twenty-four, miss. Just sign here."

Dazed, disoriented, disappointed, fingers shaking, pen wobbling, heart wrenching, Frances signed.

The tall, dark-haired man whistled "Jingle Bells" and tapped his foot while he waited. "Looks like Santa didn't forget you." He grinned at her.

Frances managed a weak smile as he gave her a quick salute, bounded down the steps and headed for his truck.

"Merry Christmas," he called over his shoulder.

"Merry Christmas," Frances echoed, but the only one who could have heard her was the cat.

She carried the package back inside, frowning slightly. It wasn't the right shape for galleys or foreign editions. It wasn't heavy enough, either. Her Christmas parcel had already arrived from her parents. Sometimes her mother sent along something extra later, but she usually told Frances to be on the lookout for it. When last she'd called, her mother hadn't said a word.

Frances shook the box. There were a few soft rustling thuds. Curious, she got the scissors and ran the blade along the taped edge of the box. Then she lifted the flaps.

Inside was another box, white and plain. No card, no note attached.

Carefully Frances lifted the lid. Small clumps of white tissue paper confronted her. She picked one up, weighed it in her palm, then began to unwrap it.

It was the figure of a man, lean and bearded, in flowing robes, staff in hand, roughly whittled out of wood. There was an expression of amazement, of awe on his face.

There was a look of astonishment on her own. Frances sucked in her breath.

Her throat tightened, her eyes ached. She stared. "Oh, Jack."

For this man could only have come from Jack. Her thumb rubbed over the smooth, polished wood, she remembered his thumb doing the same. She swallowed hard, then, fingers trembling, set the shepherd on the table and reached back into the box.

She unwrapped a woman this time. She was kneeling, head bent. She was smiling, contented, relieved. Frances set her carefully beside the man. Then, biting her lip, she reached into the box again.

There were fourteen pieces in all.

When she had finished, she had grouped on her coffee table one more rough-looking fatherly man, three men with crowns on their heads and gifts in their hands, four incredibly idiosyncratic sheep—one with what looked like a bloodstain on his gnarly fleece—an unintentionally one-horned goat, a smoothly hollowed cradle. And a child.

They were rough. They were crude.

They were Jack's.

They spoke of hope, of promise, of possibilities wholly unexpected.

And as the snow fell outside, the storm broke inside.

"Where's your faith in the power of love?" Bert had asked her.

Frances lay the child in the cradle. She looked at him and thought how unlikely his kingdom must once have seemed. She touched the tiny shepherd and knew the awe that a real shepherd must once have felt.

She started to cry.

HE HAD BEEN SMILING for seven hours. His face hurt. His jaw ached.

When he got too old and battered looking to model, he would have to go to Hollywood, he thought as he smiled yet again at a quip from Carter's date. He sure as hell could act.

He shouldn't have come. But Carter was right—he'd moped long enough. Two and a half months of moody "if onlys" were more than sufficient. He needed to start focusing on the future, not the past.

But Aspen? Aspen at Christmas? That had been a mistake.

He'd come because he'd been feeling childish and it was as good a way as he could think of to thumb his nose at Frances. It was exactly what she seemed to expect of him— glitz and glamour and gorgeous women—so he did it.

The moment he arrived, he regretted it. Aspen at Christmas seemed to be filled with every other person in the world who had spent the past two months in solitary confinement and was determined to make up for it. And most of them were women.

"Perfect," Carter had decreed. "Just what you need."

But Jack, for all that he was ready to get on with his life, hadn't found one in the three days he'd been here that he couldn't forget the moment he turned his back.

Carter, who'd found the quippy Elizabeth on the plane in from Denver, was not thrilled.

"For heaven's sake, what do you want?" he'd groused when Jack had declined to go out with them the night before. "How are you going to meet anybody if you don't get out of the room?"

"Tomorrow," Jack had promised.

But when tomorrow came, he didn't feel any more like making the effort than he had the day before.

Carter, however, didn't take no for an answer this time. He dragged Jack off to be the third wheel while he and Elizabeth made eyes at each other over dinner and drinks.

He also introduced Jack to one eligible woman after another.

So Jack smiled . . . and smiled.

But now it was late, almost midnight, and he'd had
enough. He finished his beer and shoved back his chair.

"I'm calling it a night."

Carter frowned. "I thought you were coming along to the
Hofbrau. Lots of lovely fräuleins." He winked. "You like
blondes."

"Not tonight."

"You're not lightening up, Jack, old chum."

Jack shrugged.

"Sure you won't come?" Elizabeth asked.

"No, thanks. I want to hit the slopes early."

"Suit yourself. But don't wake me," Carter said. Elizabeth whispered something to him. He grinned. "Never
mind. I won't even be there."

Jack smiled and started to move away. "Right."

"Tell you what," Carter called after him, "if I find a
likely fräulein, I'll send her along."

But Jack just shook his head. "No, thanks."

The night was cold and still, with new snow falling,
crunching underfoot as Jack walked back to the lodge. It
was a relief to be outside, away from the constant press of
humanity, the noise, the smoke. He breathed deeply, walked
slowly, in no hurry now that he'd left the bar. After all, what
was there to go back to?

He could have gone to his parents' for Christmas. His father was back in San Diego now. His brothers were going to
be there with their families. Georgia had promised to try to
fly in.

"You'll be the only one not with us, Jack," his mother
had complained.

But he couldn't face a family Christmas. All those smiling faces. All the warmth.

He wanted— Oh, hell, it didn't matter what he wanted.
He wasn't going to get it. He'd learned that much.

You didn't get love by hard work or merit or for any other reason. It was a gift, pure and simple. It could be given and, as he knew to his sorrow, it could also be withheld.

He let himself into the room, shucked his clothes and fell onto the bed. Far off he could hear midnight revelers hooting and laughing. Footsteps passed in the hallway. Soft giggles. Hoarse whispers. The heater hummed. The tap dripped.

He heard a knock.

He shut his eyes. "Hell."

A fräulein. That miserable Carter had found him a fräulein. And now he was going to have to tell her no.

No. He wasn't. He wasn't going to answer at all. That would be easier on both of them. He folded his arms behind his head and stayed right where he was.

She knocked again.

Jack sighed. He flexed his toes.

Tap. Tap. Tap.

"Go away," he muttered. "Just go."

For almost a minute there was no sound and he began to breathe easier, to smile and congratulate himself on having avoided an awkward situation when he heard it again.

Tap. Tap, tap, tap. It was as persistent as it was tentative. What the hell had Carter told her?

"Cripes." He rolled to a sitting position and waited.

Tap, tap.

Jack ran his fingers through his hair, sighed and, at the next knock, grabbed his jeans and pulled them on. He crossed the room and jerked open the door.

"Look, miss, I don't know what—*Frances?*"

It was, indeed, Frances. So pale that the freckles across her cheeks stood out like ink spots. So thin that if she turned sideways, she might disappear. So unexpected that he couldn't quite believe it was her.

"Jack." She swallowed, licked her lips, smiled. It was the same hesitant, worried smile she'd given him the first day they'd met. Only then he'd been the one knocking.

He still stared at her, unmoving.

"May I . . . come in?"

Galvanized by the notion that she might not, he jerked the door open wider, flicked on the light. "Sure. Of course. Sit down." He gestured to the bed, then to a chair. "What are you doing here?"

He wanted to hope; he didn't dare. It was probably pure luck. She'd been researching Colorado gold mines or some damned thing and had heard he was in town. Some bloody awful coincidence. Some brainless notion that maybe once more they could be "friends."

She didn't sit. She stood in the middle of the floor, her fingers knotted together around the strap of her purse. She looked right at him.

"I love you," she said.

He opened his mouth, but for once in his life no words came out. Shooting stars were going off in his mind. He stared at her. "F-Frances?" He started to reach for her.

She shook her head quickly. "I was afraid."

"Stephen," he guessed the reason.

"Partly. Mostly I was afraid of marriage."

He looked at her baffled. For all the time he'd known her there'd been a wall between them whenever the subject of her marriage to Stephen had come up. He'd wanted to ask, needed to ask, but hadn't dared.

Now he said, "Tell me."

She laced her fingers together. "We met at Harvard. Starry-eyed smart kids from the sticks in a rich privileged world. We weren't poor. Not really, just people who had to scrape and save and work like dogs to get by. People who didn't seem to fit. So we clung together. We were soul mates. At least I thought we were.

"When I finished my degree, we got married, and I taught so Stephen could go to law school. I thought he'd go into legal services or something like that. I was a great idealist." She grimaced. "Stephen thought I was nuts. He wanted the exact opposite—glamour, glitz." She paused. "Everything you have."

"I don't need it," Jack said softly.

A slight smile touched her face. "I know that. Now. I didn't then. I was afraid it would be like Stephen all over again. I couldn't take that. I loved him. I tried to please him—" her voice wobbled, then went on steadily "—but I failed."

"Oh, Fran—"

"Failed," she insisted. "Badly. It started out fine. It got worse and worse. Eventually I couldn't do anything he wanted. I wasn't letting it happen again. That was why I went to Vermont. So it wouldn't. And then you came."

A corner of Jack's mouth lifted ruefully. "Sorry."

"I didn't want you there. You were the last thing I needed. A fantasy come to life. A reminder of all the things I'd hoped for and didn't have." She shook her head in despair. "I thought you'd leave. Get bored and fed up. But you kept coming back." She glared at him accusingly.

He smiled.

"I thought we could be friends," Frances went on, her voice rising. "I thought we could have an affair. I wouldn't fail you then!"

"You never—"

"I never thought you'd want to marry me! You ruined everything."

His smile faded. "Did I?" he whispered. He wanted to go to her, to touch her, take her in his arms, wanted to make her deny it. He held back. He couldn't do a thing; the choice was hers.

Frances ducked her head, her fingers worried her purse strap.

"I thought you had," she said at last. "Because marrying you would have meant giving you the same power over me that Stephen had. It would have meant that the same thing could happen again. That I'd have to try. That I might . . . fail again."

Jack didn't take his eyes off her. His heart was in his throat. He hoped; he prayed. But he didn't *know*. "But you came."

"I came."

"Why?"

She shifted her head and met his gaze. "Because I can't only live in a fantasy world. It isn't enough. I've stopped running away. Because I love you. Because I'm willing to take the risk."

He reached for her then, hauling her into his arms, holding her against his heart, burying his face in her hair.

"Oh, God, Frances. I don't believe it. I thought . . . I thought . . ."

"I'm sure you thought I was a royal pain," Frances said, but she was smiling, too, her hands stroking down his back, her lips nuzzling his ear.

He pulled her down on the bed, casting aside her purse, unzipping her jacket, unbuttoning her shirt.

There came a knock at the door.

Frances stiffened. "Are you expecting someone?"

"Not a soul," Jack said, smiling. Carter's fräulein would have to find a welcome elsewhere. "Go away," he shouted.

Footsteps receded at once.

"Where were we?" he asked Frances.

She undid the snap of his jeans. "Right about here."

"How did you find me?" He was lying on his back feeling warm and well loved, smiling into the face of the woman who'd made him feel that way.

Frances smiled back. "It wasn't easy. If you ever planned to make me prove myself, you did a terrific job. I went to New York. I was ready to throw myself at you." She grimaced. "And you weren't there."

"I know."

"So I went to your agency. They wouldn't tell me where you were. Can't let groupies bother you, one of them said." She giggled. "Do I look like a groupie? Anyway, I skulked around until I heard one of them booking your friend Jennifer. So I went after her."

Jack stared at her, amazed. "You asked Jennifer?"

"But she didn't know, either. She said you were going skiing with some friend named Carter who owned a health-food store. So we called all the health-food stores. Do you know how many health-food stores there are in Manhattan?"

Jack didn't. He didn't care. He was laughing now.

"Anyway, we finally found it. So I called and gave some poor girl a sob story about your aunt Tillie having a heart attack..."

"My what?"

"Aunt Tillie. Writers have great powers of imagination," Frances told him.

Jack grinned. "Oh, yes?"

"Anyway, she believed me, gave me the address, and here I am."

If he'd needed anything to convince him that Frances had made up her mind, that had done it. Frances braving New York, the agency, Jennifer. He was amazed, flattered, thrilled.

But he still had to ask, "Why? You were so certain in Newport. What made you change your mind?"

She rolled over onto her stomach and propped herself on one elbow, her expression suddenly serious. "Your crèche."

"The crèche?" He stared at her. "How? I mean, it was therapy. Something to do to keep me sane."

He'd stuck to it doggedly, day after day, needing the distraction, needing, too, the link it had given him with Frances.

But he couldn't whittle sheep forever. The time came when he had to put the past behind him. And since he couldn't bear to look at it, since the memories he had were carved deeply enough in his soul without the sight of it, he had sent it to Frances. He thought she deserved some memories, too.

"It made me sane, too," she told him. "It made me see. It opened my eyes."

He cocked his head. "To what?"

Frances smiled. "To unexpected possibilities. To hope. The whole crèche, what it meant. But most especially your shepherd. He looked so amazed, as if he had his life all figured out, and then something miraculous had come along and changed it all. I was just like him." She touched his cheek, her fingers warm and gentle, loving him with her touch. "Settled. Comfortable. Hopeless."

"Hopeless?"

"Mmm. Before you came. I didn't expect anything anymore. I bet he didn't, either. We both got something we never thought we wanted. In his case, a savior in the unexpected form of a child. In my case, love in the form of a man I thought was all the things I was afraid of. I was terrified."

"And now you're not?"

"Now I'm willing to try." She kissed his lips. She touched his cheek. "I love you, Jack. More than I've ever loved anyone. And I believe that you love me."

And Jack closed his eyes, relieved, loved, justified.

He drank in the pure, complete happiness of it. And then he put his arms around her and rolled over on top of her, kissing her, loving her.

"Imagine that," he said.

HARLEQUIN
American Romance ®

COMING NEXT MONTH

#345 AMERICAN PIE by Margaret St. George

Spirited and ambitious, Polish immigrant Lucie Kolska arrives in New York on the eve of the twentieth century. Proud and daring, Dublin native Jamie Kelly dreams of feasting on his slice of the pie. But to make it, Lucie and Jamie must cast off the baggage of their old ideas before they can embrace the best of what America has to offer: hope for the future and a love that is as brilliant as the promise of the American Dream. Don't miss the first book in the "Century of American Romance"—a nostalgic look back at the lives and loves of the twentieth century.

#346 RANCHO DIABLO by Anne Stuart

Isabelle Romney couldn't escape her memories of Rancho Diablo—and the man who'd stolen her birthright. Luke Cassidy had been first in her father's heart—and for better or worse, Luke was first in hers. Isabelle swore she'd never again be vulnerable to Luke. But to do that, she had to make one last trip home....

#347 BELOVED DREAMER by Anne Henry

She'd never forgotten him. Twenty years before, Chad Morgan had asked Julie Harper to join him in a dream. Although she'd married someone else, she never forgot her first love. Now, at her high school reunion, Chad's face was the most welcome. She wondered what she would do if Chad asked her again. Would she sacrifice everything for the sake of love?

#348 PHANTOM ANGEL by Kathy Clark

The man Melora Delaney was bringing back from Vietnam had lost his youth and his memory. As a psychologist, she couldn't restore Bo's lost years, but she could help him begin life again. Melora planned two months of intensive work with her patient. When the time came—and it would—would she be able to let him go!

Take 4 bestselling love stories FREE

Plus get a FREE surprise gift!

HARLEQUIN'S "BIG WIN"
SWEEPSTAKES RULES & REGULATIONS
NO PURCHASE NECESSARY TO ENTER OR RECEIVE A PRIZE

1. To enter and join the Reader Service, scratch off the metallic strips on all your BIG WIN tickets #1-#6. This will reveal the values for each sweepstakes entry number, the number of free book(s) you will receive, and your free bonus gift as part of our Reader Service. If you do not wish to take advantage of our Reader Service, but wish to enter the Sweepstakes only, scratch off the metallic strips on your BIG WIN tickets #1-#4. Return your entire sheet of tickets intact. Incomplete and/or inaccurate entries are ineligible for that section or sections of prizes. Not responsible for mutilated or unreadable entries or inadvertent printing errors. Mechanically reproduced entries are null and void.

2. Whether you take advantage of this offer or not, your Sweepstakes numbers will be compared against a list of winning numbers generated at random by the computer. In the event that all prizes are not claimed by March 31, 1992, a random drawing will be held from all qualified entries received from March 30, 1990 to March 31, 1992, to award all unclaimed prizes. All cash prizes (Grand to Sixth), will be mailed to the winners and are payable by cheque in U.S. funds. Seventh prize to be shipped to winners via third-class mail. These prizes are in addition to any free, surprise or mystery gifts that might be offered. Versions of this sweepstakes with different prizes of approximate equal value may appear in other mailings or at retail outlets by Torstar Corp. and its affiliates.

3. The following prizes are awarded in this sweepstakes: ★ Grand Prize (1) $1,000,000; First Prize (1) $25,000; Second Prize (1) $10,000; Third Prize (5) $5,000; Fourth Prize (10) $1,000; Fifth Prize (100) $250; Sixth Prize (2500) $10; ★ ★ Seventh Prize (6000) $12.95 ARV.

   ★ This Sweepstakes contains a Grand Prize offering of $1,000,000 annuity. Winner will receive $33,333.33 a year for 30 years without interest totaling $1,000,000.

   ★ ★ Seventh Prize: A fully illustrated hardcover book published by Torstar Corp. Approximate value of the book is $12.95.

   Entrants may cancel the Reader Service at any time without cost or obligation to buy (see details in center insert card).

4. This promotion is being conducted under the supervision of Marden-Kane, Inc., an independent judging organization. By entering this Sweepstakes, each entrant accepts and agrees to be bound by these rules and the decisions of the judges, which shall be final and binding. Odds of winning in the random drawing are dependent upon the total number of entries received. Taxes, if any, are the sole responsibility of the winners. Prizes are nontransferable. All entries must be received by no later than 12:00 NOON, on March 31, 1992. The drawing for all unclaimed sweepstakes prizes will take place May 30, 1992, at 12:00 NOON, at the offices of Marden-Kane, Inc., Lake Success, New York.

5. This offer is open to residents of the U.S., the United Kingdom, France and Canada, 18 years or older except employees and their immediate family members of Torstar Corp., its affiliates, subsidiaries, Marden-Kane, Inc., and all other agencies and persons connected with conducting this Sweepstakes. All Federal, State and local laws apply. Void wherever prohibited or restricted by law. Any litigation respecting the conduct and awarding of a prize in this publicity contest may be submitted to the Régie des loteries et courses du Québec.

6. Winners will be notified by mail and may be required to execute an affidavit of eligibility and release which must be returned within 14 days after notification or, an alternative winner will be selected. Canadian winners will be required to correctly answer an arithmetical skill-testing question administered by mail which must be returned within a limited time. Winners consent to the use of their names, photographs and/or likenesses for advertising and publicity in conjunction with this and similar promotions without additional compensation.

7. For a list of our major winners, send a stamped, self-addressed envelope to: WINNERS LIST c/o MARDEN-KANE, INC., P.O. BOX 701, SAYREVILLE, NJ 08871 Winners Lists will be fulfilled after the May 30, 1992 drawing date.

If Sweepstakes entry form is missing, please print your name and address on a 3" × 5" piece of plain paper and send to:

In the U.S.	In Canada
Harlequin's "BIG WIN" Sweepstakes	Harlequin's "BIG WIN" Sweepstakes
901 Fuhrmann Blvd.	P.O. Box 609
P.O. Box 1867	Fort Erie, Ontario
Buffalo, NY 14269-1867	L2A 5X3